Praise for Susan Conant's Dog Lover's Mysteries

THE BARKER STREET REGULARS
"A study in good humor that will delight devotees of dogs and of Sherlock Holmes."
—*Boston Globe*

"Sherlockians especially will enjoy Conant's latest dog mystery. Clever and eloquent . . ."
—*Publishers Weekly*

STUD RITES
"An intimate knowledge of Alaskan malamutes isn't necessary to appreciate Susan Conant's *Stud Rites*. . . . Conant's characterizations are dead-on and her descriptions of doggy kitsch—most notably a malamute-shaped lamp trimmed with a dead champion's fur—are hilarious."
—*Los Angeles Times*

"Conant's doggy tales . . . are head and shoulders above many of the other series in which various domestic pets aid or abet in the solving of crimes. . . . Should appeal to everyone who is on the right end of a leash."—*The Purloined Letter*

THE

BARKER STREET REGULARS

A Dog Lover's Mystery

Susan Conant

BANTAM BOOKS
New York   Toronto   London   Sydney   Auckland

This edition contains the complete text
of the original hardcover edition.
NOT ONE WORD HAS BEEN OMITTED.

THE BARKER STREET REGULARS

A Bantam Book / published by arrangement with Doubleday

PUBLISHING HISTORY

Doubleday hardcover edition / March 1998
Bantam paperback edition / January 1999

ISBN: 0-553-57655-0

Published simultaneously in the United States and Canada

Bantam Book are published by Bantam Books, a division of Random House, Inc. Its trademark, consisting of the words "Bantam Books" and the portrayal of a rooster, is Registered in U.S. Patent and Trademark Office and in other countries. Marca Registrada. Bantam Books, 1540 Broadway, New York, New York 10036.

To Lynne and Dan Anderson in honor of the Alaskan malamutes they love, especially the rescued malamutes who exemplify the sweet nature and raw courage of the breed. Alaskan malamutes Jazzy, Nikki, Bones, and many others have survived exploitation, brutality, and neglect. Some, like Katy, have perished. Faced with overwhelming challenges, none has backed down. May we human beings share the strength of the dogs we struggle to save.

Acknowledgments

A number of years ago, a reader sent me a striking photograph of a gigantic dog under an even more gigantic tree. Kind reader, although I have lost your name and address, I want to thank you for suggesting the element of this book that you will recognize as your contribution. For the appearance of Alaskan malamutes Ch. Kaila's Paw Print (the late Tracker) and Ch. Kaila The Devil's Paw (Narly), a legendary grandsire and his magnificent young grandson, I am grateful to Chris and Eileen Gabriel, who will, I hope, forgive the use that Holly makes of Tracker's famous name.

Many thanks to Bruce Southworth, B.S.I., the best guide since Watson to the world of Sherlock Holmes. Any Sherlockian errors contained herein are entirely my own fault. For welcoming me to the world of therapy dogs, I want to thank Sally Jean Alexander of the Pets & People Foundation, as well as the real Rowdy, Frostfield Perfect Crime, C.D., C.G.C., Th.D., my perfect girl. For the unfailing strength that drives our little team, Rowdy and I rely on the stalwart wheel dog in our lives, her half brother and my perpetual puppy, Frostfield Firestar's Kobuk, C.G.C.

I also want to thank Jean Berman, Judy Bocock, Fran Boyle, Dorothy Donohue, Roo Grubis, Roseann Mandell, Janice Ritter, Cathy Shea, Geoff Stern, Margherita Walker, and Anya Wittenborg, as well as the editor who always takes Best of Breed in my book, Kate Miciak.

THE BARKER STREET REGULARS

Chapter One

WHEN ALTHEA BATTLEFIELD FIRST referred to the Sacred Writings, I naturally assumed that she meant the American Kennel Club *Obedience Regulations*. She didn't. What Althea had in mind—what Althea held perpetually in the forefront of her considerable intellect—was *The Complete Sherlock Holmes*. Neither *had* nor *held* is quite right, however, except perhaps in the nuptial sense of *to have and to hold*. Althea loved and cherished Holmes's adventures with a passion that admitted only the richer and the better, and entirely discounted the possibility of the poorer or the worse. As to the bit about *from this day forward*, if you count Althea's six preliterate years of dependence on parental voices, she'd been reading Sherlock Holmes for ninety years.

This is to say that soon after Rowdy and I first entered Althea's room at the Gateway Rehabilitation and Nursing Center, she and I recognized each other as kindred spirits, women with passions: in her case, Sherlock Holmes; in mine, dogs. Not that I disliked Holmes. On the contrary, the ill-used hound of the Baskervilles was one of my favorite literary characters, as I was quick to tell Althea, who pretended to bristle at the suggestion that the beast had been other than real. And not that Althea disliked dogs. Indeed, Althea's mild fondness for dogs was the reason Rowdy and I began to visit her in the first place. When she referred to my gorgeous Alaskan malamute as a "big husky," however, I pretended to take umbrage. In other words, Althea knew about as much about dogs as I did about Sherlock Holmes.

Before I say anything else about Althea or about the subsequent murder of her grandnephew, Jonathan Hubbell, I want to state outright that in taking Rowdy on pet therapy visits to the Gateway, I wasn't engaged in a mission of noble altruism. I'm ordinarily thrilled to have my self-serving motives mistaken for saintly wishes to help others, but this is a story about trickery—fakery, fraud, artifice, subterfuge, call it what you will—and I feel impelled to dissociate myself from the deliberate effort to deceive. In fact, Rowdy became a therapy dog only because I'd taken him to an obedience fun match that also offered therapy dog testing, and I'd had him tested because I knew he'd breeze through and because I thought I'd found an effortless way to get him a new title. Hah! Well, Rowdy aced the test, but as I discovered only when I registered him with Therapy Dogs International, that organization takes ferocious objection to having its initials, T.D.I., used as a title. Why? Because of an utterly irrational suspicion that certain despicably title-hungry dog owners might see T.D.I. only as an easy new title and, once having obtained it, might selfishly refuse to take their dogs on therapy visits. So there I was with a certified therapy dog and no new title when I heard about a local Boston-area group called Paws for Love, which did a thorough job of screening dogs and training handlers for therapy work, and—not that I cared, of course—would bestow on Rowdy the title Rx.D. when he had visited his assigned facility fifteen times.

Continuing in the spirit of full disclosure, I should mention my realization if I were ever to end up in a nursing home, the only thing that would cheer me up would be a visit from a big, friendly dog. I nonetheless entered the Gateway with the prejudices characteristic of most human beings and entirely foreign to dogs. First fear: The place would smell of urine. It didn't, but if it had, Rowdy would have considered the stench a fabulous bonus. Second fear: Everyone would have Alzheimer's, and ten seconds after we'd left, no one would remember we'd been there. Some people did have Alzheimer's. One was a woman named Nancy, whose body had reached a state of advanced shrinkage in which her weight in pounds equaled her age in years: ninety-three. As I learned only after our first visit to her, the Gateway staff had never before heard her utter more than a word or two. I had to be told that Nancy didn't usually speak. The first time I led Rowdy toward her wheelchair and asked whether she liked dogs, she ignored me, but croaked to him, "Beautiful! Beautiful dog! Come! Come here, beautiful dog!" Her hands were like a bird's feet. She perched one on top of Rowdy's head. He licked her face. She giggled like a child. "I love him," she said to me. "I love him."

Nancy's hearing was poor. I'd been warned to speak loudly. "I love him, too," I bellowed awkwardly. "His name is Rowdy."

On our second visit, with no prompting, Nancy called out Rowdy's name and repeated it over and over: "Rowdy. Rowdy. I love him. I love him. Rowdy. Rowdy." Licking her hands and face, Rowdy reminded me of a burly wolf tending to an emaciated feral child. Nancy suddenly looked away from Rowdy and directly at me. Her eyes were a faded hazel. She had more wrinkles than she did actual face. ''God's creature,'' she said.

''Yes,'' I agreed.

Entering the Gateway for our regular Friday morning visit, Rowdy and I always found a group of five or six sociable women in the lobby, their wheelchairs arranged in a welcoming half circle across from the elevators and next to the big dining hall. As soon as I'd signed in, pinned on my volunteer's badge, and hung my parka in a closet rather alarmingly marked OXYGEN, I'd take Rowdy to the lobby, where the women made a fuss over him and helped me to train him to offer his paw gently and never to bat at people. The elderly, I'd been advised, have thin, fragile skin. On our first few visits, Rowdy himself proved more thin-skinned than I'd expected. He whined a few times and stayed so close to my left side that an obedience judge would have faulted him for crowding. Rowdy had been around wheelchairs before, but never so many as he encountered at the Gateway. And although he was used to the chaos of dog shows, the newness of everything at the nursing home taxed him.

Leaving the first floor, we took the elevator to the third. Near the nursing station, we always found a beautifully groomed woman who owned an enviable wardrobe of handsome business suits, silk blouses, and flower-patterned scarves. She never spoke a word to me. It took me a couple of visits to realize that although she didn't want a big dog anywhere near her, she enjoyed looking at Rowdy from a distance of two or three yards. There was a tidy brown-skinned man named Gus whose wheelchair was always stationed in the TV room on the third floor. Gus liked to tell me about the German shepherd dogs he'd had. On every visit, he told me about his shepherds in the same words he'd used the last time I'd been there. Rowdy didn't lick Gus's face. Gus wouldn't have liked it. "Shake!" Gus would demand. Rowdy would offer his paw, and he and Gus would exchange a dignified greeting. Then Gus would look back at the television screen, and Rowdy and I would move on, pausing in the hallways and stopping here and there in people's rooms. In the corridors and elevators, the staff of the Gateway and people who lived there commented on Rowdy. Again and again, people reached out to touch him. There was an almost religious fervency about that need to lay a hand on him. I imagined the Gateway as a deviant yet orthodox temple and Rowdy as a canine Torah.

Big, vibrant, and boundlessly affectionate though Rowdy is, there was never enough of him to go round. To avoid overburdening Rowdy, I'd been ordered to limit my first visit to twenty-five minutes and to lengthen our stays gradually. In thirty minutes, we could have given one minute each to thirty people, five minutes each to six people, a rich fifteen minutes to two. No one got enough. No one except Althea Battlefield, who wasn't even wild about dogs.

The plastic plaque on the wall outside Althea's room on the fifth and top floor of the Gateway displayed two names: A. BATTLEFIELD and H. MUSGRAVE. Althea's roommate, Helen, was a sprightly little woman who took frequent advantage of the numerous events listed in the Gateway's monthly calendar and posted on the little kiosk in the first-floor lobby. I never found Helen napping on her bed. Rather, when she wasn't having her hair done or attending a sing-along, a coffee hour, or an arts and crafts class, she bustled around rearranging the greeting cards, snapshots, and photocopied notices pinned to her cork bulletin board. I have never understood how Helen managed to keep track of the Gateway's elaborate schedule of events. Her delight in the family photographs and cards on her bulletin board sprang in part from the perpetual novelty they held for her. The identities of the pleasant-looking people in the pictures were a mystery to her; she puzzled over the handwritten messages and signatures on the cards. The first time Rowdy and I entered Helen and Althea's room, Helen, whose bed was the one near the door, sprang from her armchair, gave an enthusiastic cry, and darted around exclaiming, "A beauty! Isn't he big! Isn't he big!"

Rowdy preened. I smiled. "You like dogs?" Although the inquiry was clearly unnecessary, I'd been trained to ask.

Helen abruptly stopped dashing and chattering to concentrate on mulling over my question. She acted more or less the way I would if someone asked me whether I liked caducei. First, I'd have to remember what they were. Then I'd have to decide whether I had any feelings about them one way or the other.

From a wheelchair positioned to give a good view out the big plate-glass window, a high-pitched, authoritative voice decreed, "Yes, but she prefers cats."

"I prefer . . ." Helen began unhappily.

"You like dogs, but you prefer cats," the voice informed her.

Although the woman by the window was seated, it was immediately clear that she was the tallest person I'd seen at the Gateway, taller than any of the men, indeed one of the longest women I'd ever encountered anywhere. Her hands were so large that in the days when she'd needed outdoor clothing, before she'd entered the Gateway, she must have had to buy men's gloves. I wondered what she'd done about hats. Her arms were tremendously long, and instead of resting her feet on the wheelchair, she stretched her legs way out in front to plant the soles of her orthopedic shoes flat on the floor. Her hair was short, white, curly, and so thin that her entire scalp was visible, as was the bone structure of her face. The skin on her forehead and cheeks had passed beyond what must have been a phase of lines and crinkles to a state of smooth translucency. Fine creases, however, surrounded blue eyes so pale that they were almost white, and folds of loose skin drooped from her elongated neck.

Althea introduced herself. Early that morning, I'd tried to think of some way to avoid using only the first names of the people I'd meet. When, as part of a group of new volunteers, I'd trailed after an experienced therapy-dog handler and her Portuguese water dog on an orientation session at another nursing home, I'd felt uncomfortable with the practice. People in nursing homes were not schoolchildren; they had grown up in a long-gone era of formality; I wanted to follow the old rules. I couldn't. For one thing, I didn't always know what people's last names or titles were. For another, I didn't want to insult the staff of the Gateway by arrogantly diverging from the universal custom. And was I to be Ms. Winter instead of Holly? After only a few minutes, though, I felt okay about using first names, which were, after all, better than none. Furthermore, as I reminded myself, everyone in the world of dogs went by first names, and plenty of the people I trained and showed with were at least as old as the people at the Gateway.

"I'm Holly," I said. "And this is Rowdy. Do you like dogs?"

Althea Battlefield thumped the padded arm of her wheelchair with an immense, bony hand. "Bring him right up here next to me, or I won't be able to see him. Closer!" Her hand groped. I used a puppy-size dog cookie to lure Rowdy into position.

"He *is* a big dog, isn't he?" Althea said. "The other one that visits here is pint size. It's what's called a bichon frise." She didn't anglicize the pronunciation, but produced a somewhat self-conscious nasal and a French *r* that would have left me with a sore throat.

I was tempted to ask Althea whether she'd ever owned a dog, but felt uneasy about raising the topic. Although I'd rapidly abandoned my resolution to shun first names, I was determined never to ask a question I'd heard from a new and well-meaning volunteer on my orientation visit: *Did you have a dog?* she'd inquired of someone. I'd cringed at the unspoken preface to the question. Indeed, *Back when you had a life, did you have a dog?*

Then, turning her attention from Rowdy to me, Althea referred to the Sacred Writings. As I've mentioned, I misunderstood her. She corrected me by pointing to a long row of hardcover books that sat on the windowsill. Arrayed in front of the volumes was a collection of objects that reminded me of the knickknacks sold at dog shows. Instead of depicting terriers, pointers, or spaniels, however, Althea's figurines showed a pipe-smoking man who wore an Inverness cape and a deer-stalker hat.

"Oh," I said stupidly, "do you like Sherlock Holmes?"

Every once in a while, of course, some dope asks *me* whether I like dogs.

Chapter Two

DURING JANUARY AND EARLY February, as Rowdy and I continued to make our weekly visits to the Gateway, I began to read the Sherlock Holmes stories, some for the first time, others, like *The Hound of the Baskervilles* and "The Red-headed League," for the second, third, or fourth. Let me make this plain, however: Just as a vast, woofy gulf separates the real dog person from the person who really and merely enjoys dogs, so, too, a great gaslit chasm stretches between the true Sherlockian and the person like me who truly and merely enjoys Sherlock Holmes. I, for example, not only own two Alaskan malamutes, Rowdy and Kimi, but am a card-carrying member of the Dog Writers Association of America. Literally! I have a card. I carry it. It identifies me as a member of the press, a bit of an exaggeration, I always think—*Dog's Life* magazine isn't exactly *The New York Times*—but then again I own a D.W.A.A. baseball cap that I'm supposed to wear when I cover dog shows, and how many *Times* correspondents can boast the equivalent? More to the point, when other dog people talk about fiddle fronts, woollies, sunken croups, good crowns, three-point majors, and the leathers of P.B.G.V.'s, I know exactly what's being said because everyone's speaking my language.

Feeling left out? If so, you know just how I felt on the Friday morning in mid-February when I led Rowdy into Althea's room at the Gateway and overheard the animated conversation she was holding with Robert MacPherson and Hugh Searles. I caught English words and phrases, sometimes whole sentences, yet entirely failed to grasp either the gist or the particulars. I teeter-tottered on the non-Sherlockian side of the gaslit chasm. For the sake of anyone who might actually be able to understand what Althea, Hugh, and Robert were chuckling and exclaiming about, I wish I'd had a tape recorder along, but I didn't. What I do remember made no sense to me. The word *callosities* stands out in my mind, as does a reference to a Crown Derby tea set, a mention of the supply of game for London, an evidently witty allusion to coals of fire, what sounded like an arch question from Althea about coins of Charles the First, and, from Robert, a riposte, I think, concerning, I swear, the extirpation of fish. At that point, everyone but me burst out laughing, and Hugh remarked that I must think they were discussing the fertility of oysters.

"Fecundity!" snapped Robert. *"Fecundity! Not fertility!"*

Callosities. Teapots. Oysters. I figured out what they were talking about only when the taller of the two men, Robert, I later learned, glanced over at Helen Musgrave's bulletin board and in a pleasant, even affectionate, tone made a passing remark about a ritual.

Feeling like the slow kid in the class who has for once got the right answer, I exclaimed, " 'The Musgrave Ritual'!" The Holmes story, which I'd just read, culminated in the discovery of a long-dead body and—oh, yes!—coins of Charles the First.

Althea couldn't see Rowdy unless he was right next to her, but she knew my voice. In a manner I now recognize as Watsonian, instead of telling Rowdy to go say hi, I said, "Althea, you have visitors. If we're intruding—"

"Intelligent company is never an intrusion," Althea scolded.

Naturally, I thought she meant my idea of intelligent company, namely, the unrivaled companionship of an Alaskan malamute. Rowdy knew better. He sank to the floor and peacefully rested his head on his big snowshoe paws. With the lobby ladies, he was a performer. Gus needed a living link to the dogs he'd once loved; Rowdy was his animate time machine. Nancy's need was raw and primitive: She suffered from the depletion of life itself. Rowdy was her donor, like a blood donor, really, but a transfuser of vitality that you could almost see and touch as it shot from him to her and restored, however briefly, her powers of speech and reason. Althea liked dogs. But what she really loved was intelligent human companionship, by which she meant, of course, a conversation with someone who would talk about Sherlock Holmes.

"This is Rowdy," I told Althea's two guests. "I'm Holly. But meet Rowdy, and you've met me. A case of identity, so to speak." That's a title from the Canon: "A Case of Identity." I can be a worse show-off than Rowdy.

Althea apologized and went on to make amends. She claimed to have forgotten my last name. It seemed to me that she'd never heard it. When I supplied my full name, Holly Winter, Althea, Robert, and Hugh exchanged little smirks, and Althea offered what was to me the bewildering assurance that there was nothing vitriolic about me. Kitty Winter, I later found out, was a nasty character, a vitriol-thrower who appeared in ''The Illustrious Client.'' By the time I happened on Kitty, I was taking the Holmes stories personally and was far from pleased to find a violent Miss Winter with what had by then proved to be a weirdly prophetic first name. But I have leaped ahead. At the time, I was mystified. Robert MacPherson and Hugh Searles, Althea went on to say, were two of her oldest and dearest friends. Neither man, I thought, was as old as Althea. Both were certainly more than seventy, probably more than eighty, but I couldn't guess their ages more precisely than that. Like active people I knew in dogs, Hugh and Robert looked vigorous and shared a liveliness that made age irrelevant. Robert, a thin, craggy, white-haired man at least as tall as Althea, looked so much like pictures I'd seen of Highland Scots that I wondered whether I hadn't, in fact, seen him wearing a kilt and playing the bagpipes at one of those Celtic music concerts that are popular in Cambridge. It was even possible that I'd noticed him ambling through Harvard Square in traditional Scottish garb. Not that a six-foot, knobby-kneed man in a skirt really stands out in the Square, which always reminds me of an eccentric dog show with heavy competition for Weirdest of Breed: kids with top-knots like the crests of exotic birds, blond-haired women in saris who've managed to pierce their noses, but haven't mastered the Indian technique of applying makeup and consequently look as if they have oozing wounds on their foreheads. I later learned that I was right about Robert MacPherson, except that he didn't parade around the Square in his kilt, but reserved it for the Robert Burns Festival, and didn't play the bagpipes, but carried the haggis, which, I should mention, is not a musical instrument, but a sheep's stomach stuffed with oatmeal and offal. It's eaten only in Scotland, where people apparently like it, and in certain rarefied circles in Cambridge, Massachusetts, where everyone hates the taste of the stuff but eats up the image.

As Robert was taking Althea to task for calling herself old and for referring to Hugh and to him as old friends, Hugh was staring at Rowdy, who had rolled onto his back on the linoleum and was waving his immense paws in the air. I translated: "He's hoping someone will scratch his chest. There's no obligation."

Hugh was a good six inches shorter than Althea or Robert, and attractively burly in the manner of people who look as if they're savoring the pleasure of the previous meal while happily pondering the delights of the next. He had yellowish hair, bright blue eyes, and a dapper mustache, which I suspected he'd grown forty years earlier in an effort to add maturity to his round baby face. In contrast to Robert, who wore a dark three-piece suit, Hugh was dressed in khakis, a plaid flannel shirt, and a tan cardigan sweater. He struck me as a man who probably liked to tinker with mechanical objects. What accounted for his staring was, I suspected, curiosity about what made Rowdy work. When I later learned that Robert had gone to Harvard and Hugh to M.I.T., I was not surprised.

"Now," said Hugh, tentatively fingering the white hair on Rowdy's tummy, "would this be an Alaskan malamute?"

"He would be," I said. "In fact, he is."

Robert lightly cleared his throat. Rising, he reached over the Sherlock Holmes figurines and removed one of the volumes that rested on the windowsill beside Althea. In making my way through the Gateway, I had noticed that almost no one was ever reading and that books were almost completely absent from windowsills, shelves, and other places where people displayed their belongings. Here in Cambridge! Book City, U.S.A.! Althea, in contrast, kept a miniature library that included several editions of the Sacred Writings. Her most prized possessions, which she stored in her nightstand, were what looked to me like nothing to brag about, just a pair of undersize paperbacks, although I'll concede that the little books were bound in leather and bore Althea's name stamped in gold. She also had a small collection of books about Holmes, Watson, and Sir Arthur Conan Doyle. In fact, she'd honored me by letting me borrow one; she'd wanted me to read a charming tongue-in-cheek essay by Rex Stout called "Watson Was a Woman." Anyway, when Robert selected the same one-volume Doubleday edition of the complete works that I owned myself, I felt terrible. I had no excuse. Althea had tried to introduce me to the science of deduction. But only now, as Robert picked up the book, removed a bookmark, and resettled himself in his chair, did I realize that Althea, the one person at the Gateway who lived amid books, had such poor eyesight that she was completely unable to read. I should have read to her. I should have scurried around finding books on tape, books, of course, about Sherlock Holmes. When I later offered to do just that, Althea refused. Robert and Hugh read to her, she explained. She had no desire to hear the Canon from the lips of others.

I got Rowdy to his feet and excused myself.

As we left, Robert began to read. *"Holmes laid his hand upon my arm,"* he began.

Hugh interrupted in a cheerful effort to continue from memory. *"If my companion would undertake it, there is no man—"*

"No!" Robert bellowed. "No, no, no! *My friend, my friend, my friend!*"

"My apologies," said Hugh.

Althea's eyes were closed. She wore a gentle smile of contentment. The exchange between Hugh and Robert, I realized, must be as familiar to her as the Canon itself.

Mollified, Robert resumed where he had left off. *"If my friend would undertake it, there is no man who is better worth having at your side when you are in a tight place. No one can say so more confidently than I."*

Robert must simply have picked up where he'd left off. Even so, it now seems to me that the passage from *The Hound of the Baskervilles* was a fitting portion of scripture for my introduction to Robert and Hugh. Among Sherlockians, the relationship between Holmes and Watson is known as "The Friendship."

Chapter Three

YOU LIVE IN CAMBRIDGE," Robert informed me, "but you did not grow up here and did not go to Harvard. You have ties to Maine. You are a dog writer. You own two Alaskan malamutes. They are your only pets. When you acquired Rowdy, he was no longer a puppy."

Robert was not, I might mention, reading my palm, which was wrapped around a coffee mug. It was the Wednesday after I'd first met Hugh and Robert. In the morning I'd finished my column for *Dog's Life,* and in the afternoon I'd gone to Harvard Square to celebrate in a typically Cantabrigian fashion, meaning that I had gone out to splurge on books. In other places, high living is French wine, marc de Bourgogne, cocaine. Here, it's hardcovers. When I ran into Robert and Hugh, I was buying paperbacks. Cambridge low life. Anyway, Althea's friends had invited me for coffee, and we were now sitting in a booth in one of those real-world coffee shops where you don't have to specify the country the beans were grown in and how long they were roasted.

"You are a linguist," I told Robert. "Your real

name is Henry Higgins. When you've finished with me, I'll be able to hold my own in the senior common rooms, and no one will ever guess that I used to peddle flowers on the streets of Portland.''

Hugh smiled. ''Robert makes a study of vowels.''

Robert nodded.

''Are you actually a linguist?'' I asked.

''Robert retired from Widener a number of years ago,'' Hugh replied, without saying whether Robert had been one of Harvard's head librarians or had just checked books in and out. ''The deduction of occupation is one of his pastimes.''

Althea later told me that Robert had been a fairly senior librarian who'd overseen a number of special collections. Hugh, she insisted, had pursued an occupation so technical that she'd never understood what it was. The friendship between the men had begun as a family connection: Their wives had been sisters. Robert's had died young and childless. Hugh, widowed ten years ago, had three children who worked in the Silicon Valley and took no interest in Sherlock Holmes, to whom Robert had originally introduced his brother-in-law.

''You met Rowdy,'' I told them, ''and Althea has heard about my other malamute, Kimi. As a matter of fact, I don't have any other animals, but I could. Plenty of people have cats and dogs, even cats and malamutes.''

''As I deduced,'' Robert responded, ''you did not raise Rowdy yourself. He is a malamute. Therefore, despite his gentleness with people—''

Hugh interrupted. ''Including, of course, Althea.''

''He is a predator,'' Robert resumed. ''Had he been brought up with cats—''

"And just how did you deduce that I did not raise Rowdy myself?"

With a smug little smile, Robert said, "Canine nomenclature merits a small monograph. The name 'Rowdy' is of an era that predates yours, my dear. Like 'Rex,' it bespeaks the twenties and thirties."

"Rowdy," I said, "is a traditional malamute name. Rowdy of Nome was the first registered Alaskan malamute." I refused to give Robert the satisfaction of admitting, first, that Rowdy of Nome had, indeed, been born in about 1928 and registered in 1935 and, second, that my Rowdy had been given his call name by a man of Robert and Hugh's generation. "You're right about the cats," I admitted. "Rowdy wasn't raised with them. Neither was my other dog, Kimi. It would be difficult for me to get a cat, but it could be done. And, okay, if I had a cat, you'd see cat hair on me, maybe, but for all you know, I could have a tank of fish. An iguana. A ferret! They've just become legal in Massachusetts and—"

"Possibly," conceded Robert with a smile. "As practiced by those such as ourselves, the science is not exact. Watson, for example, was notably unsuccessful in applying the Methods." Really, you could hear the capital letter.

I tried to remember whether I'd told Althea that Rowdy and Kimi were my only animals. Althea's roommate, Helen Musgrave, preferred cats to dogs. If I'd told Helen that I didn't have a cat, Althea would have overheard. "But I've been *thinking* a lot about a cat," I said, as if proving to Hugh and Robert that my mind, at least, was unreadable. "And I don't necessarily live in Cambridge. I could live on Beacon Hill or in Allston, Brighton, Somerville, Belmont, Brookline—"

"Denim jeans," Hugh countered. "Hiking boots. No trace of cosmetics on the face. Hair not recently trimmed. In combination with your choice of reading material? We couldn't help noticing. Indeed, we make every effort to do so."

"Everyone reads Cynthia Heimel," I said defensively. "She's the funniest woman in America."

"Unmanicured nails," Hugh responded. "Your Navajo ring."

"I didn't buy the ring. It was a present." From Steve Delaney. Steve is my vet. My lover. He lives in Cambridge, too. Come to think of it, he'd bought the turquoise ring in the Square.

Hugh, undaunted, said, "When we lamented the demise of Elsie's, you agreed."

Hugh looked so pleased with himself that I didn't bother to argue. Elsie's was a lunch place in the Square that made world-famous roast beef sandwiches. Anyone anywhere could have agreed that the closing of Elsie's was a loss to the Square. "You looked me up in the phone book," I charged. "And just because I live in Cambridge, it doesn't necessarily mean that I'm a writer," I said mendaciously. Hah! It's true that not everyone in Cambridge is a *published* writer. My next-door neighbor Kevin Dennehy, for instance, is a Cambridge cop, and he's never published anything. Being not just any cop, however, but a *Cambridge* cop, Kevin is convinced that there's a book to be written about his experiences on the force. Kevin is probably right. He just hasn't gotten around to putting the words on paper yet. "And not everyone who owns dogs writes about them," I pointed out. "Am I covered with ink and hair?"

With a languid Holmesian sigh, Robert pointed out that I was free in the daytime and walked around with a steno pad tucked in the outside pocket of my shoulder bag. "You are Holly, not Dr. Winter, not Professor Winter," he said. "Cambridge being what it is, had you a title, you would use it. Therefore, you are not an academic. You own an exceptionally well-trained dog of a notoriously difficult breed."

"Malamutes are not difficult. They're interesting."

"On Rowdy's collar," Robert continued, "Hugh observed an extraordinary number of tags. The average dog wears, perhaps, two: a dog license and a rabies tag."

"And an ID tag with the owner's address," I added, without admitting that Rowdy wore so many tags that I could hardly remember what they were: license, rabies, my name and address, his therapy dog tag, one proclaiming him a Canine Good Citizen, one from the National Dog Registry giving the location of his ID tattoo, and, oh, yes, a Saint Francis of Assisi medal I'd bought in desperation during one of the low points in our obedience career. "But I get the point."

"The collar, Hugh reports, is of fine workmanship. Yet your car, which we noticed in the parking lot on our way into that institution, before we encountered you, is old. It stood out. Bumper stickers. Cages."

I am the first to complain about the battered state of my ancient Bronco. I prefer to be the first. And the only. Robert's mother, I thought, should have taught him not to make personal remarks. Hugh's mother, too. Never mind Sherlock Holmes's.

"Crates," I corrected.

"Crates?" Hugh inquired.

"Dog people don't say 'cages.' We say 'crates.' And Maine was easy. You saw the bumper sticker. MAINE: THE WAY LIFE SHOULD BE."

"Elementary," said Robert, without a trace of self-consciousness.

"Elementary," I repeated. I might mention now, as I didn't then, that as I'd been leaving the Gateway on Friday, I'd applied my own observational skills and deductive powers. Parked two cars away from mine had been an ancient Volvo sedan in that gray-matter color favored by intellectuals determined to pass off their vehicles as mobile human brains. Without even pulling out my Sherlock Holmes magnifying glass or taking samples of the dirt embedded in the tire treads, I'd brilliantly deduced that it belonged to Robert or Hugh. It bore a single, if rather telling, bumper sticker that read THE GAME IS AFOOT! Speaking of games, two can play. Or three. "You," I said to Robert, "are intimately acquainted with libraries. Once you generated this hypothesis that I was a writer, you checked an index of periodicals. Maybe you even bought a copy of *Dog's Life.*"

With a jarring mixture of scorn and pride, Robert contradicted me by reporting that Hugh surfed the Web.

"So you're not clairvoyant after all," I teased.

"A.C.D. to the contrary," Hugh replied.

A.C.D.? To the contrary? I suppressed the urge to lapse into baffling jargon of my own. *J.H., C.D., O.F.A.!* I wanted to reply. Unfortunately, I could think of no way to turn the conversation to Junior Hunter and Companion Dog titles or to squeeze in a cryptic reference to the Orthopedic Foundation for Animals. My annoyance must have shown on my face. Its source was, as I've just said, natural resentment at being addressed in a language I couldn't follow, as opposed to justifiable indignation at finding myself the target of unwelcome snooping. Robert, however, cleared his throat and said, "We keep a close eye on Althea."

Hugh expanded. ''We prefer to know who her friends are.''

Was Althea so tremendously wealthy that gestures of apparent friendship toward her required scrutiny? Had the men suspected me of being an innovative con artist who'd hit on the scheme of identifying potential marks by cruising nursing homes with a canine confederate disguised as a therapy dog? I must have looked puzzled. In apparent response, Robert said, ''Althea is a woman of extraordinary wit.''

''And quickness,'' Hugh chimed in.

''Resolution,'' added Robert.

''In brief,'' said Hugh, ''she eclipses the whole of her sex.''

Robert glared at him. *''Eclipses and predominates.''*

I finally caught on. The adventure was ''A Scandal in Bohemia.'' The reference was to Irene Adler, *the* woman in the Great Detective's life. Not yet knowing about the late sister-wives, I said gently, ''Althea is *the* woman.''

Robert, of course, corrected me. But not about the wives. ''Is *always the* woman,'' he said.

Chapter Four

ALTHEA BATTLEFIELD'S SISTER, CECI, was ten inches shorter than Althea and her junior by ten years. It took me a minute to realize, though, that the principal difference between the sisters was that Ceci had a streak of foolishness. What briefly fooled me was that Ceci made a fool of herself over Rowdy, who is always glad to make a fool of himself over anyone. I must add, however, that fool that I am over Rowdy, I took a liking to Ceci that endured even after it slowly dawned on me that she'd pulled a fast one and that Althea knew she'd done so.

It was the Sunday after Hugh, Robert, and I had had coffee in the Square. On Friday, Rowdy and I had paid our regular visit to the Gateway. Helen had been having her hair done, Robert and Hugh hadn't been there, and Althea had had a fine time instructing me about engineers' thumbs, devils' feet, Sussex vampires, and miscellaneous other bits of Sherlockian trivia. In an oblique and tactful way, I'd tried to satisfy my curiosity about whether Hugh or Robert had ever been *the* man in her life, as she was *the* woman in theirs, and if so, which one,

Hugh or Robert, but I got nowhere, mainly because such bothersome impediments as discretion and good taste held me back from suggesting that the late Mr. Battlefield, whoever he'd been, had been other than *the* man. All I learned about Mr. Battlefield was that Althea had married him just after she'd graduated from Radcliffe and that he'd soon died of meningitis. Althea had then begun her career as an English teacher at the Avon Hill School, where she'd continued to teach even after boys had been admitted and from which she'd retired twenty-five years ago. Robert and Hugh, she told me, were fellow members of the Red-headed League of Boston, not to be confused with any of the other Red-headed Leagues in other cities or any of the three other Sherlockian organizations in Greater Boston, and certainly not to be confused with the Baker Street Irregulars. The B.S.I., I learned, was the elite, by-invitation-only society to which Althea and Robert belonged and Hugh did not. She herself was a recent inductee—the B.S.I. had been closed to women until 1991—but Hugh had been eligible for eons, and was sensitive about his exclusion.

"Politics!" Althea exclaimed.

"It's the same way in dogs," I told her.

"It's the same way everywhere," Althea said. "And what does a title mean, after all?"

"Nothing," said I, stroking the head of my Ch., C.D.X., C.G.C., T.T., soon-to-be Rx.D. companion. That's breed champion, Companion Dog Excellent, Canine Good Citizen, Temperament Tested, soon-to-be Therapy Dog, who'd also have titles from Canada, Bermuda, and elsewhere if I could afford to travel. "But what do, uh, titles . . . ?"

"B.S.I.," Althea replied. "I am a B.S.I. Robert is a B.S.I. Hugh is not." I assumed that he'd flunked a trivia test by misquoting the Canon, but to my surprise, Althea said, "And all because Hugh is an Oxford man."

As it turned out, Althea didn't mean that Hugh had gone to Oxford. As I've said, he went to M.I.T. Rather, one of the classic Problems in Sherlockian scholarship, as Althea explained to me, was a controversy about whether Sherlock Holmes's time at university, as she phrased it, had been spent at Oxford or Cambridge. Hugh's allegiance to the Oxford side of the debate was, in itself, perfectly respectable; the topic was one on which aficionados agreed to disagree. As quite a young man, Hugh, however, in a burst of excess loyalty to the Oxford side, had created a violent scene that culminated when, in the midst of a big convention of fellow Holmesians, he had punched an argumentative Cantabrigian in the jaw and sent the poor man to the hospital. The bystanders, I suspected, had been outraged at the crassly non-Sherlockian method of attack. It seemed to me that if Hugh had had the sense to whack his foe with the Master's favorite weapon, a loaded hunting crop, he'd be a B.S.I. today.

Anyway, after making our regular Friday visit, Rowdy and I returned only two days later not only because the more we visited, the sooner he got his title, but because . . . Well, I'm sure there was some less frivolous, preferably more altruistic, reason. Oh, yes. Except that it wasn't exactly altruistic. I'll have to leap ahead again here, but bear with me, because the whole business about Steve Delaney, and Gloria and Scott, honestly does have to do with the story. Steve Delaney, as I've mentioned in passing, is my lover and Rowdy and Kimi's vet, not that I get a substantial discount, in case you wondered, but he's both, although for entirely separate reasons. Until recently, I'd had no cause at all for complaint about him in either capacity, meaning that if it hadn't been for the stink Gloria and Scott were kicking up, Steve and I would have spent a torrid late-winter afternoon in bed, and then I'd have talked him into making himself professionally useful by squirting Intratrak II up the dogs' noses or at least trimming their nails. Even now, on the Sunday when I met Ceci, I still thought Steve was the best vet I'd ever used, and I knew that if a veterinary crisis befell Rowdy or Kimi, he'd rouse himself from his silent stoicism to tend to one of my dogs. As it was, he remained in the emotional co-coon he'd spun around himself in response to what I correctly insisted was outrageous harassment.

When I pressed the matter, he pointed out through locked jaws that I, too, received occasional letters of complaint. Our situations were comparable, Steve stated flatly; consumer dissatisfaction was an inevitable hazard of becoming a vet or a writer. As I told him, our situations weren't comparable at all. Yes, of course there were readers who didn't like my column or took objection to articles I published, but Gloria was plaguing him with persistent phone calls, letters, and E-mail. Further-more, she was making slanderous public accusations of malpractice. In contrast, the typical letter of complaint from one of my readers did nothing more than politely chastise me for slighting the Samoyed, the otterhound, the Gordon setter, or some other splendid breed I hadn't mentioned lately. Once in a while, *Dog's Life* heard from someone who gleefully pounced on my mistakes: "In her article on the Transylvanian Bludhund in the June issue, Holly Winter makes the egregious error of stating that this noble breed originated in Transylvania. Wrong! Had Miss Winter researched her subject in a professional manner by consulting the Transylvanian Bludhund Club of America, she would soon have been set straight!" On rare occasions, my editor got the bizarre complaint that my column in particular and the magazine as a whole had entirely too much to say about dogs. In other words, my readers' grievances were perfectly justified.

Gloria and Scott, however, blamed Steve for ruining their wonderful show dog and excellent brood bitch when, in fact, he'd saved her life. Lest I trigger a volley of the kinds of breed-loyal complaints I've just described, I'll leave Gigi's breed unspecified, but I will tell you that Gigi was short for Gloria, and I'll refrain from commenting on the kind of woman who names a bitch after herself. Anyway, two years earlier, Gigi began to have seizures, and Steve advised Scott and Gloria to spay her. They not only refused, but went ahead and bred her not just once but twice. When she developed pyometra, they finally agreed. Pyometra is a serious uterine disorder of bitches that begins as a hormonal problem and turns into a bacterial infection. Spaying is standard practice for an animal with seizures, and it's the treatment of choice for a bitch with pyometra. Indeed, Scott and Gloria thanked Steve for saving Gigi. Now, four months later, they were claiming that Gigi's surgery had been unnecessary. They didn't just blame Steve in private: They also did it in public, outside the show ring, in the grooming areas, wherever dog people gathered. If you show your dogs, you'll probably recognize Scott and Gloria.

And how did Steve respond to Gloria and Scott? Did he copy their tactics and stand around at shows to announce out loud that they'd knowingly bred a bitch with seizures? That out of greed and laziness they'd sold Gigi's puppies at six weeks instead of waiting until eight weeks? He did not. He did nothing except spend all his free time holed up in his apartment with his dogs. Furthermore, he forbade me to violate his clients' confidentiality by so much as whispering a discreet word about Gloria, Scott, or Gigi to anyone in dogs.

What really got to Steve, I must mention, was something I haven't touched on yet. Steve would have welcomed a second, third, or fourth opinion, which is to say, the opinion of a second, third, or fourth veterinarian. So, what got to Steve wasn't that Gloria and Scott had taken Gigi to someone else. No, what ate at him was that the second opinion they'd sought, accepted, and used to attack his reputation was the pronouncement of an animal psychic who hadn't even seen Gigi, if you can believe it, but had studied a photograph and, on the basis of telepathic communication, deemed the spaying unnecessary.

So I spent Sunday afternoon at the Gateway instead of with Steve Delaney, who sought only the company of his dogs. As I began to report, just after Rowdy and I entered Althea's room, her sister, Ceci Love, swept in and pulled a fast one by falling all over Rowdy while excluding and ignoring Althea. Thus she filched both her sister's therapy dog *and* the attention of someone who'd talk to her sister about Sherlock Holmes. How was Rowdy to know? As usual, we'd entertained the lobby ladies, taken the elevator, visited people, and ended up on the fifth floor. Everywhere we'd gone, I'd encouraged Rowdy to return greetings, to play up to everyone who liked dogs, to bless everyone with his great gift for making every single person feel loved and special. If some people acted a little odd? If a man we hadn't met before grabbed Rowdy's ear and had to be helped to let go? If Nancy cried out at the sight of Rowdy and wailed, ''Rowdy, Rowdy, I love him! I love him!'' Becoming a therapy dog meant learning to accept ear grabbing, tail pulling, hugs, shrieks, and moans as well as gentle pats, sweet talk, and requests to give his paw. So when Ceci screamed at the sight of Rowdy, flung her arms in the air, dove at him, and threw herself around his neck, how was he to know that he'd been recruited to participate in theft? How was I?

Rising to her feet and catching her breath, Ceci cried, "Isn't he the most beautiful thing you've ever seen? Isn't he wonderful? Isn't he a gorgeous big boy? What a handsome dog!" She paused. "Ceci Love. Althea's sister. Call me Ceci. Love is such a, well, it's such a *name,* isn't it?" Without waiting for me to introduce myself or Rowdy, she gushed, "Why, he looks like a show dog! Is he a show dog?" Before I could answer, she began to tell me about every dog she'd ever owned, most of which had been Newfoundlands. I now understand that although Ceci seemed lost in the past, she remained sufficiently oriented to the here-and-now to plant herself between Althea and me, thus blocking my route to her sister. "Kitty was a jewel, a gem, a perfect, perfect dog, our only Landseer, that's black and white, you know, all the others were black, never white, white is a Great Pyrenees, lovely breed, but give me a Newfie any day, and she never would sleep anywhere except right at the foot of my bed, if I had to get up in the night to go, well, tinkle, or get a little snack, she'd follow right along with me, and then when I crawled back into bed, she'd lie right down there at the foot and . . ."

You get the idea. I tuned out the babble. Instead, I studied the woman, who, on close examination, looked something like a diminutive version of a younger Althea, at least if Althea had slaved over her appearance. Ceci's face showed Althea's striking bone structure, but unlike Althea, Ceci wore several different shades of brown and beige eye shadow, dark mascara, eyebrow pencil, blush, and pearly pink-beige lipstick, as well as foundation and, for all I know, six or eight other facial cosmetics as well. Her champagne hair, a little shorter than shoulder length, was skillfully styled to sweep back from her face. She was dressed in lots of apricot-beige jersey—a skirt, a loose top, a matching jacket—and wore leather pumps, pearl earrings, a pearl necklace, and a bright silk scarf with a pattern of blue cornflowers that matched her eyes. I didn't have to be Sherlock Holmes to realize that Ceci was a woman dedicated to looking good. What I did not sense about her was vanity. On the contrary, I had the impression that the careful hair, the artful makeup, the attractive, flattering clothes and jewelry were meant for other people and, specifically, meant to make other people *happy*. I sensed in Ceci a little girl who had learned that the way to please people was to be good and that being good meant looking pretty.

Ceci's monologue continued. "Ah, Newfs, my husband was mad about them, too. Simon, now, Simon passed on two years ago, and for the first year, the first eighteen months, it was a terrible struggle to keep going alone, to live in that house all by myself, to rely on myself, not that I can't manage the practical details of life, I manage very capably, but there seemed to be no point whatsoever to going on at all, and of course, I missed Althea's company dreadfully. We used to go to Symphony and out to lunch, didn't we, Althea? We had lovely times together. And then, of course, everything happened all at once, one loss after another, Althea having to be moved here—"

"A fate worse than death," muttered Althea. Her wry smile made it clear that she was commenting on her sister's tactlessness rather than on her own move to the Gateway.

Oblivious to Althea's remark, Ceci went on. "And not a week later, my Simon died." Here I heard deep, genuine grief. When she said *Simon,* she prolonged the syllables. The name alone almost sounded like a question. Her voice broke.

Sympathizing with the ill-timed death of her husband, I said, "I'm sorry."

"Coal-black, he was," Ceci replied, "not a white hair in his coat, only five years old."

Althea, whose hearing was sharp, let forth a peal of triumphant laughter. "Ceci, Holly thought you meant your husband!"

"Ellis?" Ceci inquired. "Why would she think I meant Ellis? I wasn't talking about Ellis, was I?"

"No, dear," Althea assured her, "you weren't. Ceci, this is Holly Winter. She brings Rowdy to visit. My sister has already introduced herself."

Perhaps sensing the tone of the remark, Ceci took a step backward.

"How do you do?" I said while taking advantage of the opportunity to squeeze past Ceci and lead Rowdy to Althea.

As Althea administered a perfunctory pat to the top of Rowdy's head, Ceci said to me, "You knew what I was talking about when I was telling you about Simon, didn't you?"

"Certainly," I lied. Out of the corner of my eye, I caught Althea's smirk.

"Simon's name," Ceci said, "was from one of *their* stories. My late husband, Ellis, was utterly obsessed with Sherlock Holmes."

"Lord Saint Simon," Althea contributed. "Which story, Holly?"

"I haven't . . ."

" 'The Noble Bachelor.' You must."

"I will."

"It was one of their little jokes," Ceci explained

petulantly. "Our Simon was a surgical bachelor. We bought him as a pet, pet quality, you understand, excellent breeder, poor bite, and we promised to, uh, do what we did. And noble he was. The perfect gentleman."

Translation: The breeder had insisted that a dog with a poor bite be neutered.

"Ceci," ordered Althea, "enough dog talk!"

Ceci responded by accusing Althea of failing to respect her feelings about Simon. Althea replied that Simon had been dead for two years and that it was time for Ceci to stop indulging herself in prolonged and excessive grief. With genuine pain in her voice, Ceci said that Simon had been her soul mate, her dearest friend, and her constant companion. Furthermore, what kept her going now was the knowledge that his spirit was still with her.

"Piffle," said Althea.

"Conan Doyle didn't think it was piffle," Ceci snapped. "Nor, may I point out, does he now."

I had no idea what she meant. Althea looked uncomfortable. I assumed that she felt as awkward as I did about the presence of a stranger during a family spat. I tried to leave the sisters to their incomprehensible argument, but when I said goodbye and reminded Althea that Rowdy and I would be back on Friday, Ceci announced that she was leaving, too. Hugging Althea and kissing her tenderly, she said, "I love you dearly, you know."

Althea replied, "I love you, too, Ceci. Thank you for coming. You have brightened my life since the day you were born."

In the corridor, Ceci tagged along with Rowdy and me. "It breaks my heart that Althea has to be in this place," she confided, "but she was completely unable to manage. She's ninety, you know."

I pressed the elevator button. "Rowdy, wait."

"But she's as bright as ever. She was always the smart one. George, our brother, was the practical one."

"And you've always been the pretty one?" I smiled.

Ceci beamed. Then her face, which really was pretty, turned grave. As the elevator doors opened and we stepped in, she said, "The one who never gets taken seriously. Simon, for example. When I lost my Simon, all I heard from everyone but Althea was 'only a dog.'" She repeated the phrase. "'Only a dog.'"

Ceci and Rowdy and I were alone in the elevator. "I understand about Simon," I said impulsively. "Sometimes I still miss my Vinnie in the same way."

"Is he still with you?"

"She," I corrected. "Yes, she is." It was painful to talk about Vinnie, and the more vividly I sensed her presence, the more painful it became. I rested a hand on Rowdy's head. He entered my life soon after Vinnie died. He did not replace her. Rather, he came to me as my personal therapy dog.

Placing a gentle little hand on my arm, Ceci said, "They aren't gone, you know."

"They are and they aren't. I always remind myself that all Vinnie did was die. She didn't stop loving me." It was a moment of odd intimacy. As the elevator reached the first floor and the doors opened, Ceci dug into her purse, found a packet of tissues, and handed me one. I blew my nose.

"I've upset you," she said. "There's no need, really. Until six months ago, I felt the same way. Since then, I have had the great comfort of communicating with Simon and knowing for certain that his abiding presence is more than a lonely woman's foolish hope."

I cleared my throat. "I need to sign out and get my raincoat. It was very nice to meet—"

"Oh, I'll come with you." As I returned my little volunteer's badge to its place on a bulletin board in the office, signed out, and retrieved my raincoat, Ceci went on and on. Simon spoke to her, she informed me. It was a great comfort, she said again, to receive messages from Simon. I couldn't help wondering, of course, whether Ceci also communicated with her late husband, Ellis. If not, didn't the man's spirit sense her preferential treatment of the dog? Weren't his feelings hurt? But I lacked the courage to ask.

On the way out, we passed through the lobby, and I managed to shake Ceci for a couple of minutes so that Rowdy and I could say goodbye to the people gathered there, but she waited and trailed me through the doors to the parking lot. Ceci kept assuring me that what the unenlightened mistook for death was, in fact, a state of trance. Meanwhile, Rowdy devoted himself to what I assume is the exclusively earthly activity of making repeated passes at a shrub near my car and finally drenching it. The male dog's question about eternity: *Is there pee after death?* I did not ask Ceci whether she'd interrogated Simon on the subject. Simon, she said, told her that he was happy running and playing. Was that what Vinnie told me?

"My, uh, beliefs stop a little short of yours," I confessed.

"But there's no need!" Ceci cried.

"There seems to be for me."

"You do sense her presence?"

"Yes."

"Are you able to speak with her?"

I seldom discussed the subject. I especially avoided it when my friend and second-floor tenant, Rita, was around. Rita is a clinical psychologist. She already thinks that everyone is insane and doesn't need any supporting evidence from me. "Well, I, uh, I say things to her," I stammered. Vinnie was a golden retriever. She was my great obedience dog. She had a temperament from the heaven to which she has returned. Goldens are eager to please, but they aren't necessarily brilliant. Vinnie was. She was quick, insightful, observant, and intuitive. Nonetheless, when she was here with me, our verbal exchanges were a trifle one-sided, and the balance hadn't shifted since her demise.

Ceci shook her head sadly. "They have so much to share with us!"

"Vinnie gave me everything," I said in her defense.

"You'd give anything, wouldn't you," said Ceci, "to see her again."

With no hesitation, I said, "Yes. Anything."

"With the help of the gifted, our loved ones approach closer all the time." With a knowing nod, she extracted an ivory business card from her purse and pressed it on me. Then she made her way to a beige Mercedes.

I looked at the card. IRENE WHEELER, it read, ANIMAL COMMUNICATOR. The address was in Cambridge.

"I'll be damned," I said to Rowdy. "Irene Wheeler."

The animal psychic? The quack consulted by Gloria and Scott? Irene Wheeler.

I am an animal communicator. Ask Rowdy. Ask Kimi. For that matter, ask Vinnie. If you love your dog, *you* are an animal communicator. Steve Delaney is an animal communicator. For instance, he'd communicated Gigi's need to be spayed. But *Irene Wheeler, Animal Communicator?* No, no, no. *Irene Wheeler, Charlatan.*

Chapter Five

FIVE DAYS LATER, EARLY on Friday morning, I was tempted to call the Gateway to offer some trumped-up excuse to postpone our visit. I'd slept restlessly and awakened with a sense of obligations unfulfilled. Besides having to earn a living, I had to keep a dentist appointment in Newton, and I had to groom both dogs for a show the next day. I always shampoo and blow dry them before a show to make their coats really stand off their bodies, the way the standard says. The standard also says that malamutes are to be evaluated principally on the basis of their original function as sledge dogs. Whenever I get the dogs ready for a show, I feel sorry for the generations of Arctic dwellers who relied on these dogs to act as canine moving vans. What those people must have gone through to make sure the dogs would pull! I mean, unless you spend a terrible amount of time with a forced-air dryer and a brush, your dog doesn't stand a chance in the ring, so I assume that all this fluffiness the judges like must be absolutely crucial to the breed's ability to haul heavy freight. But then I thought of Gus, Nancy, and the others, Althea of course, and Helen, and I made my apologies to Kimi and took Rowdy to the Gateway.

The drive there was dismal. Everything, including the sky, was the color of dirt. Mats of leaves rotted in the gutters. Nature and artifice had cooperated to litter people's yards with broken tree branches and with scraps of sodden paper and torn plastic. The streets were thick with ice-melting chemicals and sand. Loose black sticky nuggets of asphalt lay everywhere except in the potholes they were supposed to fill. At the edges of parking lots, icy mountains of filth lingered: the unsettled graves of dead snow.

The Gateway was in Cambridge near the Belmont line, only a short drive from my house, which is the three-story red wooden one at the corner of Appleton and Concord. The Gateway was a new facility constructed of brick, concrete, and plate glass, and surrounded by foundation plantings of evergreens and rhododendrons in beds mulched with wood chips. For the previous week, we'd had mild, rainy weather, a sort of winter mud season, but last night the temperature had dropped thirty degrees, and the Gateway's parking lot was thick with fresh sand and chemicals that I tried to brush off Rowdy's feet and underbelly before we entered the lobby, which was the brightest and most cheerful place I'd seen that day.

Only one of our lobby regulars was there. In the adjoining dining hall, a man in green work clothes was running a floor-polisher over the linoleum, and the ten-thirty exercise group hadn't begun yet. At the Gateway, the day always started late. I'd been asked never to arrive before ten-thirty, when the last breakfast trays were cleared and when most people would have been bathed and dressed. When I signed in and pinned on my badge, I realized that my sweater was a depressingly colorless gray. I wished I'd worn red and tied a bright bandanna around Rowdy's neck. A staff member bustled by and, in passing, confirmed my impression that everything was running behind schedule today.

"Where are your friends today?" I asked the lone woman in the lobby.

"I don't know," she said. "Where is everyone?"

"Not dressed yet, I guess," I answered. "I'm glad you're here. Rowdy would be disappointed if he didn't get to visit."

Even after we'd spent some time with her, the morning activities in the dining hall still hadn't begun, so I decided to move up to the third floor and catch our first-floor people later. When we stepped off the elevator, I had to lead Rowdy around a man who was washing the floor. Someone was stacking trays of dirty dishes on a big cart. The TV room was empty except for a woman I'd never met before. Although she smiled pleasantly at Rowdy, when I asked whether she liked dogs, she said no, not big dogs, just little ones. Back in the corridor, Rowdy headed for 319, Nancy's room. We found the door shut. Rowdy whined softly, and I had to remind him not to paw at it and scratch the paint. A closed door, I'd learned, meant that one or both occupants were being bathed, dressed, or given some kind of medical treatment. I'd been told that it was all right to knock and wait for a reply, but I didn't want to bother anyone who might be attending to Nancy or her roommate, and I didn't want to violate anyone's privacy.

"We'll come find Nancy later," I told Rowdy. "She'll tell you how beautiful you are, won't she? And you'll give her a big kiss." She'd also moan and call out his name, and she'd have to be prevented from encouraging him to jump on her bed, where, I feared, he might accidentally crush her tiny frame, but neither her wailing nor her frailty would bother Rowdy. "I promise," I said. "She won't want to miss you, either. We'll come back later."

Having visited hardly anyone, we took the elevator to the fifth floor. There I was relieved to find Helen and Althea dressed for the day and eager to see Rowdy. Helen Musgrave interrupted her ritual sorting of the contents of her bulletin board to shake hands with Rowdy and then departed to attend some activity or event. Despite the darkness of the day, the morning light that came through the big window bathed Althea's face and made her look a hundred years old, but she was even more animated than usual, and crowed to Rowdy in a fashion that reminded me of her sister, Ceci. The cause of her excitement, I learned, was the prospect of a visit from her grandnephew, her late brother George's grandson. Jonathan lived in St. Paul, Minnesota, where he taught mathematics at Macalester College. Jonathan's father, George's only child, had died a number of years before. Except for Ceci, Althea said, Jonathan was her only living relative. He had called on Wednesday. The call alone, I saw, had been a treat for Althea. Jonathan was arriving in Boston on Saturday, tomorrow, and would stay with Ceci. Althea was getting her hair done this afternoon, and her nails, too. "Not that it matters," Althea commented, "but at my age, special occasions are to be treasured and are well worth a celebration." Just how excited was Althea about Jonathan's visit? She was so keyed up that she mentioned Sherlock Holmes only once, and the mention was no more than a passing allusion. Jonathan, she said with amusement, was interested in the binomial theorem, but she didn't hold it against him.

"Professor Moriarty?" I asked. Holmes's archenemy, the criminal genius.

''*Ex*-Professor Moriarty,'' said Althea, but I could tell that she was pleased in spite of my little mistake.

As I hope I've made clear, the visit had not a single premonitory or paranormal feature. If telepathic signals had been flashing, I might have failed to receive them. Animals, however, especially companion animals, are widely credited with psychic powers beyond those of mere human beings, and since Rowdy is an extraordinary dog in every earthly respect, I assume that he must also be able to hold his own against the competition when it comes to occult gifts. But his behavior was perfectly normal.

After I'd wished Althea a good visit with her grand-nephew, I went back down to the third floor, let Rowdy say hi to a few new people, and spent a little time with Gus. Nancy still wasn't in the corridor or the TV room, so we again made our way to 319. This time, the door was open. Long blue curtains were drawn around the bed near the door. I didn't know the name of Nancy's roommate, whose bed it was. I'd just seen her lying there looking weak, ill, and vacant. Whenever I'd spoken to her, even loudly and clearly, she hadn't responded at all. I hadn't persisted. If there'd been ten of Rowdy and ten of me, we'd probably still have short-changed the people who could have benefited from a therapy dog. As it was, I reserved Rowdy for people like Nancy.

Rowdy knew before I did. Instead of rushing bright-eyed toward Nancy's bed, he sized up the situation, turned around, and tried to head out the door. Her bed was not curtained off. It was stripped bare. Nancy's bulletin board, identical to Helen's and everyone else's, showed only a random pattern of small holes left by the pins that had held up notices she hadn't read and photographs she hadn't looked at. Her water pitcher, her

drinking glass, her box of tissues, and her other possessions were missing from her nightstand. The wide windowsill, identical to the one where Althea kept her
Sherlockiana, held nothing and looked as if it had just
been washed. Nancy owned two embroidered pillows
that usually sat on the two chairs near her bed. The
pillows were gone. So were Nancy's two stuffed animals, a fuzzy dog of an unidentifiable breed and a gray
squirrel that played a tune when you turned a key. Her
wheelchair wasn't there. I was as baffled as I'd have
been if the Gateway had been a boarding school, a summer camp, or a college dormitory. Rowdy, who'd
known immediately, pulled toward the door. I let him
lead me to the corridor, where I stood in a daze for a
few seconds until a man in white, a nurse, spotted me
and asked, "Nancy?"

"Yes," I said.

Lowering his voice, the man said gently, "Expired."

The word didn't register; I simply did not understand
it. "What?" I demanded.

"Nancy expired this morning," he said.

Far too loudly, I said in amazement, "Nancy *died*?"

The man was kind. "She was ninety-three. She was
very frail."

I signed out, returned my badge, and even managed
to exchange a few words with the people in the lobby.
Still reeling, I drove to Newton Corner and spent a mis-
erable half hour in the dentist's chair. When I left, instead of taking the fast route home along Soldiers Field
Road, I impulsively took the little North Beacon Street
Bridge, cut across to the Watertown and the Cambridge
side of the river, and turned onto what's rather grandly
called Greenough Boulevard, but is a narrow, unpreten-
tious road that runs along the Charles River. That section of the boulevard is a parkway, I suppose. Trees,

weedy bushes, and a chain-link fence separate it from a vast parking lot and a long stretch of massive brick buildings that used to be a federal arsenal. Large parts of the old arsenal are now a shopping mall. One building houses a health maintenance organization. Another has become an apartment complex. The old arsenal is, however, uphill from the river and almost out of sight, at least if you don't look for it, and in warm weather, Greenough Boulevard gives a pretty view of the river, provided that you keep your eyes on the water and not on the far bank, unless, of course, your idea of a pretty view is an International House of Pancakes, a discount office supply store, and Martignetti's Liquors. But I'm not the only one to find the little stretch of road appealing, at least by city standards. There are small parking areas and, by the water, wooden benches. Even in good weather, people sit alone in their cars sipping coffee from cardboard cups. I always imagine that these are unhappy spouses who don't want to go home and have nowhere else to go but Greenough Boulevard. The car-proud spend hours there polishing their vehicles with paste wax. The athletic skate on the sidewalk, ride bikes, or jog. Lots of people walk dogs there. In the spring, Harvard, Northeastern, and other local university crew teams practice on that stretch of the river, and recreational rowers propel one-person shells through the water. Kevin Dennehy, my cop friend and neighbor, distrusts the area. He maintains that it is a dangerous place for a woman. He's warned me never to go there alone even with my big dogs.

On a cold Friday afternoon, in full daylight, though, I felt perfectly comfortable in driving along the road. Rowdy was in his crate in the back of the car, but if the engine quit, I could get him out and walk safely to a telephone. Kevin was wrong, I reflected. He knew

Rowdy so well that he'd forgotten how the dog appears to strangers. Despite the recent warm spell, patches of ice floated on the river. It was too early in the season for crew practice and much too cold to sit on the benches. No one was skating. I passed a solitary cyclist headed in the other direction. That's how I thought of the woman, as a solitary cyclist. The phrase was Conan Doyle's. It was the title of a story. A ragged couple pushed a shopping cart that probably contained everything they owned. Nancy's belongings wouldn't have filled half the cart. She'd been ninety-three. And frail. Althea was only ninety. How old was that French woman, Jeanne Calment? A hundred and twenty? Althea could easily have another thirty years. Helen Musgrave could have forty or more. Gus, my lobby ladies, all the others? I couldn't shake the feeling that if I'd only been alerted, I could have rushed Rowdy to the Gateway, and Nancy would still be alive.

Parked in a turnout was a dark panel truck, a van with no windows except the two by the front seats and, of course, the windshield. My eye caught the flash of something white near the riverbank. I naturally assumed that it was a dog and slowed down to see what kind. My brain cells identify any unknown object as canine. I'm always easing on the brakes to get a good look at paper bags blowing in the wind. But there was no wind today, and the white object wasn't at ground level, but in the hands of a tall, lean man standing by the river and wrestling in a peculiar, scary-looking way with what I now saw was definitely not a white dog. Still, the white thing wiggled and squirmed in a way that looked animate. Kevin's warnings about this stretch of Greenough Boulevard had made me suspicious. And I was mindful of death. The man had a furtive look. The white thing was struggling. At the risk of making a fool of myself, I pulled over, slammed on the brakes, cut the engine, and, leaving Rowdy in his crate, leaped out of the car without even closing the door. As I sprinted toward the man, I yelled, "Hey, what are you doing?"

The thought flashed across my mind that I was accusing a kind and innocent reader of trying to drown today's *Boston Globe*.

But I wasn't. The man must have been so preoccupied with his task that he hadn't paid attention to the sound of my car, and, of course, I hadn't slammed the door. Startled, he flung the white thing onto the ground, gave it a brutal kick toward the water, cursed at me, and made a dash for the dark panel truck. As he backed out of the turnout, he hollered, "Hey, bitch, it's not even my fucking cat!"

I wished afterward that I'd imprinted every detail about that truck on my memory. I had no excuse. I'd been reading Sherlock Holmes every day for weeks. Still, I didn't notice whether the panel truck was black or dark blue, and I can almost never tell one make of car from another unless I'm close enough to read "Dodge" or "Chevrolet." I did not get the plate number, didn't even look at it, had no idea whether it was even a Massachusetts plate. But I got a good look at the man. He was in his thirties, I thought, six feet or so, thin, with brown hair that somehow looked expensively cut. The sides were short, and the hair on top hung in what I had some idea might be known as a shingle. It occurs to me that shingles is a disease. Anyway, his hair, I thought, might have been cut in an effort to disguise his most memorable feature, which was a prominent bulbous forehead. He had on the kind of fashionably loose-fitting suit that I see mainly on actors in movies set in California. The suit was dark green. On a freezing February day, he wore nothing over the suit, no coat, no parka. He must have thought it would take him only a second to drown what indeed proved to be a cat.

Chapter Six

THE WHITE OBJECT THAT lay on the ground at the river's edge was a pillowcase fastened shut with rough twine. Before picking up the pillowcase, I explored it quickly with my gloved hands. The animal inside squirmed, fought, and yowled. I had to remind myself that it would be no kindness to release the creature and let it dash off to starve to death or be killed by a car. My fingers found what felt like, and subsequently proved to be, a smooth rock about the size of a football. I hoped the man had smashed his toes on it.

I am still not sure how I transported the cat, the bag, and the rock to my car. My intention was to support the rock with one hand and the wiggling animal with the other. The poor thing might already be injured; the man had, after all, hurled the pillowcase to the ground and kicked it. If I simply picked up the pillowcase and carried it, the stone might do additional harm. I ended up, I think, half dragging the pillowcase to the tailgate of my Bronco.

Rowdy's crate, occupied by close to ninety pounds

of perpetually hungry predator, was just in back of the front seats. Kimi's empty crate was at the rear. I unlocked and opened the tailgate, then briefly left the pillowcase and its contents on the ground. Hurrying to the still-open driver's side door, I fished around on the floor behind the seat, found an old dog blanket that I always carry, and hastily shrouded the back and sides of Rowdy's crate. In the big covered cage, he looked like a gigantic, furry parakeet. "Within seconds," I warned him over the caterwauling from the pillowcase, "I am going to put a cat in the back of this car, and I don't want your opinion on the subject. Is that clear? Good boy." So far, at least, he was doing nothing except looking interested.

After trotting back to the rear of the car, I opened Kimi's crate and did my best to support the little animal as I lifted the pillowcase. Once I had cat, bag, and stone inside the crate, I tried and failed to untie the twine and had to go dig my Swiss Army knife out of the glove compartment. By the time I returned to the rear of the car, Rowdy was shuffling around and thumping in his crate. The poor frantic cat was momentarily silent. With one hand, I held the pillowcase shut, and with the other, I used one of the knife's four or five blades to cut the twine. Then, holding the crate door shut, I tucked the knife in my pocket. My eyes had moved from the crate. When I looked back at it . . . Well, sorry, but the cat was out of the bag.

To prevent the rock from slamming into the cat as I drove, I had to reach back in the crate and retrieve the pillowcase. The cat was now huffed up in a ball of enraged, hissing fur in a far corner of the crate. The poor thing wasn't much to look at. From the head down, it wasn't too bad. It was short-haired, and its body was uniformly black. Its face, however, was disfigured by an irregular white splotch that might have been cute, I guess, except for the presence of a squiggly pink and brown birthmark that meandered down the splotch and spilled all over the cat's nose. One of its ears was intact. The other was badly ripped and looked infected. From its eyes oozed a greenish-yellow discharge. When I eased open the door of the crate and reached in for the pillowcase, the cat suddenly lashed out with one paw and gave me a deep scratch. "Damn it! Ouch!" I screeched. But I managed to shut and latch the crate. "Rowdy, no more noise! Enough! And you, cat, no more noise from you, either." I slammed the tailgate shut, thus giving myself about three seconds of silence. Alaskan malamutes don't exactly bark. Rather, they express themselves. Rowdy's self-expression took the form of eager, high-pitched whining interspersed with deep rumbling and percussive body slams against the sides of his crate. Meanwhile, the cat, instead of meowing in some species-appropriate fashion, bawled and wailed like a human infant. In desperation, I popped the first tape that came to hand into the tape deck, turned up the volume, and blasted the animals with Hank Williams's classic rendering of "You Win Again."

According to the clock on the dashboard, the trip home took twelve minutes. That's impossible. It took at least twenty-four hours. Furthermore, once I got home, it took what felt like another full day to settle the animals. I started by taking Rowdy into the house. Then I dragged two big dog crates from the cellar, set them up in what is supposed to be my guest room, and incarcerated the dogs. "You," I said sweetly to Kimi, "I trust even less around this poor cat than I trust Rowdy, and that's saying something. This cat is a temporary visitor in our home, it has just survived a terrible trauma, and we are going to be kind and gentle and considerate to it until we can find somewhere else for it to go. UNDER-STOOD?''

Congratulating myself on my wisdom in occupying the ground floor of the house instead of installing myself in the second-floor or third-floor apartment, I made another trip to the cellar, rummaged around, and finally found a puppy crate that would do for the cat. It was an old airline-approved carrier that had been sitting disassembled in the basement for so many years that I had to carry it up, put it in the bathtub, scrub it, and then fasten it together before I could use it for any animal, even a scraggly, ugly, and probably diseased cat that had given me a scratch that was still bleeding. I will skip over the experience of transferring the cat from Kimi's crate in the car to the puppy crate to my kitchen except to state the obvious, namely that cat scratches really, really sting and that even the world's most hideous and ungrateful cat deserves to be rescued from drowning. ''Now,'' I murmured gently to the cat as I deposited the carrier on the kitchen table, ''I'm going to fix you a lovely dish of tuna, and we're going to get you out and take a good look at you.'' Muttering soothing remarks about poor, hungry little kitties and the evils of cruelty to animals, I opened a can of tuna. The sound of the electric can opener and the smell of raw protein got the dogs going, but I promised them lots of attention later, reminded them that they'd both get to go to a show tomorrow, avoided the subject of baths, and shut the guest-room door. Returning to the kitchen, I dished out the tuna and placed a nice smelly bowl of it on the table in front of the puppy crate. Slowly, calmly, and quietly, I opened the crate. Through its door whizzed a streak of black that sent the Pyrex bowl flying to my new quarry tile floor. Shards of glass lay in a pile of tuna. The cat had vanished. Until I found it, I couldn't let the dogs loose.

It was now three-thirty in the afternoon. I hadn't eaten lunch, hadn't had any caffeine since breakfast, hadn't written a word. Nancy was dead at ninety-three. Althea was ninety. Some vicious s.o.b. had put this poor cat in a weighted pillowcase and tried to drown the animal in the river. And I hadn't even gotten the number of his license plate. My hands were bleeding. The dogs were fussing. The cat was hiding somewhere. Where? No matter where, Rowdy and Kimi would sniff it out. I still had both dogs to bathe and groom, and in a few hours, Steve would arrive, if you could call it that, in the same state of stoical unavailability he'd been in since the beginning of the whole mess created by Gloria, Scott, and the so-called animal communicator, Irene Wheeler. Without even cleaning up the tuna and glass, I took a seat at the kitchen table and burst into tears.

Only a few minutes later, my second-floor tenant and dear friend, Rita, rapped on the door. If Rita weren't a therapist by profession, she'd still be the kind of person everyone talks to, mainly because she has endless curiosity about people's inner lives. Rita will spend eight or ten hours listening to her patients, arrive home exhausted, pour herself a drink, put her feet up, and then ask you how you're feeling and really want to know. Now, however, the last thing I wanted was to tell Rita how I was feeling. All I wanted was not to feel it at all. I opened the door for Rita, anyway. She wore a new red coat and matching heels. Her hair had been freshly trimmed and lightly streaked. She looked so un-Cambridge, so New York, so groomed and manicured, so stylishly dressed, so accessorized, as she says, that by comparison I felt like the pile of broken Pyrex and dead fish still lying on the floor.

"What's wrong?" she asked. "The dogs! Did something happen to one of your dogs?"

"No, they're fine, they're in their crates, and I can't let them loose because there's a cat in here somewhere. Rita, someone kicked it and tried to drown it, and . . . This has been a horrible day from the second I woke up. One of my people at the nursing home died. She was ninety-three, but—"

"But you still didn't want her to die," Rita said. "Holly, I'm sorry, but I can't talk now. I have a patient, and I have to run. I was just going to pop in to ask what you know about finding lost dogs."

"Willie?" Willie is Rita's Scottie. "He was barking twenty minutes ago."

"A dog of one of my patients. She's frantic. I thought you might have some idea of how she should go about—"

Ordinarily, I'd have told Rita to have her patient call me, and I'd have swamped Rita with advice about posting photographs, informing every dog officer in the state, advertising in the papers, organizing brigades of friends, and alerting those champion finders of lost dogs, neighborhood children. Now, I just went into my study, found a handout on the topic, gave it to Rita, and said that I hoped her patient found the dog. After offering another apology for having to leave, Rita rushed off.

Rita is a natural therapist. After her departure, I began to pull myself together. I swept the floor and vacuumed up every bit of broken glass. The dogs, I realized, didn't have to remain in their crates. I led them, one at a time and on leash, to the door to the fenced yard. I made myself a sandwich out of the New York sharp cheddar that I use to train the dogs. The cheese was manufactured for human consumption, I reminded myself; I hadn't yet descended to lunching on liver treats. I had a cup of strong coffee that fortified me for a systematic search for the cat, which I finally found in the first place I should have looked: the long, narrow space between the head of my king-size bed and the wall. When Kimi steals food too big to wolf down in one gulp, it's where she dens up to gnaw her booty. I can usually lure her out with a combination of food and the word *Trade!* spoken in an enthusiastic, talking-to-dogs tone of voice. If there's a talking-to-cats tone, I haven't mastered it. Lying flat on my stomach, I peered in at the cat, whistled softly, made stupid clucking noises, drummed my fingers lightly on the floor and offered bits of cheddar and tuna. I got nothing for these efforts but a kink in my neck and a couple of loud hisses.

"The thing about making a fool of myself with dogs," I told Kevin Dennehy a half hour later, "is that I get results. Now here I am stuck with this cat under the bed, and I can't get the damn thing to come out."

Kevin was seated at my kitchen table sipping Bud out of the can. Indeed, it occurs to me that I can introduce Kevin, and Cambridge, too, as Caesar introduced Gaul. Thus all Cambridge is divided into three parts, of which one drinks mineral water, the second imported wine, and the third what in Kevin's language is called Bud, in mine beer. In this context, as one writes in Cambridge, let me add that the connection between Kevin and the Romans isn't just random. Rather—surprise, surprise—the association has to do with dogs and specifically with the mastiff, a breed found by the Romans in England and subsequently taken home to such cozy spots as the Coliseum, and the breed with which Kevin has an obvious anatomical and temperamental affinity. True! Giant breed, weight of adult male up to about two hundred pounds, massive head, short coat, natural protectiveness, unmatched loyalty . . . Except that Kevin has red hair and freckles and that if you set him down in the middle of Dublin, no one else there would look Irish at all. There is, however, an additional point of similarity: The mastiff has a kind nature.

"It's a darling little cat, too," I said. "Practically a kitten. And desperately in need of a good home. Once Steve checks it out and gives it its shots, it'll be a ready-made perfect pet."

Yes, I tried to con a cop. In the Holmes stories, Lestrade, Gregson, and other members of the force are usually slow-witted foils for the Great Detective. They have to be, really. If Conan Doyle had made them superbright, Holmes would have been stuck home fiddling and doing drugs.

"No," said Kevin.

"Well, you could at least find this bastard who tried to murder the poor thing," I replied. I'd already given him a detailed description of the man. "I'd definitely recognize him. I'll be happy to testify against him. And I have the pillowcase and the big rock that was in it and the twine that was used to tie it up." I rose from my seat and retrieved the items from the kitchen closet. To avoid contaminating the evidence, I'd stored the stone, the pillowcase, and the twine in a brown paper grocery bag. Now I rather dramatically lowered the bundle to the kitchen table and revealed its contents. "You see? It's a really smooth stone. You'll get a beautiful set of prints from it."

Kevin eyed my carefully preserved evidence with less enthusiasm than I might have wished.

"And," I added, pointing at the stone, "for all we

know, this is some rare kind of rock that an expert could identify instantly.''

"It's granite," Kevin said.

"Well, to you maybe it looks like ordinary granite, but granite isn't all the same, is it? You must have geologists you could ask. And for all I know, there's someone in the state crime lab who specializes in being able to take one look at a lump of rock and know exactly where it came from. The pillowcase and the twine are admittedly pretty ordinary-looking, but think about trace evidence! Put this stone and the pillowcase and the twine under a microscope, and you'll probably find fibers and maybe even little flakes of skin or whatever that you can test for DNA. I mean, if we get lucky, maybe he slept with his head on the pillowcase. Maybe he had a cut on his hand and bled on the twine!''

Instead of rushing to use my phone to summon a team of crime-scene technicians, Kevin reminded me that he'd warned me about that stretch of the river.

"I was just driving by. I didn't intend to stop. But obviously it's a good thing I did. So what are you going to do about it?''

Kevin shrugged. "It's M.D.C." As the signs on Greenough Boulevard announce, the agency in charge is the Metropolitan District Commission. The M.D.C., for reasons I don't understand, maintains and polices a lot of parks, skating rinks, pools, and other recreation areas in Greater Boston.

"You know people at the M.D.C.," I said. "And the crime took place in Watertown. I'm sure you know people there, too.'' I didn't mean just any old people, of course. "And I know I should've noticed the license plate.''

"Make and model of—''

"Kevin, it was a perfectly ordinary van. Panel truck.

With no windows. The kind plumbers drive. Electricians. Or like a delivery van, but with no sign on it, no lettering or anything. Just a plain van. I'm not Sherlock Holmes. I didn't see anything distinctive about it."

"Hey, hey," said Kevin. " 'Quick, Watson, the needle.' I got no use for that."

For the past week, Kevin, together with the state police and someone from the D.A.'s office, had been investigating the brutal and highly publicized murder of a Cambridge drug dealer named Donald Lively. Lively, who'd been in his early thirties, had been bludgeoned to death in the parking area behind his lavish condo in East Cambridge, only a few blocks from the courthouse. According to the papers, he'd been operating an elite cocaine operation that catered to software millionaires, wealthy foreign students, and other beautiful people with runny noses. Because of the proximity of Lively's headquarters to those of the law, the case had received lots of media attention. Kevin and a couple of other investigators working on it had had their pictures in both Boston newspapers and had appeared on the TV news. Kevin was, however, atypically silent about the progress of the investigation. Today, he looked preoccupied and discouraged.

"That's some Hollywood version," I said defensively. "In the stories, Watson doesn't approve, and eventually, Holmes gets cured. Anyway, Kevin, I want you to find this guy who tried to drown the cat."

"You call the M.S.P.C.A.?" The Massachusetts Society for the Prevention of Cruelty to Animals.

"Yes, but they're obviously not going to do anything. They did ask about his van, but they had no interest in examining the evidence. And if his foot hit this stone when he kicked the pillowcase, he might be limping! That would help. Even apart from that! Kevin, I could identify this man.'' I tried to talk Kevin into letting me go to the station to look through mug shots. Anyone vile enough to commit assault and attempted murder on an animal would surely have his picture on file in connection with other crimes, too. Kevin didn't disagree, really. He just said that he'd think about it. He left without the stone, the pillowcase, and the twine.

After Kevin's departure, I ran to the local convenience store for cat food, litter, and a disposable cat litter tray that I filled and installed in my bedroom. This time, instead of trying to entice the cat out, I shoved a bowl of smelly canned cat food into its den, firmly closed the bedroom door, and got to work on the dogs. Kimi is easier to bathe than Rowdy. I did her first and then tackled Rowdy, who considers water a form of sulphuric acid that will burn through his skin on contact. He managed to leap out of the tub only once, but as usual, he shrieked the entire time, and when I'd finally finished rinsing him, he shook hard before I'd grabbed a towel, and the whole bathroom got sprayed with damp dog hair.

When Steve arrived, the kitchen table was shoved against a counter, and the grooming table and my new high-power blower occupied the center of the floor. Kimi, I must brag, looked fabulous. My wrists ached from brushing her. Rowdy was now on the table, the blower was roaring, and the kitchen looked like what it had become: a grooming shop. Although more tiring and messy than assuming the lotus position to chant *ohm* and envision irises, grooming is nonetheless a form of meditation in which subject and object, you and the dog, achieve a state of mystical communication and blissfully transcendent unity. When you're done, you look like hell and feel wonderful.

Steve didn't feel wonderful. For once, he didn't even

look wonderful. He wore green scrubs, which usually bring out the green in his eyes, but he was spattered with drops of blood, his eyes were a flat blue, and his face was expressionless. I turned off the dryer and needlessly asked how he was doing. Instead of answering, he just said he needed a shower.

"I haven't cleaned the bathroom yet," I admitted. "It's still filled with hair. I'll do it now."

"Don't bother," he said.

"I don't mind. And don't open the bedroom door. There's a cat in there. I need you to take a look at it. There's no hurry."

"Good." He opened the refrigerator door, got a glass from the cupboard, and started to pour himself some milk. Before drinking it, he stuck in a finger and removed what must have been a dog hair. "You couldn't do this somewhere else?"

"I always groom here in the winter."

"At seven-thirty on Friday night?"

"It's not seven-thirty. Is it? I lost track of time. The dogs haven't even eaten yet."

"Neither," said Steve gloomily, "have I."

Three hours later, the dogs were in their crates in the guest room, and Steve and I were in bed. He was asleep. I was reading Sherlock Holmes. Holmes hadn't had a sex life, either, I was thinking. Abstinence didn't seem to have done him any harm. I put the book down, turned off the light, passed out, and had erotic dreams. In the middle of the night, I was awakened by a soft noise or perhaps by the crack of light that showed through the half-open door. Steve wasn't in bed. I threw on a bathrobe and padded barefoot toward the kitchen, which was now clean. In deference to Steve's fastidiousness, I'd vacuumed everything and washed the floor. I'd also cleaned the bathroom, taken a shower, and made some pasta and a salad. While we were eating, I'd told Steve about the cat. In return, he'd said almost nothing. Uncharacteristically, he hadn't even wanted to peer into the cat's hiding place to take a look at it.

Now, in the middle of the night, I peeked into the kitchen. All the lights were on: the overhead light, the one over the sink, the one in the hood above the stove. The kitchen table was padded with a layer of newspaper. In the center, Steve had neatly spread one of the clean old towels I keep for the dogs. The emergency kit he always carries in his van sat open on a chair. Smack in the center of the towel was the ugly cat. Its eyes were gooey with ointment. In front of it was a small bowl of semimoist cat food. It was eating. Steve was bent over the cat, gently palpating and stroking it. The damned thing was purring loudly.

Chapter Seven

AT THE SHOW ON Saturday, which was just that, a conformation show, with no obedience, my beautiful Kimi got a three-point major, and my wonderful Rowdy took the breed. If you don't show dogs, you probably imagine that Kimi sank her teeth into a sort of low-ranked version of a four-star general and that Rowdy literally swallowed the competition. I'll translate. Kimi earned three of the fifteen points and one of the two major wins she needed for her championship, a "major" being a win worth three or more points. And Rowdy went Best of Breed. Speaks for itself, doesn't it? Maybe not quite. By 10:30 A.M., the rest of the malamute owners were free to take their dogs home. Rowdy, however, having won his breed, would need to appear in the Working Group ring, and the group judging wasn't scheduled to start until 3 P.M. Poor Holly! Stuck hanging around all day. Too bad for her that the judge liked her dog. Whoops! Maybe I need to explain this "group" business. It's easy. American Kennel Club breeds are divided into seven groups: Sporting Dogs, Hounds, Working Dogs, Terriers, Toys, Non-sporting

Dogs, and Herding Dogs. After the individual breeds
have been judged, the Best of Breed winners compete
against the other Best of Breed winners in each of the
seven groups. Working Group: one Akita versus one
Alaskan malamute versus one Bernese mountain dog,
and so on. Thereafter, the seven group winners compete
for Best in Show.

Anyway, after Kimi's and Rowdy's triumphs in the
first phase of the process, my cousin Leah and the dogs
and I lingered near the ring to accept congratulations
and socialize with other malamute people. Also, I had
photos taken. Rowdy appears with his professional handler, Faith Barlow, and Kimi with Leah, who amateur-
handles her very capably indeed. The judge, Mrs. Ring,
is in both pictures, of course. No, I didn't invent the
name. Just as the real world of Conan Doyle aficionados
is peopled with actual, live individuals with made-up
sounding Holmesian names like Musgrave, so is the
dog fancy populated by a staggering number of Wolfs,
Foxes, Pasterns, Springers, Handlers, Cockers, Kerrys,
and Bassets. I'd noticed the phenomenon years earlier;
you can't miss it. Robert and Hugh, however, had given
me a term for it: the *nomen omen*. There are limits. So
far as I know, the fancy doesn't yet have any Mrs.
Highjumps or Mr. Showleads. But do we ever have
dumbbells. Gloria, for instance. Scott. As I shall now
explain.

After the photos and the chitchat, Leah and I crated
the dogs and left them under Faith's vigilant eye while
we ate lunch. The show site, I might mention, was a
trade center about two hours from home. The cafeteria,
which occupied one corner of the exhibition hall, served
relatively decent food, at least by dog show standards.
You didn't have to poke a fork into Leah's ham, green
beans, and mashed potatoes to identify them as such;

my tuna casserole had clearly not been prepared with cat food. Having made the mistake of deciding to eat lunch at lunchtime, Leah and I were lucky to find places at one of the long, crowded tables. Lots of people smiled, waved, and said hello. Leah and I show quite a bit in breed and obedience, I'm a dog writer, of course, and Leah's appearance is so striking that everyone always remembers her, if only because of her long, curly ruby-gold hair, which is in a red-headed league all its own. So we were seated opposite each other innocently eating lunch. On the way to the show, I'd told Leah about the cat, which, by the way, I'd last seen at dawn when I'd awakened to find it asleep on Steve's pillow, purring in his ear.

"I tried to pat it," I now told Leah. "But all it did was hiss at me."

"It associates you with a traumatic experience." Leah was, need I say, taking introductory psychology. Rita, who is a Ph.D. psychologist, agreed with me that the rate of Leah's mastery of the subject was astounding. After two weeks of lectures and readings, there was absolutely nothing about psychology that Leah didn't know. Rita also informed me that freshman obnoxiousness was an understudied trait, less because it spontaneously disappeared than because no researcher wanted to have to put up with the know-it-all subjects who displayed it.

"If it weren't for me, that cat would be dead," I pointed out. "If it were a dog, it would be *grateful*." After pausing to pull my chair forward to make room for someone taking a seat directly behind me, I added, "Well, at least it's a female. I won't have it spraying all over my bedroom until I find it a home."

"Some female cats spray," Leah informed me.

"Is that true?"

"Yes. And if it's ugly and sickly and unfriendly, who's going to——?"

Before she finished, a loud, raspy, penetrating, and all-too-familiar voice bellowed almost in my ear, "Crooks, all of them! Out to do nothing but empty your wallet. And the worst of them is that Delaney. You heard about our Gigi?"

Leaning across my tuna casserole, I whispered to Leah, who knew all about the trouble poor Steve was enduring. "Say nothing!" I ordered. "Not a word!"

She mouthed silently, "Gloria?"

I nodded.

Behind me, Gloria continued. "Spayed her! Ruined my bitch! Spayed her! What am I supposed to do with her? She's no good to me now."

In Cambridge, no one remarks on Leah's clear voice or perfect articulation. Althea Battlefield spoke with the same precision and in the same ringing tone. For reasons I've never quite fathomed, it's highly educated women who always sound as if they want to make sure that hearing-impaired foreigners seated across the room won't miss a single word. The men, in contrast, sometimes murmur so softly that I have to lean forward and strain to understand them. Oh, yeah. Maybe that's the idea. Anyway, ever since I'd first started taking Leah to dog shows, I'd been trying to convince her that if she simply couldn't help projecting her voice to the most distant reaches of the show precincts, she should either keep her mouth shut or watch what she said. In particular, not until we were safely back in the car headed home was she permitted to utter an even mildly derogatory comment about anyone's dog. Indeed, the word she now enunciated had nothing to do with anyone's precious female show dog. *"Bitch!"* Leah sang out. At a dog show, thank heaven, *bitch* is utterly unobjection-able; it's practically every other word you hear.

Oblivious to Leah's assessment, Gloria switched from slandering Steve to extolling the powers of Irene Wheeler. "She could of fixed up Gigi, only by the time we got to her, it was too late. An animal communica-tor's what she is. Better than all of those vets combined. Ought to be stuck with their own needles, if you ask me."

Over my left shoulder, I heard loud male guffawing. "You tell 'em, Gloria," said Scott.

Egged on, Gloria added, "If you ask me, all that Delaney cares about is what he can rip you off for."

I'd heard all I could take. So, I suspected, had Leah. Her freckles had disappeared into the crimson that suf-fused her cheeks.

"All done, cousin?" I asked brightly.

In disgust, Leah balled up her paper napkin and pitched it into the remains of her lunch.

"Nothing," I reminded her in a whisper. *"Do noth-ing."*

As we rose and carried our trays away, I was careful to avoid looking in Gloria and Scott's direction. The sight of the pair would undoubtedly shatter my control over the impulse to upend my plate and deposit the remains of my casserole on Gloria's head. Also, I didn't need a refresher on what the vile couple looked like. They were in their mid thirties, I suppose. Somewhere on Gloria, something always glittered where no glitter belonged: fake rubies on a T-shirt, sequins on sneakers, gilt flecks in a thick layer of green eye shadow. At no more than five two, she was about ten inches shorter than Scott, but she was almost as starved-looking as her hollow-cheeked husband. His scrawny face always wore a smile that suggested hidden knowledge of dirty secrets, maybe his own, maybe other people's. His hair was lank, and he had dandruff. Perhaps because he favored western-cut polyester shirts and often fingered things—his earlobe, his belt, his wife's neck—I always imagined that Scott played incompetent guitar in what tried to pass itself off as a hillbilly band.

"This is monstrous," said Leah as we left the cafeteria. "But I can't believe that anyone listens to her."

"You'd be surprised. People don't always consider the source."

"I'll bet they have awful dogs," Leah said hopefully.

"Wrong. Their dogs are quite decent. None of this is the dogs' fault."

"Steve won't do anything?"

"Leah, he's entitled to deal with it in his own way. And at least he isn't here to have to listen to her."

Ah, but at about one-thirty, Steve turned up. He found me in what could hardly be called a romantic setting. Been to a show lately? No, not Broadway. A *real* show. A dog show. If so, you've undoubtedly noticed that old-fashioned chewies like bones and rawhide are being rapidly displaced by the moderately gruesome and, in some cases, by the outright macabre. The trend started with pig ears. Then it was hooves and cow ears. Then what are called "muscle chews." And what *are* muscle chews? Hunks of cattle neck. Ligaments. Muscles. Yes, body parts cooked in their own gravy. Ick! And now it's tracheas, great big dead-white tracheas removed intact from beasts of heaven knows what species and—enough!

"The problem with these tracheas," I said to the vendor, "is that they look *human.* Are you sure they're . . . ?"

"A hundred percent digestible," the vendor assured

me without actually answering my question. "And dogs love them."

Just as my right hand rose protectively to my throat, Steve appeared at my side. Although he'd been up in the night with the ugly cat, he looked more rested than he had for a week. He wore new jeans and a navy sweater I hadn't seen before. I love being seen with him. Superficial? Yes. But then I love being seen with Rowdy and Kimi, too, and there's obviously no question about the depth of my devotion to them. I ran a hand over Steve's cheek. He'd shaved today.

"Caressed with fingers fresh from tracheas," he said.

"Sterile tracheas. What are you doing here?"

He has the most beautiful smile. I tried to remember the last time I'd seen it. "Leading a normal life."

I smiled back. "Good."

"I heard Rowdy took the breed. Someone called Buck, and he called to leave a message for you. I thought I'd drive out and watch the group."

Translation: the judging of the Working Group.

"He isn't coming, is he?" I was filled with alarm. Buck is my father. Even if he weren't, he'd still be *the* most mortifying person to be seen with on the liver-littered surface of the dog-show world. If he were small, quiet, introverted, and mortifying, it wouldn't be so bad, but Buck's appearance, demeanor, and voice are over-whelming in a remarkably mooselike fashion. He crashes through life as if it were underbrush. He bellows. Worse, everyone not only knows him, but knows whose father he is or soon finds out. If I'm in the ring, he looms just outside radiating paternal pride and criti-cizing every move I make. The one time he didn't do it was the day he stood outside the obedience ring and watched my Vinnie score a perfect 200. I expected him to lecture me about the handler errors the judge had missed, but he didn't. He said, "Well, I guess that's all right." His behavior toward me is a little like Robert's toward Hugh. He considers himself a member of an elite group from which I've been excluded, and he scrutinizes me for the equivalent of misquotation.

To my relief, Steve said, "No such luck."

"Rowdy's not going to go anywhere in the group," I said.

"Then why stick around?"

"Because I'm a good sport. Besides, he just might. So, where's your new cat?"

"At the clinic. Under your name. They're working on that ear, and I want to keep an eye on her for a couple of days."

As we made the rounds of the booths, I wondered whether to warn Steve about Gloria and Scott, but decided against it. After the hullabaloo they were making about how he'd ruined their show dog, he obviously knew that they might be around. With luck, they'd gone home by now.

They hadn't. It was outside the ring during the judging of the Working Group that we encountered them, if that's the right word for suddenly hearing Gloria holler from only a yard or so in back of us, "Jesus Christ! Hey, you! You, Delaney! You got a nerve showing your face here."

Standing next to Steve, I could feel his whole body tighten. But he kept his eyes on the ring and on Rowdy, and said nothing, even when Gloria muscled her way through the crowd and planted herself right next to him. "You deaf or something?" she demanded. "You didn't hear me saying you got a nerve showing your face here?"

"It's a dog show," I informed her. "Not a face show. If it were, you wouldn't have been allowed in."

I was immediately sorry.

"Oh, yeah?" Gloria roared. She reminded me of the gruesome dog treats. She looked like an emaciated sow that had sacrificed its ears.

Steve gently took my elbow and, murmuring gentlemanly apologies to everyone we passed, moved me away from the ring and out of Gloria's range. "Rowdy looks good," he said placidly.

"The judge doesn't think so," I grumbled.

"You ought to handle him yourself. He responds better to you than he does to Faith."

"Faith is a thousand-times better handler than I am. Rowdy adores her."

As if to vindicate me and retain his handler, Rowdy surprised me by going third. Kimi's win? Rowdy's Best of Breed? Now, a group placement? It takes a lot to ruin a day like that. Well, Gloria almost succeeded. As I thanked Faith and took Rowdy's show lead and ribbon from her, I noticed Gloria making her way from person to person. She was handing out cards. For once, her voice was quiet. And I assure you that people were listening to her. She was talking about Irene Wheeler. She was handing out Irene Wheeler's business cards. I didn't need a card, of course. Ceci Love had already given me one. I intended to use it. Tomorrow, I vowed, I'd make a phone call. I'd make an appointment. Gloria lacked the brains to plan the campaign she was carrying out. I wanted to meet the power behind her. Who was that power? Irene Wheeler. No shit, Sherlock.

Chapter Eight

I WAITED UNTIL NOON. For all I knew, psychics lolled in bed on Sunday mornings. Or did they go to church? Besides, I didn't want Steve to overhear. As I puttered around killing time until he left, it occurred to me that when Holmes undertook an investigation, he never had to hang around until Watson departed or worry that his partner would tell him to mind his own business. On the contrary, whenever Holmes announced that the game was afoot, Watson sprang up like a walk-hungry dog at the sight of a leash. Rowdy or Kimi, I decided, would make a far better Watson than Steve. My game, after all, was seldom afoot. It was almost inevitably a paw. Sorry about that.

I got Irene Wheeler's answering machine. Her message was disappointing. "This is Irene Wheeler," said a pleasant, ordinary voice. "I can't come to the phone right now, but please leave your name and number after the beep." What did I expect? Weird background music, that's what: silver trumpets, creepy violins, harps plucked by angelic canine loved ones. Just how was the caller supposed to know that the angelic harpists were canine? Irene Wheeler was supposed to say so. "Irene Wheeler," I wanted her to whisper breathlessly, "cannot come to the phone because she is fully occupied in marketing the hope of eternal companion-animal life while practicing veterinary medicine without a license." I hung up without leaving a message. I didn't want my call returned when Steve might answer the phone or overhear me as I made an appointment.

Frustrated in my effort to schedule a consultation with Irene and thus to meet the damned troublemaker face-to-face, I decided to settle for secondhand information. Last Sunday afternoon, Ceci had been paying what might be a regular weekly call on her sister, Althea. With no encouragement, Ceci had been voluble about Irene Wheeler's psychic powers. Maybe I'd find Ceci at the Gateway today. If so, I'd pump her.

When Rowdy tried to bound ahead of me into Althea's room, I came to a halt, heard a male voice, and finally remembered that on Friday, Althea had been eager to see her grandnephew. What was his name? Jonathan. Her late brother's grandson. Calming Rowdy, I decided to step in, say hello, and assess the situation. If I found Althea engaged in a happy reunion with Jonathan, Rowdy and I would make a swift departure; maybe Jonathan read Sherlock Holmes, and he and Althea were having a cozy Holmesian gossip. On the other hand, maybe Ceci was preventing Althea and Jonathan from enjoying exactly that kind of exchange. If so, I'd persuade Rowdy to distract Ceci, and then I'd lure her aside and get her to tell me everything about Irene Wheeler.

I found neither Althea's sister nor her grandnephew, but Hugh and Robert, whose chairs faced Althea's wheelchair. The male voice had been Robert's. He was speaking now, but not of Sherlock Holmes. Missing from Robert's tone and from the faces of the three old friends were the quickness and lightness I'd admired when Althea, Hugh, and Robert shared their passion for Conan Doyle. When the three had exchanged their scholarly banter, their expressions had turned playfully grave. Questioning me about my homework, as I thought of it, Althea could play the stern English teacher. I remembered our discussion of the tongue-in-cheek "Watson Was a Woman." Rex Stout's error? Althea had demanded. Had I spotted it? No, I'd confessed, I hadn't. In fact, I'd just been tickled by the essay. Althea had frowned, clicked her tongue, shaken her head, and assigned me "The Dying Detective," in which, I was to note, we are indeed shown Holmes in bed.

Now, all three old faces were serious. My first thought was that Althea was dying. On our next visit, Rowdy and I would find her room as depersonalized as we'd found Nancy's, stripped of the person and her few belongings. Worse, we'd find here someone other than Althea. But didn't the dying belong in bed?

Recovering from my lapse, I prevented Rowdy from pawing Hugh, who rose from his chair, stroked his pale mustache, absently thumped Rowdy's head, and said, with a note of suppressed excitement, "There's been a death in the family. We were asked to break the news."

"Ceci?" I asked softly. "I'm so sorry."

Hugh dismissed my condolences. "No, no, not Ceci. Nothing the matter with her except the usual." He rolled his eyes.

Evidently annoyed by Hugh's slowness in breaking the actual news, Althea said, "My grandnephew, Jonathan, is dead."

Tactlessly, I said, "I thought he was a young man."

"He was," she answered. I found her response impossible to read. She certainly wasn't crying.

Robert seemed to speak for her. With a hint of drama, he announced, "Jonathan was murdered in Ceci's yard."

"Ceci asked us to inform Althea," Hugh added, as if there were a need to explain his presence and Robert's.

"I'm so sorry," I said again. "We'll go. This is no time—"

Althea protested, but I felt an internal pressure to leave. As I was about to excuse myself, Althea surprised me by asking me to bring Rowdy to her. He nuzzled her hand and solemnly rested his chin on the arm of her wheelchair. She placed the palm of her hand on top of his big head and kneaded his dense coat almost as if he were a mother cat and her huge, ancient fingers a litter of bony kittens. Watching her, I was jarred to realize that it would be all wrong for me to offer her the hug that, under these circumstances, I'd have given to a stranger my own age. Althea's husband, the shadowy Mr. Battlefield, had died soon after she'd married him. Since then, her physical contact with other human beings must have been limited to Ceci's sisterly embraces, the pokes and prods of doctors, the handshakes of friends and strangers, and, lately, the ministrations of the Gateway staff. Or so I imagined. Maybe she'd actually had torrid affairs with Hugh, Robert, and dozens of other Sherlockian men.

Hugh accompanied Rowdy and me to the door of Althea's room and followed us a few steps down the corridor, where he gestured to me to wait a moment. After clearing his throat, shuffling his feet, smoothing his mustache, and making what seemed to be an effort to compose himself, he whispered very loudly, "There's more that no one said!"

"Does anyone know who murdered him?" I asked. "Do you have any idea what happened?"

"As yet, very little." Hugh's eyes sparkled. His plump middle moved in and out as he breathed. He licked his lips. "But I must tell you that near Jonathan's body were found"—here he paused for what I knew was effect—"the footprints of a gigantic dog."

I suppressed the Robert-like urge to correct him. *Mr. Holmes,* I wanted to say, *they were the footprints of a gigantic hound.*

Chapter Nine

ROWDY AND KIMI BEING the models of canine perfection that they are, I had a hard time dreaming up an excuse to consult Irene Wheeler. Yes, if I left a bowl of fruit on the counter, they staged a raid and scattered orange rinds and banana peels all over the house, and yes, I'd had to get rid of my bird feeder because Kimi caught songbirds on the wing, but who'd hire a clairvoyant to find out that malamutes were malamutes? Besides, to unmask Irene Wheeler as the fraud I knew she was, I'd do better to claim that one of the dogs was sick. Raw superstition held me back. How would I feel if my deception succeeded and, a week later, Rowdy or Kimi fell ill? Alternatively, I could blurt out the truth about missing my wonderful Vinnie and aching for one more glimpse of her. It felt wrong, however, to profane my bond with Vinnie by pretending that our spiritual connection depended on some joker who promised access to the Netherworld Web in return for this world's currency. I'd settled on a compromise. When Irene Wheeler answered her phone on Monday morning, I was prepared to burble about my concern for the dogs' karma, auras, spirits, souls, and any other occult entities I could conjure up.

No explanation was required. On the contrary, Irene Wheeler seemed to take it for granted that I required professional help to understand my dogs. In a cordial, businesslike manner, she wasted no time in offering me an appointment at three o'clock that afternoon. The presence of the dogs, she explained, would be unnecessary. Indeed, she worked most effectively from color photographs. Irene Wheeler's fee for an initial consultation was precisely what Rita charges for a fifty-minute hour of psychotherapy. Rita, however, bills her clients; she doesn't ask for cash up front. Also, Rita doesn't work from photographs.

Once having committed myself to being ripped off by Irene Wheeler, I employed myself in the manner of a hardworking freelance writer by taking Rowdy and Kimi around the block, refilling their water bowl, making fresh coffee, and reading the morning paper. The New England News Briefs column—truly that's what it's called, "Briefs," just like underwear—carried a paragraph about the murder of Althea and Ceci's grandnephew, Jonathan Hubbell. I read:

Newton Joggers
Discover Body

NEWTON—Law enforcement officials are investigating the death of Jonathan Hubbell, 31, of St. Paul, Minnesota, whose body was discovered early Sunday morning by two Boston College students as they jogged through the Norwood Hill section of this quiet suburb. The deceased was reportedly on a visit to his great-aunt, Mrs. Cecilia Love, 80. The joggers made their find in Love's yard. Traces of a white powder believed to be cocaine were found on the body. Preliminary reports indicate that death resulted from head trauma.

New England News Briefs: not just underwear, but skimpy underwear, practically a g-string. For example, there was no mention of the paw prints of the gigantic dog. Or had Hugh and Robert imagined them? In spite of the scantiness of the newspaper account, I drew the obvious conclusion that this cocaine-dusted grand-nephew, Jonathan, had used his elderly great-aunts as an excuse to come to Boston for a drug deal and that he'd been murdered when it had gone wrong. Althea and Ceci had both deserved better than what this Jonathan had inflicted on them. Althea had been eager to welcome the only relative she and Ceci had left. For Ceci, too, the impending visit had probably been a major occasion. I could almost see her fussing around planning special meals and rearranging the pillows and the knickknacks in her guest room. And if this damned grandnephew had to do drugs and get murdered, couldn't he have been considerate enough of Althea's reverence for the Canon to pick an abusable substance other than Sherlock Holmes's very own cocaine?

The phone interrupted my work. I'm always afraid not to answer it. I'm on the list of Alaskan Malamute Rescue people who get calls about dogs in trouble. If I don't pick up, a malamute owner who wants to dump a dog may not bother to leave a message or may have the dog euthanized before I can return the call. Alternatively, the owner may give the dog away free to the kind of "good home" that beats him, sells him to a research laboratory, uses him in the so-called sport of dog fighting, or simply dooms him to years of neglect tied outside on a rope or cable.

This call, however, was from one of Steve's vet techs, Rowena, who cheerfully informed me that my cat was ready to go home.

"It's not *my* cat." A call about *any* Alaskan malamute is a call about *my* dog.

"There must be some mix-up," Rowena replied. "We have her here under your name."

"It's like Winnie the Pooh," I said, "living under the name Sanders. Remember? Pooh had a sign over his door that said Sanders. Well, that cat is living under the name Winter." *Living* under my name. Instead of dying underwater. "I'll pick it up this afternoon," I said grudgingly.

"If you don't pick her up by noon," Rowena said apologetically, "we'll have to charge you for another day."

Twenty minutes later I was standing at the tall counter in Steve's waiting room as Rowena entered my name in the computer, found the cat's file, and asked whether I'd come up with a name for her yet. Three or four people with cats in carriers or dogs on leash waited on the benches. I felt ashamed to have them hear me admit that I was the kind of heartless person who doesn't name a pet.

"It's not my cat," I said. Suddenly inspired, I gave Rowena a big smile. "Maybe *you'd* like it."

Shaking her dark curls, she returned the smile. "Sorry, but I've got three already. The doctor wants to talk to you before you leave. He's with a patient now. Could you wait a couple of minutes?"

Instead of taking a seat, talking to the human and

animal clients in the waiting room, or gritting my teeth at Steve's mother's embroidered and framed depictions of what are supposed to be terriers, I paced around, looked behind the counter, craned my neck, and scanned the notice board near the phone. Posted on it were business cards of dog trainers, contact information for humane societies and animal shelters, a list of obedience clubs, and notes and fliers about lost and found pets. Could I take the cat to an animal shelter? Every no-kill shelter I'd ever heard of avoided euthanasia by accepting young, healthy, adoptable animals while rejecting the old, the needy, and the difficult. The cat would never pass the screening. If I handed it over to one of the other facilities, it would probably be dead before I drove out of the parking lot. I was a person who rescued animals *from* shelters, at least from shelters where the staff really cared about the animals and called when a malamute came in. In contrast, a certain animal rescue league in Boston inexplicably refused to work with breed rescue groups. When the shelter manager told me that the policy was to euthanize dogs rather than to turn them over to rescue groups, I was insulted. I still am. Is a malamute better off dead than with me? And the organizations devoted to rescuing cats were so overwhelmed with stray and abandoned animals that I couldn't bear to add another to the existing burden. No, I'd place the cat myself.

The lost-and-found notices suggested a wonderful new possibility. The despicable man in the dark van had yelled that the cat wasn't even his. If he'd been telling the truth, maybe someone actually wanted the poor ugly thing back. Most of the lost animals whose descriptions and crudely photocopied snapshots were posted by the phone were dogs: a beagle mix, a terrier mix who looked like Benji, a Great Pyrenees, a Doberman. A rabbit was missing. The only cat was a long-haired calico.

When Rhonda, another of Steve's staff, ushered me into an empty exam room, she looked sad. "How do you think he's doing?" she asked. She meant Steve.

"He's holding up," I said. "He's making an effort. I wish he'd talk about it, but he won't."

"He got another letter from that woman today."

"Gloria."

Rhonda nodded.

"What did it say?"

"He tore it up. I didn't see it."

The swinging door opened, and Steve came in with the cat in his arms. When he's about to discuss an animal, he always wears a serious expression. A stranger might not have noticed the tension in his jaw or the fine lines around his mouth. As he gently placed the cat on the metal exam table, he began to deliver one of his clear, maddeningly slow descriptions of the animal's condition. A white bandage wrapped around the cat's head covered the torn ear, but highlighted the foolish splotch and birthmark that disfigured its face. From what Steve was saying, I gathered that the cat had lost a piece of the ear. I already knew that the missing piece wouldn't grow back. Steve demonstrated how to apply ointment to the cat's eyes. I was also supposed to put drops in the unbandaged ear twice a day.

"We had to assume that she'd never seen a veterinarian before," Steve said, "so we went ahead and immunized her. Her feline leukemia test was negative, so we gave her . . ."

On the wall behind Steve was a huge poster that depicted dozens of breeds of domestic cats. My eyes drifted to it. A few months earlier, I'd happened to see a cat-food commercial on television that had made a powerful impression on me. The feline star was a large, incredibly beautiful short-haired gray cat with what I'd later described to Steve as immense deep-yellow eyes. I'd told him everything about the gorgeous cat in the ad in the hope that he'd identify the breed so I'd know what it was I wanted if I ever decided to get a cat. He said it sounded like a Russian blue, but when I looked up the breed on the poster and in a book at the library, the Russian blue was somehow different from my immense gray cat with its stunning amber eyes.

". . . most common birth defect in the domestic cat," Steve was saying severely.

I hadn't been listening. "You mean the birthmark?"

"Double paws." Eyeing me, Steve delivered a short lecture about the presence of an extra toe. Then he asked whether I knew how to trim a cat's nails.

"I've owned cats," I said defensively. "Vinnie was absolutely wonderful with cats. So was Danny. So was Rafe. And if I do dogs' nails, I can do cats'. Besides, at the risk of repeating myself, let me point out that *this is not my cat.*"

Ignoring the disclaimer, Steve explained that if I failed to give the cat regular manicures, the nails on the extra toes would grow in big circles and work their way back around and into the flesh of the toes. He'd trimmed the cat's nails for me, but I was to remember to do it regularly. Also, the cat had roundworms and several other internal parasites for which it had received initial treatment, but I was to pick up medication on my way out. As to her teeth, which were in poor condition, he'd take care of those when he spayed her.

"You must be kidding," I said. "How old is this cat?"

He shrugged. "Six, maybe. Eight."

"Steve, it's a hideous cat. I'm covered with

scratches from it. All it does is hiss at me." I reached toward it. It cooperatively hissed. "You see? It's missing half an ear, and now you're telling me it has worms and bad teeth, it needs to be spayed, and it's six or eight years old? Who on earth is ever going to adopt this thing?"

"You are," he said. "Make an appointment in a couple of weeks for me to spay her and take care of her teeth. We don't know what she might be harboring. I don't want to take the risk now."

"The dogs will kill it," I said.

Steve smiled. "Not with you around."

Chapter Ten

I EXPECTED TO FIND IRENE Wheeler in a shrouded sanctuary seated before a crystal ball. Or maybe her office would be a sham version of Steve's, and she'd wear a white coat or even green scrubs. In fact, I encountered a thin, bright-eyed woman in a conservative navy wool suit who welcomed me to the front room of a pleasant, light apartment that occupied the ground floor of a three-story house almost identical to my own. My house is barn red, hers was white, and since I don't have clients, I don't have the kind of cupboard-size waiting room Irene Wheeler did, but if I furnished my living room as a prosperous Cambridge professional's home office, it would look just like Irene's. My own office, my study, occupies what was originally a small bedroom. Everywhere are pictures of Rowdy, Kimi, Vinnie, Danny, and lots of other dogs; and ribbons and trophies old and new. A gold-framed copy of Senator Vest's Eulogy on the Dog hangs near my new computer. "Faithful and true," proclaimed Senator Vest, "even to death." A wooden urn containing Vinnie's ashes rests on a bookcase. Her collar is looped around her earthly remains. I finger it now and then, and read her tags almost as if the information on them might have been updated since the last time I looked. I would dearly love to know her present address. Like most other rooms in Cambridge, however, my study serves principally as a repository for books, periodicals, and reams of photocopies and clippings, some in three-ring binders, some in folders, some in plastic file boxes, many, the unjudged, teetering in semipermanent purgatory in a precarious stack on top of a filing cabinet next to the wastebasket, their fate in the hands of God. Surveying Irene's uncluttered office, I envied what was obviously her gift of prophecy. I wished I could forsee what I'd want someday and what I could safely throw away. Sherlock Holmes, I recalled, docketed everything. He was confident that he'd always want to be omniscient.

By city ordinance, Cambridge requires each household to maintain a minimum of one wall of books per person, including babies. Dogs and cats are exempt. The floor-to-ceiling shelves behind Irene Wheeler's desk thus contained what was for Cambridge an ordinary number of books, with a run-of-the-literary-mill ratio of paperbacks to hardcovers, say fifty-fifty, but incredible though it may seem, and astonishing though it was to me, I swear that she owned more books about the occult than I do about dogs, and that's saying something. The titles of my books follow a somewhat repetitious pattern: *The Complete Alaskan Malamute, The New Complete Alaskan Malamute, This Is the Alaskan Malamute, Your Alaskan Malamute, Successful Obedience Handling, Expert Obedience Training for Dogs, Schutzhund Obedience, The No-Force Method of Dog Training, Improving the Obedient Dog.* A few of Irene Wheeler's titles followed a similar pattern. She had *Ani-*

mal Talk, What the Animals Tell Me, and *Stories the Animals Tell Me.* Although she also had *Strange Powers of Pets,* most of her books seemed to be more about the former than the latter: telepathy, channeling, past life regression, etheric bodies, ancient healing arts, eternal spirals, cosmic pyramids, flower remedies, the energies of gems. The names of the books gave the only visible clue to Irene Wheeler's profession; in other respects, these might have been the premises of a freelance computer consultant or a psychotherapist in private practice.

Unless the polished stones on Irene Wheeler's chunky necklace exuded some mystical force invisible to me but visible, perhaps, to the psychically gifted, the only mystery about her appearance was how anyone managed to stay so thin. Mindful of her fees, though, I was reminded of the Duchess of Windsor's famous remark that you can't be too rich, either. Like the late Duchess, Irene Wheeler had the build of a sight hound, and her shoulder-length fawn-colored hair would have looked at home on a saluki's ears. Her eyebrows, however, were overplucked, and I noted a nervous awkwardness about her gait; in the ring, she'd have been faulted for a subtle lack of refinement. When we shook hands, hers felt like a bony paw. Probably because of self-starvation, she was very pale. She couldn't have been more than thirty.

She took a seat behind the big desk, which was the kind you see in warehouses that sell discount office furnishings: yards of wood veneer designed to impress at first glance and to be ignored thereafter. "You're here for a reading."

"For two dogs." Heaven forbid that one of the two be rivalrously marooned in whatever state of psychic frustration might result from an unread mind.

Luckily, Irene Wheeler assured me that she charged a flat fee for an initial reading. I fished in my bag, counted out a painful number of twenty-dollar bills, and said, "Ceci Love recommended you. She gave me your card."

Rita and the other Cambridge therapists I knew through Rita were obsessed with client confidentiality. Steve, for that matter, didn't blab about his intimate knowledge of the innards of particular dogs, cats, and ferrets. Irene, however, said, "Oh, Ceci! And Simon, of course. He has had a great deal to share with her. It's been tremendously satisfying to channel his messages. She was really a mess, you know."

I nodded in what I hoped was a meaningful and even conspiratorial fashion.

"Ceci was bereft without the ties they shared. She had lost all sense of perspective and purpose."

"She must be terribly upset again now," I said. "You do know that her grandnephew was just murdered?"

As if giving a factful report on a recent conference call, Irene Wheeler assured me that she and Ceci had already been in touch with Jonathan. "Jonathan is, of course, in a temporary state of considerable imbalance," Irene informed me, "but a radical change at the physical level is far easier to accept when seen in its spiritual context. Ceci is finding great comfort in the continuation of contact."

"I didn't know you did people," I said. "I thought—"

"What I *do*, as you put it, is cosmic balance. We are a hierarchy, you see, each of us with a particular place, each perfect in that place, provided that it is known and cherished." She paused. "And your pets?"

The word always throws me. In my cosmic hierarchy, dogs occupy the pinnacle. *Pets* always makes me think of creatures incapable of such splendidly unique canine accomplishments as precision heeling and perfect empathy. I mean, did Senator Vest deliver a Eulogy on the Goldfish? Well, there you have it. Without protest, however, I presented Irene Wheeler with two color photographs. One showed Rowdy and Kimi on a pebble beach by the ocean in Maine. The other had been taken indoors at home. Its quality was so-so, but I'd caught the dogs in a characteristic pose, stretched flat on the kitchen floor facing each other, their forepaws almost touching. "Rowdy and Kimi," I said. "Rowdy is the male, and—"

Irene Wheeler put a finger to her lips. "They will speak for themselves." Resting a hand a few inches above each photograph, she closed her eyes. I kept mine open and thought about what Rowdy and Kimi were undoubtedly thinking about, namely, the cat, which I'd locked in my study to prevent if from reclaiming its refuge under my bed.

Irene opened her eyes. Her face bore a mildly accusatory expression. "Their color is not blue."

"Oh." Had I said that it was? Casting my eyes downward, I realized that I'd dressed for the appointment by wearing a blue denim skirt. I usually wear jeans. Blue jeans. With pockets full of cheese, roast beef, and liver. If blue made the dogs feel anything, the anything was hungry.

"They wish to be children of light."

A primordial longing for the midnight sun? Nonsense. What dogs care about is not color, but odor, the worse the better. If consulted about my wardrobe, Rowdy and Kimi would advise me never to change my clothes.

"They are close to nature," Irene continued.

"That's true," I admitted. "The closer, the better."
The dogs are especially crazy about chasing down nature when it's small and furry. If pressed, however, they'll settle for feathers.

Abruptly switching topics, Irene announced that she was sensing something about teeth.

"*What*?"

"Teeth," she repeated. She apologized for not being more specific.

"There's nothing wrong with their teeth," I said.

"It's the message I'm receiving," she said. "I have no doubt whatsoever. Teeth."

I was startled. The dogs have wonderful teeth, strong, white, and clean. Because my father thinks that fluoride is part of a Communist conspiracy, I, however, grew up without it and have to go to the dentist all the time. The weird thing was that my teeth look fine. The psychic couldn't have noticed anything. And the dogs and I are genuine kindred spirits. Was it possible that they or I had somehow radiated vibrations about my teeth?

"Teeth," I said. "Well, I'll bear it in mind."

In another abrupt shift, Irene said, "These animals are ancient souls."

Give me a break. One look at malamutes, and you can tell they're ancient souls, the essence of dog primeval.

Irene then launched into a lecture about—and I'm not making this up—dogs and the solar plexus, of all things. Let me repeat: solar plexus. According to my definition, the solar plexus is the place in your middle that hurts if it gets punched. But according to Irene Wheeler, the solar plexus of the dog radiated cosmic energy that united with human consciousness and raised it to new levels of constancy, loyalty, and bliss. What was special about dogs was that their solar plexuses were cosmically better than anyone else's. I'm always happy to hear a new theory about the benefits of dogs, of course, but frankly I'd have been equally willing to believe that the power of dogs sprang from the pasterns, the stomach, the pancreas, or a really likely spot such as the brain or the heart.

Unasked, Irene then began to tell me about myself. I liked navy blue. I responded positively to challenges. I was experiencing a conflict in my love life. As I've said, I was wearing a blue denim skirt and, as I haven't said, a navy sweater embellished, I might add, with undercoat Kimi had just started to shed. My parka was also navy blue. Anyone with two malamutes is by definition someone who likes a challenge. As to my love life, whose is without conflict?

So, I was ready to dismiss Irene's powers entirely when she startled me by tapping on one of the photographs of the dogs. I stood and peered. One of her thin fingers was rapping on the picture taken by the ocean and, specifically, on Rowdy's face. Closing her eyes, Irene murmured that this one was of special interest to her. Since her eyes were shut, it didn't seem to matter where I stood or what I did. I loomed over her and stared. This one had great force, she asserted. He was deeply connected. "Yes!" she cried out.

I sat abruptly.

"Yes!" Her voice vibrated. "This one is a special gift. He is a gift from one who had departed. Here is a connection! Here is a guide!"

Rowdy, in fact, entered my life soon after Vinnie left. I had never told any human being, not even Steve or Rita, that Rowdy had always felt like a gift from Vinnie. The idea had always seemed too crazy to speak aloud to anyone but a dog. I'd never told Kimi. I hadn't wanted to hurt her feelings. I had told no one on earth but Rowdy. I caught my breath.

Opening her eyes, Irene Wheeler gazed at me and then again at the photographs. Tapping Rowdy's picture, she murmured, ''Both are ancient beings. This one, however, has the purer soul.''

I felt enraged. Purer, indeed! Kimi is my dog, too. Furthermore, *Kimi* is short for *Qimissung*, which means snowdrift, as in ''pure as the driven,'' damn it, and I do not like to hear her disparaged. Purer soul! Irene Wheeler was, I decided, a complete fraud.

Chapter Eleven

HUGH SEARLES HERE." The Holmesian's voice on the phone was brisk. As if taking me up on an any-old-time offer to borrow my car, Hugh added pleasantly, "We want Rowdy at once. Let's say we'll pick him up in half an hour. Would that be convenient?"

It was five-thirty on that same Monday. Rowdy and Kimi had eaten dinner, and I had no plans. Even so! "Pick him up?"

"In the manner of Pompey," Hugh said hurriedly. "Toby."

I felt myself inducted into what's known as the Great Game: the playful pretense that Sherlock Holmes had been a real-live person and that Watson's tales were accounts of actual events. By now, I'd read or reread maybe three quarters of the stories—whoops!—three quarters of the factual reports. Missing from my personal version of the Canon were the tales I'd never read at all or had unforgivably, even sacrilegiously, forgotten. Deliberately deleted from my version were a few tales I just didn't like. I knew, however, that Toby and

Pompey were tracking dogs rather blithely borrowed by Sherlock Holmes. In the Great Game, those dogs were as real as Holmes and Watson. Ah, but in which adventures? For once, my near-total recall for dogs had deserted me, and I was unable to dredge up the sort of subtle acknowledgment of comprehension that would have pleased Hugh. Although I had no intention of trying to pass myself off to Hugh as any sort of Sherlockian, I felt oddly ashamed of my inability to return what would be, in effect, the correct password or secret handshake, some countersign of forceful commitment to the Canon.

Without spoiling the game by announcing that even the Master Detective himself wouldn't be allowed to help himself to one of my precious dogs, I explained that Rowdy was, as I tactfully phrased it, something of a handful. "He doesn't necessarily listen to anyone but me," I said, without adding that he doesn't necessarily do more than take my opinions under advisement. "What do you need a dog for?" I asked.

Robert and Hugh, it emerged, had seized on the murder of Jonathan Hubbell to play the Great Game in real life or—and here's what troubled me—in real death. The police, Hugh informed me, had finally finished their so-called examination of the crime scene, doubtless after destroying vast amounts of valuable evidence. Despite "the depredations of the Gregsons and the Lestrades," as Hugh phrased it, Ceci's property might contain important clues about Jonathan's murder. Ceci was being most obliging in the matter. Although Ceci was, according to Hugh, a functional illiterate, her husband, Ellis, had been an active member of the Red-headed League of Boston. And Ceci was, after all, Althea's sister. Rowdy was to play Toby or Pompey to Robert and Hugh's Holmes and Watson. For all we knew,

Hugh asserted, the murderer, accompanied by his gigantic dog, had arrived and departed on foot. A mere forty-eight hours or so later, the trails of the two were surely fresh enough for another dog to follow. Furthermore, Ceci had no idea what had prompted Jonathan to leave the house. When she'd gone to bed, he'd been listening to music. She was certain that he'd made no plans to go out. That Saturday night had been brutally cold; Jonathan obviously hadn't just gone out to enjoy the night air. And if he'd decided to use Ceci's car, without her permission, of course, or to take a cab or even to go for a walk, he'd have left by the front door, and he'd have closed it after him. As it was, a French door at the rear of the house had been found ajar, and his body had been discovered in the backyard. Between the time Jonathan left the house and met his end, what had his movements been? Hugh and Robert were determined to put a dog on Jonathan's trail.

"What you're looking for," I told Hugh, "is a highly trained search and rescue dog. Every single thing you've mentioned is an extremely difficult task." As I was about to say that Rowdy would be absolutely useless, it hit me that in taking the request seriously, I was playing into the Great Game. In the case of a real murder, the pretense struck me not as a harmless pastime, but as a morbid and ghoulish confusion of fact and fiction. If Kevin Dennehy had been silly enough to ask for Rowdy's assistance as a tracking dog, I'd have told him to find a canine with an educated nose. But Kevin was the real thing, a police lieutenant; he'd never have made such a request. Hugh and Robert, in contrast, would probably go marching off to the crime scene with deerstalker hats on their heads, magnifying lenses in their hands, and the Sherlockian cliché on their lips: "The game is afoot!" They didn't need a tracking dog; all they wanted was one more stage prop. What prevented me from refusing to participate in this mockery was, of all things, Hugh's touchingly genuine faith in the methods of Sherlock Holmes. As if reading my mind over the phone line, Hugh said, "You must imagine that we're a pair of old jackasses having fun at the expense of this unfortunate young man."

Precisely.

"Not at all!" I countered.

"We may be a pair of old jackasses," he said proudly. "Well, I may be one. I can't speak for Robert. But there is nothing asinine about the methodical collection of empirical evidence. And I assure you that we see this murder for the horror that it is."

"Yes," I said.

"Perhaps I could persuade you to accompany Rowdy."

I gave in, but insisted on driving to Ceci's myself and also substituted Kimi for Rowdy. Kimi was anything but a real tracking dog—I'm not claiming otherwise—but I'd taken her to a couple of tracking workshops, where she'd shown considerable aptitude for the sport. With her tracking harness on, she might satisfy Hugh and Robert's desire for a Toby or a Pompey by putting her nose to the ground. To Rowdy, a harness meant *pull.*

After digging out Kimi's red tracking harness and an old thirty-foot army-green tracking lead, I bundled up in my parka and then remembered that I had to check on the cat. After locking the dogs in my bedroom, I eased open the door to my study, slipped in, and quickly shut the door without giving the cat a chance to escape. As it turned out, the cat hadn't been hanging around looking for the opportunity to bolt. Rather, it had installed itself, appropriately enough, on the mouse pad next to my new computer. At the sight of me, it glared, hissed, and then vanished in the tangle of cables under the printer. The mouse pad was covered with cat hair and oily medicine. "Nice little kitty," I said hypocritically. Then I produced those stupid squeaking noises that no self-respecting person makes to a dog that weighs over five pounds. Not that I don't like cats. Not that I'm superstitious about them, even about really hideous black cats like this one. But cats are not my special mission. *Dog* spelled backward? Yes. But *cat*? Tac? I don't see the cosmic significance.

Nonetheless, instead of following Hugh's precise instructions for getting to Ceci's house in Newton, I stayed on the Cambridge side of the river, took a right onto Arsenal Street, and then made an immediate left onto the strip of Greenough Boulevard where I'd saved the cat. I did not, of course, expect to come upon the tall, evil man with the bulbous forehead. I certainly didn't expect to catch him abusing another helpless little animal. It occurred to me that in Kevin Dennehy's mind, that stretch of road represented a sort of Great Grimpen Mire, the haunt of the hound of the Baskervilles. Remember the famous message sent to Sir Henry Baskerville at the Northumberland Hotel? *As you value your life or your reason keep away from the moor.* Well, Kevin had never come out and warned me about valuing my life and my reason, but when he mentioned the area, he spoke in sinister tones, and his wholesome freckled face took on a sort of Baskervillian expression. Anyway, as I drove slowly along what actually was a dire-looking stretch of road, I wondered why Kevin had wasted his time scaring me when he could have been calling the Metropolitan District Commission or writing to the Boston newspapers to demand the installation of streetlights along the presumably dangerous stretch. As it was, the only illumination came from the big lights in the parking lot of the shopping mall; the area by the river was utterly black. I relied on my headlights to see that only a couple of cars and one pickup were parked in the turnouts; there was no sign of the evildoer's dark van. The pointless detour left me feeling guilty. If the cat had been a dog, wouldn't I be doing more to find out who'd tried to drown it?

After crossing the river, I pulled over to consult the directions that Hugh had dictated. Ceci lived in a section of Newton called Norwood Hill. Following Hugh's instructions, I cut through Brighton and, just after entering Newton, veered sharply uphill in more senses than one. Brighton was apartment buildings, triple deckers, and shops that sold lottery tickets, potato chips, and not much else. As a tangle of streets ascended Norwood Hill, the size of the houses increased with the gain in altitude, and dim gaslights replaced the bright electricity of the lower regions. At a four-way intersection of narrow streets, I came to a stop to figure out where I was, but couldn't read the street signs in the darkness and realized that the gaslights carried a message: If you didn't already know your way around, you didn't belong in this neighborhood at all. After crossing the intersection, I pulled up, dug a flashlight out of the glove compartment, got out of the car, and found a small street sign that told me I was almost at Ceci's. Another gaslit block and a couple of turns put me on Norwood Road, which, as Hugh had said, soon split into Lower and Upper Norwood. Bearing right on Upper Norwood, I passed a baronial stucco minipalace, a rambling brick Victorian, a Cape that looked little and cosy by comparison with its imposing neighbors, and, on my left, a colonial that obviously dated not to New World imperialism but to the twentieth-century colonization of the suburbs. Beyond that colonial was a second, this one big, white, and square, with three gables and two massive chimneys. To the right of Ceci's house was a detached garage, and in the driveway that led to it was a car I recognized from the Gateway lot, the old Volvo with the bumper sticker that read THE GAME IS AFOOT.

I hadn't even turned off the ignition when the front door opened. Robert, tall and dignified, came down the walk bearing a big battery-powered lantern. I noticed that he, like my father, had an exceptionally large head. Looped around his neck was the wide strap of a camera that clunked against his chest. To my relief, he wore neither an Inverness cape nor a deerstalker hat.

At his request, I left Kimi crated in the car and followed him into the house, which was all high ceilings, brocade chairs, shiny mahogany tables, oriental rugs, and dark wood floors. Ceci, dressed in layers of pinkish-beige jersey, was fluttering around offering tea and sherry.

Hugh looked up from an assortment of paraphernalia that he was removing from a cardboard box and arranging on the floor of the spacious front hall. Robert, as usual, wore a suit. Hugh had on a plaid flannel shirt with pens and pencils stuck in the breast pocket. Exchanging glances with Robert, he looked like a carpenter consulting an employer about which door he wanted rehung. Hugh rose to his feet, assured himself that I'd brought a dog, and immediately put on a padded canvas jacket. Robert donned a heavy black wool coat that made him look like an undertaker. Then the three of us followed Ceci into a living room the size of a banquet hall. At its far end, the room became a sort of miniconservatory: a series of French doors overlooking the backyard formed a large bay or alcove. A forerunner to today's sun spaces, the area had a floor of burgundy tiles, tubs of potted palms, and the kind of natural-colored rattan furniture that obviously hadn't been bought at some discount department store's spring sale on wicker. The two chairs and an ottoman had cushions covered in a deep green and rose floral prints: fat peonies about to turn blowsy. The low table was topped with glass. Robert and Hugh trailed after Ceci as she made her way to the alcove and began to question her about Jonathan's movements. Where had he been when she had gone to bed? Had she no premonition of evil? What had she observed the next morning?

Turning a rheostat that lowered the lights in the bay, Ceci said, "I feel that Jonathan left this way."

"You *feel*?" Robert inquired. "And what grounds do you have for—"

"Ceci, dear," Hugh interrupted, "which of these doors did you, in fact, find unlocked?"

Pointing to a French door in the center of the alcove, Ceci said, "Ajar. Ever so slightly open. It was really very naughty of Jonathan to have done that." She talked on. I didn't follow what she said. Indeed, so transfixed was I that I didn't even follow her to the alcove. I stared at an immense oil painting that hung over the baronial fireplace in the living room. The painting was a beautifully executed life-size portrait. Its subject posed right in front of this same fireplace. During his lifetime, when he'd actually sat on the hearth directly beneath his portrait, he must have given people the uncanny impression that they'd been struck by double vision on a giant scale. Maybe the artist had intended precisely that effect. In any case, as rendered in oil, the subject was a handsome, noble fellow. The portrait was illuminated from above by a small light mounted on an elaborate gilded frame. The bottom of the frame bore a brass plate that read LORD SAINT SIMON.

An end table near the fireplace held a collection of crystal knickknacks and china shepherdesses arrayed around a small photograph in a correspondingly small silver frame. The frame wasn't cheap-looking—nothing in Ceci's house was—and it was tasteful, but it was only about two inches wide and four inches high. Like the massive gold frame over the fireplace, it displayed a portrait. This one showed a bald-headed man with wire-rimmed glasses. The man wore a morose expression. I assumed that he was Ceci's late husband, Ellis Love. If so, he had a right to look slighted.

Chapter Twelve

HUGH AND ROBERT HAD brought what I suppose
should be called a scene-of-crime kit: Robert's
camera, two powerful lanterns, tweezers, small
paper envelopes, paper and plastic bags, labels, indeli-
ble markers, little glass jars and test tubes, measuring
tape, a yardstick, plaster of Paris or perhaps of somewhere else, a fingerprint kit evidently purchased at a toy
store, a laptop computer that sat like a mechanical bird
in a homemade-looking nest of insulation, and exactly
the kind of oversize magnifying glass depicted in car-
icatures of Sherlock Holmes. With misogyny worthy of
Holmes, they forbade Ceci to go anywhere near the
equipment arrayed on the floor of the immense central
hallway of her house. I, they decided, might make myself useful by lugging gear, but would probably drop it.

I felt a senseless urge to prove myself worthy of a
key role in the charade. "Toby," I announced, "was
spaniel and lurcher. *Lurcher*, as you probably know,
refers to a sighthound cross, usually greyhound. The
term connotes—"

"Poachers," Robert said.

"Gypsies," I finished.

Hugh was tinkering with the laptop computer. Robert pointed menacingly at it and apologized for Hugh's insistence on wasting time.

"The neatest and most orderly brain," quoted Hugh, peering up, *"with the greatest capacity for storing information—"*

Robert interrupted. "Not *neatest*! Not *information*! *Tidiest*! *Facts*! *The tidiest and most orderly brain with the greatest capacity for storing facts of any man."* He added emphatically, *"Man! Not machine."*

Pressing the power button on the laptop, Hugh cryptically replied, "Jupiter nonetheless arises."

Robert was livid. *"Ascends! Jupiter nonetheless ascends!"*

"Pay no attention to them," Ceci advised me. "I never do. Ellis was just the same. I put up with it from him for a great many years, and—"

"Fifty-nine," Hugh said. "You and Ellis were married for fifty-nine years, Ceci. We attended your Golden Wedding anniversary."

In an odd voice, Ceci said, "Jonathan was there." She sounded puzzled, as if some unreliable person were trying to convince her of her grandnephew's presence on the occasion. "I had entirely forgotten, well, almost entirely, until the subject came up in our"—her voice dropped to a whisper—"recent communications." Brushing a hand lightly across my sleeve, she murmured, "And you? Have you sought Irene's assistance?"

Before I could answer, Robert broke in to warn me not to get Kimi, or Toby, as he called her, until the first stage of the investigation was complete. Ascending like Jupiter, I suppose, Hugh announced that it was about to begin. It started where Jonathan had evidently left the

house: at the large plant-filled alcove at the far end of
the living room. As Robert quickly sketched the area on
a sheet of paper fastened to a clipboard, Hugh drew it
on his laptop. I just looked at it. The alcove, I observed,
was formed by sets of French doors. Those on each end
were windows, really, and angled to create the bay. The
doors gave onto a brick terrace. Ceci flipped a switch
that turned on large lights that must have been mounted
high on the back of the house. Peering out, I saw a vast
yard that sloped downward and disappeared into darkness.

Leaving Ceci indoors, I zipped my parka, pulled on
gloves, and followed Hugh and Robert onto the terrace,
which was elevated about two feet above ground level.
It was about ten feet wide. A flight of brick steps led
from the terrace to the rear of the property. On the
sides, the terrace stopped abruptly where the alcove
ended. Systematically casting back and forth on the
empty terrace, Robert reminded me of an advanced obedience dog working his scent articles. The examination
of the terrace seemed like a waste of time. Not so much
as a stray leaf was visible, and any outdoor furniture
Ceci kept there, a wrought-iron table and chairs, perhaps, had been stowed elsewhere for the winter.

Undiscouraged, the Sherlockians next turned their attention to the garden beds that ran along the foundation
of the house. I should explain that if you faced the back
of the house, to the left ran a brick walkway that eventually passed between the house and the garage, and led
to a white wood fence with a sturdy gate. The flower
bed to the right of the terrace ran parallel to the back of
the house, turned the corner, and ended at another
length of the same high white fence. Robert and Hugh
hovered over the path to the garage and the flower bed
next to it. I observed nothing except a thick layer of fir

bark, the leafless branches of small azaleas, the emerging shoots of daffodils, and the foliage and blooms of dozens of crocuses and snowdrops, their blossoms tightly closed, as if the February night had forced the harbingers of spring to fashion makeshift parkas out of pastel petals. Nothing seemed out of the ordinary. That mulch is ubiquitous in the suburbs, where expensive lawn services convince homeowners that bare earth, dirty as it is, should never be seen unclothed.

On the other side of the house, however, the corresponding bed of fir bark, dormant azaleas, daffodil shoots, and early bulbs drew enthusiastic exclamations from Hugh and Robert: "Features of interest!" In my skeptical eagerness to see whether the men had found a genuine clue, I had to be shooed away so I wouldn't trample the flowers, if not the evidence. As it turned out, mashed blossoms and squished daffodil shoots *were* the evidence. Along most of its length, this mulched bed looked identical to the one on the garage side of the house. Near the angled French door that formed this end of the alcove, however, broken foliage lay flat on the fir bark. I found myself in agreement with Robert and Hugh: The appearance of the ground honestly did suggest that someone had stood there to peer through the glass.

As Robert was taking close-ups and distance shots, one of the French doors opened. Ceci, apparently alerted by the flashes of the camera, appeared on the terrace. Her fluttery manner hinted at the sort of dissociated woman who cloaks herself in full-length dead animals, but has hysterics at the sight of the furry corpses the cat drags home; I had the sense that practically from the moment she'd been born, everyone around her had engaged in a conspiratorial, if unconscious, program of operant conditioning that systematically reinforced that kind of internal split. If so, maybe Ceci's dogs had made her whole again. She wasn't wearing fur. Rather she had all but vanished inside a long, thick quilted coat, heavily padded boots, Polartec mittens, and a matching tam-o'-shanter. She was dressed to walk a dog on a cold night.

"Has my Simon been back?" She was childishly eager.

Robert, who seemed to specialize in dealing with Ceci, replied, "Someone or something has stood or been placed near this angle between the window and the wall of the house. The damage to the vegetation appears recent."

"My Simon," said Ceci indignantly, "would be most unlikely to tromp down my flowers." With hurt feelings, she added, "And he's never been this close to the house before." As if mouthing someone else's words, she said hopefully, "He is not yet ready. The time will come."

"The hypothesis," Robert said severely, "concerns the presence of a human being."

Flinging a mittened hand toward the lower part of the yard, she said, "The police spent all their time below, where Jonathan had his accident."

"Ceci," Robert said firmly, "Holly is beginning to feel the cold. Take her in and give her a cup of hot tea."

Ceci agreed, but as I climbed the steps to the terrace and followed her through the open French door, she made the justifiable complaint that Hugh and Robert treated her like an imbecile. "I am perfectly competent. I went to Wellesley, you know, just like Madame Chiang Kai-shek, not that I stayed long, girls didn't in those days, you know, I left to marry Ellis, girls did that back then, but Ellis made sure that I understood practical matters, he was a stockbroker, you know"—I hadn't—"and I have always had my own checking account and reconciled my bank statements and taken care of my charge cards. You see, in his business," she continued as I trailed after her into the kitchen, "he saw a great many women who suddenly lost their husbands and didn't know how to make out a deposit slip or cash a check, never mind understanding investments, and he was determined not to leave me in that position. We'd no sooner returned from our honeymoon, Niagara Falls, less trite then than now, when Ellis sat me down and said, 'Ceci, buy and hold!' " Filling a teakettle, she concluded, "*I* am no imbecile!"

"Of course not," I said. As I was reflecting that if I were in Ceci's financial position, I'd forget Ellis's dictum and sell enough to update the old-fashioned kitchen, Ceci hunted through a cupboard, extracted a box of graham crackers, and with an exasperated click of her tongue complained that Jonathan had polished off all the nice lemon wafers. Worse, Ceci said, instead of replenishing the supply, Mary had gone and bought graham crackers. Ceci went on to lament Mary's insistence on leaving at three in the afternoon. "And," Ceci said, "she positively will not work weekends. But I must admit that she's the first one I've had for longer than I care to remember who doesn't smash the china, and when she *is* here, she's a hard worker."

Watching Ceci resentfully arrange a teapot, cups, saucers, spoons, a sugar bowl, a creamer, and a plate of the unsatisfactory graham crackers on a wooden tray, I sensed a gap between us that was as generational as it was financial: From Ceci's viewpoint, why remodel a kitchen? Why spend money on the domain of the hired help?

If we were going to drink something, shouldn't it be decaffeinated coffee? Brandy? Ovaltine? But tea was what Robert had suggested. I took Ceci's compliance as a sign of suggestibility. We did not, of course, have our tea in the kitchen. Ceci politely rejected my offer to help with the tray. With no apparent effort, she lifted it herself and carried it across the kitchen and hall, and through the living room to a side table in the alcove. The potted palms, the bone china, the whole scene gave me the bizarre sense that I should be wearing white gloves and a perky little hat with a decorative veil. After sitting, I crossed my legs at the ankles.

"It's rather drafty here," Ceci apologized, "but it's where Irene receives best." Ceci could have been talking about a radio.

"Yes?" I prompted, thinking, *Oh, so Irene makes home visits.*

"Naturally, Simon comes back to his own yard. How many sugars?"

When she'd served me and poured for herself, I asked when Simon had begun to reappear.

Ceci glowed. "Exactly one week ago today. Monday. Of course, I've been communicating with him for the past year, and it has been a great consolation, not that I ever for a second believed that Simon had *ceased to exist,* if you understand me, but I was blocked by the wall that isn't there."

"Does Simon . . . ?" I fished for a serious-sounding alternative to *bark* or *woof.* "Does Simon speak to you, uh, directly?"

With touching sweetness, Ceci explained that Simon spoke *through* Irene. "I ask him a question, and he responds through her." She sounded as I would if I had to explain the simplicity of E-mail to a Rip Van Winkle whose idea of high-tech communication was the carrier pigeon.

Consequently, it seemed better to focus on the content than on the technology. "Questions like . . . ?" I asked.

"Well, naturally, one of the first things I wanted to know was why on earth he died! And why *then*, when Ellis had passed on only a year before and I'd just had to put Althea in the nursing home. It was no time to leave! And as soon as he answered, I felt like such a selfish fool!"

It seemed to me that with investments bought and held, daily help, and more than enough room for Althea in this palatial house, Ceci damned well ought to feel selfish. Not that Althea complained about the Gateway. But has anyone ever really wanted to move to a nursing home?

"And what did Simon say?" I felt ridiculous.

"Well, it's really quite obvious, but Ellis needed him, you see, because he was having difficulty in adjusting to the Great Transition." She sipped her tea and remarked lightly, "Ellis always did hate to travel. After he passed on, everyone kept telling me I ought to fly off to Europe, now that I could, but I didn't want to leave Simon, and I was very busy, very active in the church, and Althea and I were always going places in those days, symphony, out to lunch, and there's a very pleasant group of people who get their dogs together at one of the parks near here, and I took Simon there to play with his friends, and I had no desire to go dashing off to some foreign country all by myself. And then after I lost Simon, before I found Irene, I could barely . . . There were weeks when I never left this house. I let myself go completely. I could think of nothing, you see, except all my departed ones, my baby, Willie, who lived only two days, and my Nancy, who was such a beautiful girl—she's been gone thirty years now—and all my beautiful dogs, and then my Simon. I was in a terrible state, you see. There didn't seem to be any point to anything anymore, with everyone *gone*."

"Yes."

"So one of the very first things I asked Simon was, what was I to do?"

"And?"

Ceci deftly placed her cup in its saucer. "Simon quite simply ordered me to pull myself together. He was distressed and Ellis was distressed at the way I'd let myself go. It made them feel rejected and unloved, you see, that I'd stopped caring about my appearance. So, straight away I got my hair done, and I bought a new suit and a few other odds and ends, and not in black, either! Simon does not like to see me in black. On a Newfoundland, it's one thing, of course, but on me, he finds it very depressing."

"How often do you, uh, hear from Simon?"

"Well, at first, it was only once or twice a week, when I had to go all the way into Cambridge to Irene's office, but then Simon communicated his wish to come home here to Norwood Hill, and Irene was very obliging."

I'll bet she was, I thought. "And now?" I asked.

"Simon is always *with* me," Ceci replied, "just as your dear what's-her-name is always with you."

"Vinnie," I said.

"But for several months now, I've arranged to communicate with him almost daily."

At Irene's fee? Plus, I guessed, a premium for at-home consultation.

As if reading my thoughts, Ceci continued, "That's what irritated Jonathan, of course. He was very, very annoyed with me, and unpardonably rude to Irene, well, not unpardonably, after all, forgiveness is forgiveness, but really very rude."

"In his, uh, recent communications?" I was surprised. I'd always imagined the dead as more courteous than the living, why I'm not sure. Did the Book of Judgment have an appendix devoted to etiquette?

"No, no, no. All is forgiven now. Jonathan simply did not understand, and Irene naturally has extensive experience in coping very tactfully with the ignorance and hostility of skeptical materialists."

"So Jonathan actually met Irene? Before, uh, his—"

"Before he *died.* Once one comprehends the word in its true sense, Holly, there is no longer any need to avoid it. All events have their place in the great hierarchy of the cosmos. Death, too. Of course, *passing on* does express the literal truth. But death, you see, is not death as the agnostic understands it. It is but a trance state. Or as Sir Arthur Conan Doyle so beautifully phrased it, the door is not shut, but merely ajar."

I was astounded. *"The* Sir Arthur Conan Doyle?"

"Spiritualism was the great passion of his existence in this sphere. Those silly detective stories were simply a diversion. Once he made the Great Discovery, he devoted himself to spreading the joyful news."

"The *same* Sir Arthur Conan Doyle?"

Put out, Ceci said, "From the moment he departed this life, he has communicated very generously with those who listen. I certainly don't find anything so surprising about it. After all, *When you have eliminated the impossible, whatever remains,* however improbable, *must be the truth."*

"I suppose so," I said.

"Would you care to see Simon's footprints?" Ceci asked.

Chapter Thirteen

BUNDLING HERSELF IN HER winter dog-walking outfit and arming herself with a flashlight, Ceci implored me in hushed tones to use common sense, as she phrased it, by keeping mum about what she'd just told me. "The unenlightened," she confided, "readily misinterpret the experiences of those who truly see." She continued, in an apparent non sequitur, "Take this Baker Street Irregulars nonsense. When you think about it, it's childish, isn't it? Pretending those imaginary people are real? These people are, after all, adults, and there they are giving themselves these silly nicknames—the Science Master, that's Robert—and playing all those games about *trivia*! Not that Althea is brainless, far from it, and neither was Ellis, who has, of course, come to view all that foolishness in perspective now, naturally, but a woman beyond the blush of first youth"—she pulled on the tam-o'-shanter—"is terribly vulnerable to misinterpretation and can be robbed far too easily of the opportunity to communicate with those who have passed beyond."

"Yes," I said.

"And stripped of her right to control her own life. And finances. Not that a guardian or whatever isn't necessary for someone in Althea's condition. Fortunately, Jonathan had her power of attorney, not that she has anything, really, but she's as blind as a bat, you know, and if she fell into the clutches of some unscrupulous person, she'd sign any sort of document that was put in front of her, speaking of which, for goodness' sake, who is going to manage Althea's affairs now? There can't be much more to it than writing checks to the nursing home, I suppose, but I really cannot be expected to deal with her affairs as well as my own. Where was I? Oh, in any event, it's dreadful enough to have Althea locked up in that place, but there was no choice, really, and my own competence is perfectly evident, but one never knows what misunderstanding may arise, and I'm sure you'll agree that one shudders to contemplate ending up in an institution merely because one has passed through the doors closed to, well, closed to closed minds."

With that, Ceci opened not the sort of door she was discussing, but one of the French doors to the terrace. "The path leads straight down," she remarked. This time, the reference was not metaphysical. Ceci briskly marched down the steps from the terrace to a bluestone walk that did, indeed, run straight down the sloping yard toward an area on which Robert and Hugh were now concentrating. The camera flashed.

"Now, watch that you don't trip the way Jonathan did!" Ceci called out. To me, she said, "We'll have to go beyond the gate."

Of the pearly variety? But as we approached Hugh and Robert, I pulled out my flashlight and trained it directly ahead. I saw, framed by an evergreen hedge, a black chain-link fence with an earthly wrought-iron gate. To the right of the path, a few yards from the hedge, stood a granite sundial. Robert and Hugh were busily examining an area a few feet from its base. Adding the beam of my flashlight to the light from their lanterns, I saw a roughly dug hole that suggested someone's premature and abandoned attempt to plant a small shrub in the frozen lawn.

"That," said Ceci, pointing to the shallow hole, "is where poor Jonathan caught his foot."

Robert cleared his throat. Hugh grunted.

"And," Ceci continued, "he reached out for the sundial to catch his balance, you see, but missed it. His hand slipped, and he fell and injured his head."

The scenario Ceci proposed was outright impossible. The hole, in which someone really might have tripped, was so close to the sundial that if Jonathan had caught his foot, lost his balance, and fallen in the direction of the sundial, he'd have bruised his upper thigh, perhaps; to have hit his head, he'd have had to be the height of a small child.

"Jonathan sensed Simon's presence, you see," Ceci explained, "and felt suitably ashamed of himself for saying those cruel things to Irene. I have never been so humiliated in all my life! As I told Jonathan when I shared my joy about Simon, all transactions are exchanges of *energy*, you see, and Irene's time, as well as her gifts, of course, are *her* energy, and she is perfectly entitled to receive energy in exchange. It's only fair."

I said, "But Jonathan didn't see it that way."

"I should never, *ever* have told him about Simon," Ceci agreed. "It was just that when Jonathan happened to call—he was really very good about staying in touch—I simply couldn't keep the news to myself. Simon had just made his first material appearance, just the evening before, and I was so absolutely thrilled! And, of course, I couldn't tell Althea, of all people. Althea does not understand at all.''

"When was this?" I asked.

"Well, Simon first came back on Monday. So, it was Tuesday that Jonathan called.''

Three days later, on Friday morning, Althea had been excited about her grandnephew's impending visit. The sequence made sense. On Monday, Irene stages Simon's appearance. On Tuesday, Ceci can't help telling Jonathan all about the wonderful psychic whose daily consultations have culminated in the material return of a dead dog. By Wednesday, Jonathan has made plans to come to Boston. He calls the sensible greataunt, Althea. He arrives on Saturday and meets Irene. At his insistence? According to Ceci, he is unpardonably rude to Irene; in other words, he charges her with conning his elderly great-aunt. Soon thereafter, he dies a violent death. And my hypothesis about a drug deal? I tried and failed to work in the cocaine. White powder, the paper had said. Instead of doing the coke indoors, Jonathan goes outside? Where the wind might be blowing? All I could think of was the sneeze scene in *Annie Hall*.

"Jonathan had an officious streak," Ceci told me. "In retrospect, I can see that it was most unwise of me to say a word to him. Not, of course, that my affairs were any of his business.''

As Ceci talked, Robert and Hugh arranged numerous little evidence bags in a long, narrow box meant for index cards. As they worked, they exchanged cryptic Sherlockian references. I was proud to catch an allusion to "The Dancing Men." In the story, mysterious little stick figures, the dancing men, had been drawn, among other places, on a sundial. And what clues *had* Hugh and Robert found? Blobs of ectoplasm? Wasn't that what spirits came back as? Gelatinous matter, chilled and slippery, like flavorless Jell-O. Had psychic zealots had the guts to taste this glop? Not that I expected them to substitute it in a recipe for molded lime salad. I mean, to a spiritualist, ectoplasm is human remains, of a sort, and consuming it might accordingly be considered a form of cannibalism. But if intrepid psychic researchers had gone ahead and sampled this stuff, strictly for the sake of science, "flavorless" probably wasn't how they described it. Rather, they probably gave the report you always hear about everything from frog legs to rabbit to human flesh: It tastes like chicken, only not quite.

"Ceci," Robert demanded, "what is this hole doing here?"

"I was concerned," she replied with dignity, "that Simon was repelled to find himself out here all cold and by himself. He lived in the house, of course. You remember, don't you? He was my constant companion. He had the free run of the yard whenever he wanted to go out—the fence goes all the way around—and at the time I thought, well, he belongs, really, out here in the fresh air. That's why I bought the sundial, you see. I simply couldn't tolerate the prospect of a gravestone. It's so depressing, so *un*-Simon, if you see what I mean, so . . ." Ceci continued to discourse on Simon's warm, sanguine disposition and the unsuitability of cold ground. She then moved to the topic of Boatswain, who, as Hugh and Robert probably did not realize, was a Newfoundland dog and the subject of a poem written by his bereaved owner, Lord Byron, for inscription on the dog's tomb.

" 'Are deposited the remains,' " Ceci quoted, " 'of one who possessed Beauty without Vanity.' "

" 'Strength without Indolence,' " I continued, " 'Courage without Ferocity, And all the virtues of Man, without his vices.' "

"You *do* understand," Ceci said.

"So you buried Simon's ashes here." That's in Byron's poem: ashes. "And then?"

"Then last week, we had that warm spell, you remember, which was deceptive. How was I to know? So I got out a shovel and started to remedy my error, but just below the surface, the ground was frozen, and the task was considerably more arduous than I ever expected. So"—she pointed to the hole—"that's as far as I got."

"Simon's remains are in an urn?" I asked.

"Of course! I wouldn't just—"

"Ceci," Robert interrupted, "what did you do with the shovel?"

"I left it right here."

"Did the police take it?" Hugh asked.

"No, no, it was gone. I've wondered if it might not have been stolen by those young people who found Jonathan. But never mind that! I was about to show Simon's paw prints to Holly." Making her way to the gate, Ceci explained, "They're perfectly preserved, you see, because Simon was here every day last week during the warm spell, when it was so damp, and then, of course, it suddenly turned cold, so you can still see them where the mud froze."

With more seriousness of purpose than I'd have expected, Hugh and Robert followed Ceci and me through the gate, which led to the dead end of a dark street. Reaching the dead end, the joggers who'd discovered the body must have reversed direction, taken a breather, and succumbed to the temptation to peer through Ceci's iron gate into the private precincts of the wealthy. I wondered whether the sight of the corpse had permanently cured the joggers of their snoopiness or whether, on the contrary, they would forever after feel compelled to sneak glances into hidden gardens on the chance of again uncovering one of the unexpected secrets of the rich.

"Lower Norwood Road," Robert informed me.

Here, a few gaslights were spaced at wide intervals. The one near the rear of Ceci's yard was out. Her property, as I hope I'm making clear, ran all the way from Upper Norwood Road, where her house was, to Lower Norwood, as did the lot next to hers. On the side of Lower Norwood opposite her back gate loomed a dark mass.

"Vacant house," Hugh remarked.

Robert was quick to correct him. *"Empty* house! *Empty.*" That's the title of one of the adventures: "The Empty House."

With undiminished pleasure, Hugh said, "He is everywhere," meaning, as Holmesians mean, Sherlock Holmes.

The house next to the empty one was a brick Tudor with bright windows, a light over the front door, and carriage lamps set on pillars on either side of the front walk. "The Franklins must be home from Florida," Ceci remarked. Then she trained her flashlight on her own side of the street, where a wide strip of rough grass and dirt took the place of a sidewalk. "Right over here, near these bushes. There! You see? All along here! The best ones are just to the right of the gate."

Shining my own flashlight on the area, I saw what were unmistakably the paw prints of a very large dog. How large? Rowdy weighs close to ninety pounds. He's a heavy-boned boy with big snowshoe paws. But these prints were longer, wider, and deeper than any I'd ever seen in the mud of my own backyard. For an unnerving moment, I wondered whether everything I understood about death was wrong. Had Simon really come back? Then I realized that Lower Norwood Road must be on the route of some local dog walker who owned . . . ? A Newfoundland? A living one, that is, or a mastiff, a Great Dane, or maybe one of those so-called giant malamutes that get sold through ads in the dog magazines for staggering sums of . . . well, energy exchange. Caveat emptor. Just my humble opinion, of course, backed by a lifetime in dogs and by the official standard for the Alaskan malamute. Have I digressed? Not really.

Anyway, if I couldn't identify the breed that had left the prints, Ceci couldn't be sure that they belonged to a particular Newfoundland who'd been dead for two years. But she *felt* certain, and the feeling satisfied her, as did Robert and Hugh's close examination of her evidence. On his knees, Hugh was going over the prints with his Sherlock Holmes magnifying glass. Ceci was triumphant. "There! You see? Now, am I letting my imagination run away with me? Am I seeing things? I know my Simon when I see him. Holly, wouldn't you know your Rowdy or your Kimi anywhere?"

"Yes, I would," I said truthfully.

"Well, you see? And I know my Simon. I've seen him just as clearly as I see his paw prints."

"Ceci," Robert demanded, "what color was Simon?"

I replied for her. "Black. His portrait is over the fireplace."

"Embedded here," said Hugh, "and observable in small quantities in the lower portion of the yard are hairs that, pending further research, we have tentatively identified as coming from a dog.''

Ceci clapped her mittens together in delight.

"The hairs," Hugh continued, "are not black. On the contrary, without exception, these hairs are uniformly *white*."

Chapter Fourteen

WITH HUGH AND ROBERT'S permission, I finally got Kimi and her tracking gear from the car. Kimi "got dressed," as Ceci phrased it, in the house. I should mention that Kimi's dark facial markings make her look intimidating. In particular, the goggles around her eyes create a permanent Lone Ranger mask. Ceci wasn't put off. To a Newf person, a seventy-five-pound malamute was practically an over-size Pomeranian. "Isn't she just the sweetest little girl?" Ceci cooed. "Isn't she a darling? Isn't she a love?"

I sometimes wonder: If you talk like this to an Alaskan malamute, what do you have left to say to a parakeet? Not that Kimi isn't sweet; she is. One of my most profound glimpses into her character, however, occurred when I watched her tackle and pin a male Great Pyrenees twice her size. As far as I could tell, she did it just on the off chance that he was wondering who was top dog. She didn't hurt him, and he obviously understood that she didn't mean to. In other words, Kimi is not everyone's idea of the ideal house pet. But then the average person's idea of the ideal house pet is a stuffed animal. In any case, I'm not the average person: My only absolute requirement of my dogs is that when I look into their eyes, I see God. I felt that in that sense, Ceci and I were kindred spirits.

"And all dressed up in her pretty red harness?" Ceci went on. "Oh, what a little sweetie pie she is!"

Ceci's fussing over Kimi annoyed Hugh and Robert, presumably because it impeded their effort to cast Kimi in the role of Toby or Pompey. I sympathized. Did Holmes and Watson have to put up with having Mrs. Hudson or some other female ramble on about how darling and sweet and adorable *their* tracking dogs were? But Toby and Pompey actually were tracking dogs, whereas the chance was slight that Kimi would make a half-decent pretense of scent-discriminatory night tracking on an old, heavily contaminated trail. Kimi's expression, however, is always intelligent, and in her red harness, she looked the part. When Ceci produced the only possession of the late Jonathan's not confiscated by the police, a Black Watch scarf he'd left in her front hall closet, I accepted it with as diligent and serious an attitude as I could muster.

"Now, Ceci, dear," Robert said, "when you retired to bed, Jonathan was listening to 'Bali Hai.' "

"And drinking Ellis's cognac," she concurred.

"What?" The word jumped from my lips.

"Cognac," Ceci repeated.

"No. Uh, 'Bali Hai'? From—"

"*South Pacific,*" Ceci said irritably.

Let me now apologize for inflicting on you the merest mention of "Bali Hai." It pains me to realize that the song will run through your head for the next quarter century. But, look, I had to mention "Bali Hai" because, hey, has anyone ever listened to it while snorting cocaine? Not that I'm an expert on cocaine. What I knew about it consisted mainly of what I'd read in newspapers and learned from the old Dave Van Ronk song, which was still popular in Cambridge among would-have-beens in their forties and fifties who now regretted having wasted the sixties getting their doctorates instead of making productive use of the era by smoking dope and hanging around coffeehouses in Harvard Square. Ah, the touching effort to make up for lost hipness that never was! Also, of course, I knew what Dr. Watson and Kevin Dennehy had told me. Their perspectives were a lot more like what I read in the papers than what I heard from Dave Van Ronk, who appeared to share the opinion of Sherlock Holmes. On one point, these sources agreed: An effect never attributed to the drug was anything remotely like a mad compulsion to listen to *South Pacific;* the eerie strains of Holmes's violin had not foreshadowed ''Bali Hai.''

''And was Jonathan drinking heavily?'' Robert inquired.

Ceci bristled. ''I am thoroughly tired of hearing aspersions cast on Jonathan's character! And while we are on that subject, let me say that far from being one of those *drug* people the papers are always going on about, he was . . . Now, I've gone and forgotten the word for him. I was telling Mary all about him as we were fixing the guest room for him, and she told me some word the young people use. Now it's slipped my mind. I was telling her all about his activities on behalf of the Young Republicans and about his *stamp* collection, you see, and about what a nice young man he was. And she said that the young people have a word—''

''Nerd?'' I blurted out.

''Nerd! That's it!'' Ceci was as delighted as if the lost word had turned out to be *prince.*

"Didn't he teach at Macalester?" I asked. I'd been there once. It's in St. Paul. Steve grew up in Minneapolis, and one time when I went there with him, his mother drove me so crazy that I developed an acute attack of homesickness two days after leaving Cambridge. Steve treated my near-collapse by buying me a Stephen McCauley novel at a bookstore called The Hungry Mind, which obviously imported its air from Harvard Square. After one paragraph and a few breaths, I was cured. Anyway, The Hungry Mind is almost on the campus of Macalester, which is the most politically correct college in the United States. Posted everywhere were announcements of events promoting disarmament, abortion rights, lesbian awareness, multiculturalism, rain forest preservation. A coming-out day was scheduled to coincide with parents' weekend. At Macalester, a Young Republican philatelist who listened to *South Pacific* would surely have been as out of place as a Chihuahua mistakenly entered at a Great Dane speciality, which is to say that Jonathan must have felt like a political hors d'oeuvre.

Hugh and Robert had Ceci show me where Jonathan had been seated when she'd last seen him alive.

"Well," said Ceci, pointing to the miniconservatory where we'd sat, "contrary to my wishes, he was here, and when I pointed out that it is rather drafty, he just said that it was thirty below zero in St. Paul. And he refused to move."

I asked, "Why was it contrary to your wishes?"

"Because Jonathan had done damage enough already, thank you very much. He was perfectly horrid to Irene, who, I must say, was very gracious in the face of his insults. And then after she left, when we were having dinner, prime rib, if I'd known, it'd've been meat loaf, he was extremely condescending and high-handed, and instead of sharing my happiness and accepting the evidence . . . Do you realize that Jonathan absolutely refused to look at Simon's paw prints? And he exuded hostile forces that were driving Simon away, which was why here by the French doors was positively the last place I wanted him. But here he planted himself. And he refused to budge.''

The chair she identified as the one where Jonathan had sat was the one I'd used. Since Saturday evening, when Jonathan had been there, Ceci and others might also have sat there, and the apparently thorough Mary had probably vacuumed its cushions as well. To please Hugh and Robert, I nonetheless directed Kimi to the chair, made a display of presenting her with Jonathan's Black Watch scarf, and issued what I hoped was a credibly professional-sounding order to track.

Kimi emerged as the Meryl Streep, if not the Toby or Pompey, of malamutes. She was far more convincing than Rowdy'd have been. If offered the scarf, Rowdy'd have taken it in his teeth and administered a death shake. Kimi, however, having been given the opportunity to take the scent, preceded me through the French door that Hugh held open. Once outdoors, she chose the route that Hugh, Robert, Ceci, and I had taken, probably the one followed by Jonathan and subsequently by the detectives, crime scene technicians, and other official investigators of the murder. Somewhat to my disappointment, Kimi did not keep her nose to the ground. Still, the combination of her characteristic self-confidence and the long, taut tracking lead fastened to her harness created the happy impression of a dog who knew what she was doing. It's remotely possible that she did. Technically, a tracking dog follows footsteps step by step, and a trailing dog works near the track, but an air-scenting dog goes after scent wherever it's available, on or above ground, and doesn't fit the Hollywood image of a bloodhound at work. The sense of olfaction, of course, is thousands, millions, or even billions of times more acute in dogs than in human beings. According to those who believe in the occult, all objects, inanimate as well as animate, retain information about everything they've ever been exposed to. Walls not only have ears, but can speak to those gifted with the power to hear, especially, if you ask me, if those gifted with the power to hear are paid lots of money and convey interesting messages about the exalted or fascinating personages their clients were in past lives. The only thing no one was in a past life is boring. You have to wonder whatever happens to dull souls.

Anyway, to the nose of the dog, all objects really do communicate history. Or at least relatively recent history. There was no question that Kimi was perceiving my scent, the trails of Hugh, Robert, Ceci, the authorities, and Jonathan, too, as well as the myriad scents of everything from dormant insects underground to the aromas of the dinners recently cooked and consumed by Ceci's neighbors on Norwood Hill. I had no faith that Kimi was discriminating between Jonathan's scent and each of a zillion others.

"Air scenting," I remarked . . . well, airily.

Ceci's property, as I've explained, sloped down from Upper Norwood Road, where her house was, to an evergreen hedge and the gate in the fence that opened to Lower Norwood Road. Jonathan's body had been found near the bottom of the yard, by the sundial that marked the burial place of Simon's ashes. It seemed to me that if Kimi actually was looking for Jonathan or anything that bore his scent, she should veer off the bluestone path and make for the area near the sundial where his corpse had lain. According to one theory of how dogs track, what the animal follows isn't the odor of the breathing, sweating person, but the scent of the microscopic flakes of skin that fall off all of us all the time and subsequently get eaten by bacteria and decompose. It seemed to me that if we, the living, went around repulsively scattering this dandruff that reeked in our paths in a manner we'd all prefer to ignore, well, what about corpses? I mean, most bodily functions don't rev up and switch into high gear after death. Shedding, I thought, should be an exception. As in "shuffled off this mortal coil"?

I was pondering the inspiration for the image—did Shakespeare have a dog? a pet snake? dandruff?—when Kimi abruptly turned off the path and headed for the sundial. As she neared it, her demeanor changed. She slowed her pace, lowered her head, and put her nose to the frozen grass. Instead of casting about in some body-shaped area near the sundial, however, she worked her way to within an inch of its base. Ears alert, nostrils twitching, she concentrated intently on the ground. Then with an air of fascinated deliberation, she patiently sniffed her way up the stone pedestal to a height of about a foot and a half. There, her nose lingered briefly before beginning its delicious descent. A year or two earlier, I'd watched a TV show about the ritual banquet of a society in France called *La Confrérie des Chevaliers du Tastevin*. What struck me was the familiar expression of rapture on the faces of the chevaliers as they savored the bouquets of their wines. With an almost snobbish sense of pride, I realized that when it came to ecstasy in olfaction, the Chevaliers du Tastevin had nothing on Rowdy and Kimi. In case you've never walked a dog, I should perhaps say explicitly that the bouquet Kimi relished was not that of wine.

I translated for Hugh and Robert. "There's been a

dog here.'' To prevent Kimi from overmarking, as it's called, I took hold of her collar and gently moved her away from the sundial. In the beam of my flashlight, the granite pedestal showed not the slightest stain. ''A big dog,'' I went on. ''Tall enough to leave a mark as high as Kimi sniffed. Probably but not necessarily a male. Probably high-ranking in the social world of dogs.''

''Recently?'' Robert asked.

''It's hard to say. How long scent lasts depends on humidity, temperature, and some other factors.'' I imagined myself the author of a work comparable to Holmes's monograph on however many distinct varieties of tobacco it was. A contribution to the scientific literature on dog urine, however, felt rather undignified and not really comparable at all, even though my subject had the obvious merit of not causing lung cancer.

''Let's say,'' I ventured, ''that the dog was here within the past week. Probably more recently. Kimi is pretty interested in it, so it's probably fresh.''

''Consistent with the white hairs,'' Robert remarked. Hugh nodded.

''The yard is fully fenced.'' I pointed toward the gate. ''Is the fence this high all around?''

The men agreed that it was.

''Six feet or so,'' I said. ''An escape artist dog might jump it or climb it to get out, but it's unlikely that a loose dog would've gone to the trouble of scaling the fence to get in, not without some strong motivation.'' I refrained from citing the obvious example of a bitch in season. ''One of the gates could've been left open,'' I continued. ''For Simon? But Newton enforces the leash law, so the chances are slim that there would've been a stray dog around here. What I really think is that someone deliberately brought in a big dog. I think it was part of an effort to convince Ceci that Simon is returning in material form.''

At Hugh and Robert's suggestion, I led Kimi through the gate to Lower Norwood Road. Still holding her tracking lead, I released my grip on her collar and let her explore. The pruned evergreens inside the fence formed a tidy hedge. Here, masses of shrubs were tall and wild. Kimi snuffled around without paying special attention to anything. To satisfy Hugh and Robert as well as to sate my own curiosity, I directed Kimi's attention to the gigantic paw prints preserved in the frozen mud and ordered her to track. Kimi, of course, could virtually see the big dog who'd left those prints. But did she understand what I wanted? For the thousandth time, I resolved to get serious about the sport of tracking.

Kimi dutifully put her nose down. She kept it down as she took a few steps, hesitated, took another step or two, and came to a puzzled halt near the blacktop. Numerous tire tracks were visible on the wide verge of dirt and weedy grass that stretched from the asphalt to the ragged hedge. The road was narrow. Anyone driving here for any reason could have run a tire off the paved surface. Hugh and Robert, however, were thrilled. Toby, they decided, had successfully followed the big white dog to the spot where he had entered a parked car and been spirited away.

No pun intended.

Chapter Fifteen

ACCORDING TO ECCLESIASTES, a living dog is better than a dead lion. As I said goodbye to Ceci, I couldn't help wishing that Ecclesiastes had gone on to assert that a living cat is better than a dead dog. Lacking a biblical pronouncement on the topic, I failed to convince Ceci that a darling little kitty would make the perfect addition to her household.

The next morning, while running errands, I tried to foist off the cat on the employees and customers at the dry cleaner's, the local used-book shop, the hardware store, and—drat!—the proprietor of the fish market, who obviously would have offered a delectable home. In the afternoon, the cat had to endure my presence in my study for the three hours it took me to keyboard and revise a book review for *Dog's Life* that I'd drafted by hand. Before I dared to step into my office, I had to put the dogs in the yard in case they squeezed past me and nailed the cat. When I entered, the cat was curled up on my mouse pad. At the sight of me, it hissed. I'd discovered by now that the easiest way to get it to move was to offer affection. As soon as I reached out to pat it, it dove off the desk and disappeared. I'd cleaned the litter box that morning. The odor lingered like the grin of the Cheshire cat.

After proofing and printing the rave review—*The Domestic Dog: Its Origins, Behavior, and Interaction with People* edited by James Serpell—I dashed to the post office counter at Huron Drug, where I mentioned the cat to six people who weren't interested. At the Fresh Pond Market, I pounced on a promising-looking adopter, a psychotherapist friend of Rita's whose shopping cart held a bag of cat litter. Sounding offended, she said she was buying the litter to absorb oil that had leaked around her burner. In self-congratulatory tones that reminded me of my own when I talk about my dogs, she said, "Besides, I'm allergic to cats."

The part about the oil may have been true, but the smug bit about the allergy struck me as a pitifully inadequate effort at a local form of status seeking. In normal places, when someone asks how you are, you're supposed to say *fine*, right? What's mandatory among Cambridge psychotherapists is a volley of complaints about physical illness, mental distress, or both, preferably accompanied by tips about traditional and alternative remedies that others might try should they, too, luck into the same maladies. Lower back pain is now passé, as are Achilles tendinitis, chiropractors, and acupuncture. Depression is still worth your social while, but the prestigious new class of afflictions now sweeping the Cambridge psychotherapeutic valetudinarian community consists of allergies. Out with pain! Out with sorrow! In with sneezes, blotches, watery eyes, gastrointestinal symptoms, or, best of all, diffuse sensations of discomfort accompanied by heart palpitations, difficulty in breathing, and a radical drop in blood pressure, a syndrome preferably triggered by pervasive and unavoidable allergens like air and water, for example, that cause no reaction in ordinary people, but reserve their provocation for the ultrasensitive and ultraspecial. A Cambridge psychotherapist with nothing better to brag about than an undistinguished allergy to something as unimaginative as cats was probably suffering from such low self-esteem that she'd soon regress to lower back pain. The cat, I decided, deserved a better home than this woman could provide.

"They're worse than dog people," I was saying to Rita a half hour later as we sat in my kitchen. "At least we have ribbons to show for our wins."

"She's a perfectly nice person," Rita replied in defense of her colleague. "It's just that her practice is down. She's been hit hard by managed care." That's Rita's allergy: health maintenance organizations, the demise of private practice. "It's too bad she didn't want the cat."

"If she's going to be out of work, it isn't too bad at all. Besides, her oil burner leaks. Her house could catch fire. And I don't want the cat exposed to environmental toxins. You want some coffee? Tea? Are you done for today? You want a drink?"

"Yes. My six o'clock canceled. Speaking of my clients, you remember the one whose dog is lost?"

With my head inside the refrigerator, I said, "Still lost? I'm really sorry. Maybe I can think of something . . . But let me get you your drink. We have Nut Brown Ale, Sam Adams, and Kevin's Budweiser, and there's white wine here, but it's been opened. Scotch? Gin? Absolut?" Absolut vodka is what therapists here started to drink at about the same time the allergy fad began. It's possible that they're all, in fact, allergic to Absolut. Its main appeal, if you ask me, is that it permits Cambridge therapists to play mugwump: It looks as clear and pure as mineral water while packing ten times the wallop of imported wine.

I poured an Absolut for Rita and a Bud for myself. There you have us: her silk blouse, good wool suit, stockings, pumps, rings, earrings; my jeans, running shoes, and a faded blue sweatshirt and new white socks decorated with black paw prints, deliberately, that is, bought that way, not, for once, embellished by Rowdy and Kimi.

Settling myself at the table, I apologized to Rita for having been so unresponsive to the problem of her client's lost dog.

"You weren't unresponsive," Rita said generously. "She found the material you gave me very supportive. She'd already called a lot of shelters and dog officers and vets' offices, and she'd put up posters, but she's got an ad in the paper now, and she hadn't thought of asking children." *Yes, she, she, she.* Rita avoids revealing the names of her patients.

"Children really are worth enlisting," I said. "They notice dogs. They notice a lot. Sherlock Holmes had the right idea. The Baker Street Irregulars. Neighborhood urchins. Street Arabs."

"Child labor," Rita decreed. "Unfortunately, she still hasn't found her dog, and the problem is compounded by her irrational conviction that the whole episode was her own fault."

"Was it?"

"It's a good thing you didn't try to become a therapist," Rita said. "She took the dog running with her, and when she got back to her car, she noticed she'd dropped one of her gloves. She'd taken them off only a minute or two before, so the glove had to be somewhere nearby. And then she did something that was nothing worse than a little careless. She'd hitched the dog to a park bench so she could do her stretching exercises without having the dog run off. When she went back to look for her glove, instead of taking the dog with her or putting him in the car, she left him tied there. Then she retraced her steps and found the glove. When she got back, the dog was gone.''

''And?''

''And it's been more than a week, and she hasn't seen him since.''

''I meant, had he slipped his collar? Was his leash still there? Does she have any idea what happened?''

''His leash was gone. It was an expensive new leash, and she'd looped it around the bench. She doesn't think it could've broken, he wouldn't have chewed on it, she's ninety-nine percent sure it was really fastened to the bench, and so on, all of which leads her to the conclusion that it was her fault. And in desperation, she's gone and consulted some pet psychic, who's at least kept her hopes up, which is as therapeutic as anything I'm doing.''

''Irene Wheeler,'' I said coldly.

Rita nodded.

''Irene Wheeler is a crook.''

''What harm can it do? 'There are more things in heaven and earth,' Holly, 'than are dreamt of in your philosophy.' '' Rita sipped her vodka. ''Besides, my client is taking action instead of passively accepting misery as her due, which is a definite advance. And the psychic assures her that the dog is safe, well, and nearby. Without that assurance, my client would probably feel too crushed to pursue the practical steps of actually looking for the dog.''

''If you go out and look for the dog, and then you find it, it's because you looked. It isn't because you swallowed some psychic's sugar pill. Rita, you know those people, Scott and Gloria, who are harassing Steve? This Irene Wheeler is the same person who told those people that Steve shouldn't have spayed their bitch. She conned these people into believing that she could've cured their bitch, and she simultaneously conned them into acting as her unpaid publicists. You go to a show, and there's Gloria handing out Irene Wheeler's business cards and talking her up at Steve's expense. Gloria is, admittedly, malicious, but she's none too bright. On her own it would never occur to her to carry out this kind of organized scheme. It would never occur to Scott, either. Mostly he does what Gloria wants. The driving force there has to be Irene Wheeler. But the real con job she has going is worse than that."

I filled Rita in on everything I knew about Ceci's involvement with Irene. "Rita, this Irene Wheeler is not harmless," I concluded. "She saw Ceci's loneliness and vulnerability and gullibility. Most of all, she saw Ceci's money. And she stalked, and she pounced, just like a cat after a bird. To take advantage of Ceci like that is *evil* in itself. But there's also Jonathan's murder. From what I can piece together, Ceci blabbed to Jonathan about Simon's return, and he immediately caught on that she was being conned, and he came here to put a stop to it. Jonathan met Irene. Irene went to Ceci's house. And according to Ceci, Jonathan was very rude to her, meaning, I assume, that he told Irene to leave Ceci the hell alone. That same night, Jonathan was murdered. One and one?"

Rita was stern. "Holly, you need to talk to Kevin."

"I will. I'm not keeping it a secret. But when I got home last night, all the lights in the Dennehys' house were dark. I didn't want to wake anyone up. And I haven't been able to reach Kevin today. But I have left messages."

"Now," Rita said with annoyance, "I don't know what to do about my client. She—"

The pronoun was starting to get on my nerves. I wished that Rita would relax her professional ethics and spit out the name of her client. I interrupted Rita to say so.

Rita glared at me before continuing. "*She*, I repeat, *she* is really in agony, and I've been trying to support the reality part of this, taking steps, and so forth, and also working on her terrible sense of blame, which has to do with other issues in her life. And I saw the psychic, really, as a therapeutic ally. Although, I must say, so far, she's done my client nothing but good."

"She's slick," I said. "I consulted her myself."

"*You?*"

"I wanted to get a firsthand impression, which was—and is—that she is smooth. That's the hitch about the murder. This murder doesn't gibe with my take on Irene Wheeler. I can easily see her as a con artist. In fact, that's how I *do* see her. But I can't see her bashing someone over the head with a shovel. That's apparently what the murder weapon was. Ceci left a shovel in the yard. It disappeared. Anyway, the murder weapon was a blunt instrument, and blunt is not Irene Wheeler's style. Sharp, subtle, something that could go undetected— that's her style. Gloria is the blunt instrument type. She's coarse. She's blatant. You practically get a concussion just from listening to her."

"Maybe her involvement with this psychic goes deeper than you realize."

"Maybe it does," I said.

But Rita, of course, always thinks that everything goes deeper than I realize.

Chapter Sixteen

HEY," SAID KEVIN DENNEHY, "I'm not asking how much they took you for on that vacuum cleaner for dogs." His gaze rose innocently and sanctimoniously to the overhead light fixture in my kitchen. Now and then, ex-acolyte Kevin Dennehy still locks baby blues with heaven.

"Miss Manners would be proud of you," I said. "But it isn't a vacuum cleaner. It's a blower. My old one quit, and I had to replace it. You can't show-groom a malamute without one. It is an absolute necessity."

I might as well not have spoken.

"And why is it," Kevin continued rhetorically, "that a representative of the law stands idly by and keeps his mouth shut when a poor helpless citizen is being victimized by some door-to-door salesman out peddling vacuum cleaners for dogs?"

"Kevin, really! I did not buy it from a—"

"Because," Kevin barreled on, "it's your money, and you've got the right to throw it away on any crazy thing you want, that's why. Take my mother."

The offer sounded genuine. "Are you planning a yard sale?" I asked.

Kevin cracked a smile. "Trying to slip in ahead of the dealers?"

"My own mother was enough for one lifetime. I'm not bidding on yours."

"A lot of people might consider my mother a crackpot," Kevin said, eyeing me. "Good Catholic lady, raises her kids to be good Catholics, goes to Mass every day of her life, and boom! Out of nowhere, she's a Seventh-Day Adventist."

"Your mother had a conversion experience. She wasn't duped. There was no coercion. And when I spend money on my dogs, it's my choice. No one is taking advantage of your mother or me. The situation with Ceci is totally different. Ceci is being *had*."

As we talked, Kimi had been peacefully dozing on the new tile floor at Kevin's feet. A few minutes earlier, Rowdy had vanished to my bedroom to engage in one of his favorite pastimes: sorting through the big basket of highly assorted dog toys to pick the exact one that suited his fancy. Now, with an air of calm satisfaction, he wandered back into the kitchen bearing a fuzzy stuffed dinosaur and happily settled himself about a yard from Kimi. Because these polyester fleece creatures were billed as chew toys, I'd special-ordered squeakerless versions that would be safe in malamute jaws. Neither dog, however, had tried to rip open the dinosaur or its kin, which included a duck, a featureless man, a teddy, and a lion. Kimi, in fact, was relatively uninterested in the fleece toys. Rowdy, however, took immense pleasure in the little stuffed menagerie, pleasure that seemed to consist mainly of simple possession. After carefully selecting just the right toy, he'd stretch out with his treasure between his forelegs and close to his chest, where he'd rest his chin on it, savor its scent, and nibble now and then like a puppy with a full stomach who still enjoys being close to Mama. And that's how he settled himself now with the dinosaur until Kimi opened her eyes, rose, stretched, strolled over to him, snatched his toy, and casually returned with it to her original spot.

"Why does he let her get away with that?" Kevin demanded.

"She's no threat to him. It's a game she plays. He indulges her. I assume that in some way, he thinks that this is the price he pays for having her around." I paused. "In other words, they both know what's going on, everything is voluntary, and no one is being taken advantage of."

Wearing what I'll admit was a hangdog expression, Rowdy patiently eyed Kimi, who clasped the dinosaur between her forepaws and eyed him back. "You are a good boy," I told Rowdy. "You want another toy? I'll get you one."

When I returned a few seconds later with a second toy dinosaur identical to the first, Kevin asked, "This old lady, she mentally competent?"

"Ceci? Here, Rowdy, here's *your* toy. You are a very good dog." Peace between malamutes is not something I take for granted.

"She know who she is, where she is?" Kevin was still pursuing the subject of Ceci. "What day it is? Whose money she's spending? On what?"

"Yes, absolutely, except that what she's spending it on is—"

"Her own business," Kevin said. "She got any complaints?"

"No, she's overjoyed. There isn't a more satisfied consumer in the entire Commonwealth of Massachusetts. She's totally delighted. And, Kevin, I understand that there's nothing illegal about psychics. I don't think there should be. I think that most psychics genuinely believe in their own powers and probably do a lot of good. But this business with Ceci isn't about psychics in general, it's about Irene Wheeler. And Irene Wheeler is a fraud. She isn't just conveying spiritual messages that she might honestly believe were coming from the dog. What she's done is to convince Ceci that the dog is appearing in the flesh, and if you ask me, *that's* fraud. Furthermore, she is preying on loneliness and grief and love. And *that* is evil.''

Slowly moving his big head back and forth, Kevin said, ''If I gotta go and arrest everyone who's out there promising resurrection, I'm—''

''Be serious! Kevin, there is no comparison. Irene Wheeler has been deliberately staging the so-called materialization of Ceci's dog in an effort to get more and more money from her. There is nothing religious about it. The whole enterprise is a travesty. If anything, it's heresy.''

''Lady left the gate open. A dog came in and peed.''

''And, minor point, a man was murdered, a man who was trying to defend his elderly great-aunt from a con artist. You know, Kevin, there's a pattern here, as Rita would say. This is the same thing you did, or refused to do, about the evidence I carefully preserved when I rescued the cat. I kept the pillowcase and the twine and the stone for you to send to the police lab, I showed those things to you, and for all you've done, I might as well have thrown them in the river. I do not understand why you are taking such an obstructionist attitude lately.''

Huffing himself up, Kevin said, ''Hey, obstructionist? Me? Is the lady being conned? Damned straight she is. But let me give you a couple of facts. First of all, when what you've got is a case that's got nothing to do with religion, you still got trouble. Phony charities. Get-rich-quick schemes. Romance. Geez, Holly, the lonely people out there. Half the world's a charter member of the Eleanor Rigby Social Club. Pretty housekeeper convinces her elderly gent he's Cary Grant, marries him, he knows it's for love, and what's his family do? Drag it into court? Yeah, some of the time. She says she loves him, he says she loves him, family looks like a pack of piranhas. End of story. Or a smooth talker convinces an old lady to sign over her estate to build a palace for homeless pussycats.''

''Where?'' I asked.

Kevin ignored my interruption. ''Old-timer fancies himself a whiz at crossword puzzles, only these days he's a couple of blanks short of an answer. Opens his mail. Special invitation to enter a crossword contest. All's he has to do to enter is complete this puzzle and, by the way, send a check. Five dollars. Ten dollars. One across: three letters, furry pet that says meow. He's still a genius. Writes the check. Mails it. Gets a letter back. Congratulations! He's won. His prize is he gets moved up to the expert level. Entry fee: twenty dollars. Forty dollars. One down: five letters, four-legged animal that says neigh.''

''Through the mail? That must be a federal offense. If it isn't, it ought to be.''

''You want it straight? In ninety-nine percent of these cases, you can't prove a thing, and if you can, you can't catch the perp, and even if you do, ninety-nine percent of the time, he gets off, and if he goes to jail, he's out next week. Most of the time, no one hears a thing, because when these guys are good, hey, everybody's happy, at least for a while. You used to be a lonely old nobody, or a lonely not-so-old nobody, and now all of a sudden, you're a winner, you're a financial wizard, you got the satisfaction of feeding starving kids in Boola-Boola Land, or you got romance back? Complaining is the last thing that's going to cross your mind.'' Kevin's voice dropped. ''For a while. And if you catch on, you're going to knock yourself out making sure your relatives don't find out, because if they do, you're going to end up somebody's ward, and where you're going to end up is in a nursing home.''

''Ceci is aware of that possibility,'' I said, ''except that she doesn't see herself as a victim. What she's afraid of is misunderstanding. That's what she thinks about Jonathan, the grandnephew, the one who was murdered. What I think is that Jonathan got the full picture.''

''Maybe Auntie did him in.''

''*Ceci?* I really don't . . .''

Although Kevin had no connection with the official investigation of Jonathan's murder, I couldn't bring myself to say anything incriminating about Ceci. I couldn't help thinking, though, that the murder weapon had presumably been the shovel she'd admitted to having left in her yard. I remembered how effortlessly she'd lifted and carried the heavy tea tray. Most of all, I thought of how dependent Ceci was on Irene Wheeler and how pitifully eager for a reunion with her beloved Simon. As to risk, it seemed to me that half the people who lived at the Gateway might've risked jail to stay out of the nursing home.

''When it comes to murder,'' said Kevin, ''one thing you can forget is this pet psychic who's conning the old lady. These vultures who prey on the elderly are dirt, they're filth, you can't touch them, most of the time you don't even know they're there, but if things start to go wrong, the world's full of sitting ducks, and all's they do is move on to a new one. These bastards are the scum of the earth, but there's one thing they're not, and that's violent.''

Chapter Seventeen

MY CONVERSATION WITH KEVIN took place on
Wednesday. Over the next few days, one little
incident after another echoed his disheartening
message that no one would nail Irene Wheeler.

The first incident consisted of my checking out and
reading a tattered old library copy of a book published
in 1924. Its title was *Memories and Adventures*. It was
the memoirs of Sir Arthur Conan Doyle. If I'd hoped to
find proof that a belief in spiritualism was any indication of lunacy, I'd have been deeply disappointed in the
book. It was the warm, charming, utterly cogent autobi-
ography of a sane person whose assumptions about the
possible and the impossible differed radically from
mine. The creator of Sherlock Holmes had been a man
bursting with energy and interests: crime and detection,
of course, politics, war, friendship, love, travel, the sea,
the Arctic, and that marvelous new invention, the bicycle. Gregarious and industrious, Conan Doyle was an
incredibly prolific writer who penned his works while
talking with family and friends. On several occasions,
he'd played Sherlock Holmes; he'd investigated real

crimes. Only at the end of his memoirs did he turn to what ultimately became the grand and generous passion of his life: his determination to share with the world the joyous news that the spirits of the dead could communicate with the living. His fervor was more technological than evangelical. A few weeks earlier, I'd heard Nicholas Negroponte preach on the radio about bits and bytes. Negroponte: the Billy Graham of computers. Half of Negroponte's claims sounded more farfetched than Conan Doyle's. I believed Negroponte; I'd experienced the miracles myself. Conan Doyle, of course, had persuaded millions of readers to accept Sherlock Holmes as a virtual reality. Yet he didn't convert me to spiritualism. He did, however, convince me of his sincerity and his sanity. I'd have liked to consult him myself. I wondered what he'd make of Irene Wheeler. He'd encountered fraudulent mediums. Would he spot her as one? If so, as a man of vigorous action, he'd certainly expose her fakery. Furthermore, he'd devise an ingenious plan to identify and punish the scoundrel who'd tried to murder the poor cat that now occupied my office. As the perfect ally, Conan Doyle had only one drawback: He'd been dead since 1930.

The second incident occurred on Thursday night after services, which is to say at the end of the evening's dog training at the Cambridge Armory. I'd left Rowdy home and taken Kimi to the advanced class. Steve had been working his pointer, Lady, in Novice, more to build her self-confidence than to prepare her for obedience competition, I might add. Anyway, after class, out on the sidewalk in front of the armory, Kimi checked out Lady, who immediately curled up in a quivering ball of submission at Kimi's feet. Steve's shepherd bitch, India, is a superb obedience dog. What's more—and the two don't always go together—India is wonderfully obedient in everyday life. She is utterly devoted to Steve and quietly protective of him. India is one of the least neurotic animals I have ever known. Lady, in contrast, actually leaps in fear at the sight of her own shadow. Terrified, love-starved, and unbelievably sweet, she was brought to Steve for euthanasia. With more justification than she realizes, she regards him as her defense against a world that is trying to kill her. It seemed to me symptomatic of Steve's state these days that he'd shown up with Lady and left his tough-minded protector at home.

Without preamble, I said, "It's harassment. You could at least talk to a lawyer."

"These aren't the first dissatisfied clients I've had. They won't be the last. They're entitled to take their business elsewhere. There's no more to it than that." He paused. "Negative attention can be reinforcing, too. I don't need to tell you that."

It's true. Take barking. *Yap, yap, yap, yap, yap.* The owner springs up, dashes to the dog, and yells, "Now, Fang, enough of that! No more noise! I am sick to death of listening to that racket all the time, and so is everyone else! Stop! Quiet! No——more——barking!" Now consider the opposite behavior, namely, not barking. When Fang is a good, quiet boy, what does the owner do? Nothing. And from a dog's point of view, almost anything is better than nothing, and a dramatic display of attention is radically better than nothing. In fact, it's such a big treat that Fang wants more. *Yap, yap, yap, yap, yap.*

"Gloria and Scott don't care about your response or nonresponse," I told Steve. "They're getting plenty of positive reinforcement elsewhere. Irene Wheeler is getting free publicity. This is not some minor behavior problem that is going to vanish if you ignore it. If a dog goes for your throat, you defend yourself. You don't just stand there trying not to reinforce the behavior. Besides which, you are not the only person being hurt here.''

''All I'm doing, Holly,'' he said pointedly, ''is minding my own business.''

That's how we parted for the evening.

The third incident emerged from a series of minor episodes evidently presented for my viewing by some Higher Power who wanted to teach me a lesson in the difficulty of distinguishing between truth and make-believe. The incident itself, to the extent that it was one, was strictly internal and consisted of my concluding that I couldn't make the distinction myself and couldn't tell whether anyone else could, either.

On Friday morning, Rowdy and I arrived in Althea's room at the Gateway to find Robert and Hugh engaged in fantastic Holmesian speculations about Jonathan's murder. In today's episode of the Great Game, Robert and Hugh took turns playing the Great Detective.

''Has there ever been,'' Robert interrogated Althea, ''a family connection with Australia?''

Bending toward me, Hugh said in an undertone, ''The possibility of a missing heir, you understand.''

''None whatsoever,'' replied Althea. ''The return of long-lost kin from anywhere at all is entirely out of the question. Jonathan was Ceci's heir and my own, and we are his, too, for that matter. He told me so himself. You see, there are no other family members.'' As if in response to my unspoken speculations about who would inherit now that Jonathan was dead, Althea added, ''Except ourselves, of course. I myself am now Ceci's heir, I suppose, although the matter is strictly hypothetical. Ceci is a relatively young woman. As for me?'' Here, Althea produced a mischievous smile that took sixty years off her face. Wagging a finger at Hugh and Robert, she said, ''As for me, I suppose I'd better be careful if the two of you install yourselves in the next room and suspend a bellrope near my bed!''

Delighted with myself, I said a bit too loudly, '' 'The Speckled Band'!''

Remember that one? Dr. Grimesby Roylott? His stepdaughters? The ventilator? The bellpull? And the deadly snake, the swamp adder, that *is* the speckled band.

Hugh and Robert greeted my interjection with glances of withering scorn. Resuming the interrogation, Robert asked whether Jonathan had been in a position to reveal the shameful secrets of some highly placed personage. I struggled to sense how light the banter really was. Althea, I was certain, understood the game as just that; in pretending that the Canon was the true record of the exploits of Sherlock Holmes, she reveled in what she knew was fantasy. Of Hugh and Robert I felt less certain. At some level, they could tell fact from fiction. It seemed possible, though, that just as I could imagine Holmes and Watson as real people, so Hugh and Robert could conceive of them as historical beings. Why not? Didn't the entire world *believe* in Sherlock Holmes?

''Jonathan did not move in the circles of the illustrious,'' said Althea.

Narrowing his eyes, Hugh demanded in low tones, ''Freemasonry?''

As Althea was shaking her head, I felt like asking what Conan Doyle had had against Freemasons. In his work, they were always portrayed in a hideously sinister fashion that I'd never been able to comprehend. A reference to Conan Doyle as a writer of personally biased fiction would, however, have seemed like a spoilsport's effort to ruin the game. Furthermore, although Hugh and Robert were successfully distracting Althea from what might otherwise have been gloomy thoughts of the demise of her family and the restrictions of her life at the Gateway, the strained atmosphere of forced gaiety and the scorn that had greeted my own contribution made me reluctant to say anything more. Responding to my discomfort or perhaps to the oddity of the whole situation, Rowdy grew increasingly restless. Instead of playing up to Althea, Hugh, or Robert, he focused exclusively on me. For the first time since our initial visits to the Gateway, he whined noisily in what I heard as a plea to go home. I didn't linger, but excused myself by claiming that he needed to go out, as in a sense he did.

Once we left Althea's room, Rowdy stopped his noise and seemed in no hurry at all. As we waited by the elevators, an attendant, Ralph Ryan, according to his name tag, appeared from around the corner with an ancient, emaciated man in a wheelchair. Rowdy gave the frail-looking man his usual happy tail wag. "Do you like dogs?" I asked brightly. To Rowdy, I whispered, "Wait."

The man said nothing. It occurred to me that he may not have heard me. When I'd found myself in similar situations on previous visits to the Gateway, I'd tried to read the person's facial expression and body language. Now, I found nothing to read. The attendant, Ralph, was almost as unresponsive as his charge. I hated to seem like the kind of person who acts as if people in wheelchairs can't speak for themselves ("Does he like dogs?"). Some people at the Gateway, however, really were unable to speak for themselves. Most of the employees would tactfully let me know when someone couldn't see or couldn't hear and whether the person did or didn't welcome the attention of a therapy dog. Ralph yawned and checked his watch. Rowdy and I might have been invisible and inaudible. When one of the two elevators arrived, I let Ralph and the man have it to themselves. In the absence of information about the old man's wishes, it seemed best not to trap him in a small enclosed space with a big dog.

As Rowdy and I waited, a woman wearing a bright red dress and baby blue bedroom slippers joined us. She said how beautiful Rowdy was, but declined my invitation to pat him. He was too big for her, she said; she'd always had toy poodles. When the elevator finally came, she followed us in with no hesitation. The second the doors closed, she began to complain about the Gateway. The elevators took forever, she said. The food wasn't what it used to be, and neither were the activities. There was a shortage of staff because everyone was underpaid. Furthermore, these days, the Gateway wasn't in the least fussy about who got hired. "They'll take anyone who'll work for almost nothing," she said. "And with what it costs to be here? Scandalous!" She went on to say that when she'd moved to the Gateway, it had been just like a hotel. Now, no one did anything for you. "And it used to be spotless!" she exclaimed indignantly. "How that's changed! Yesterday, a cockroach crawled right across my windowsill, and I couldn't get a soul to do a thing about it." As the doors opened to the lobby, she lowered her voice and confided, "They pretended they didn't believe me. They do that here, you know. It's one of their favorite tricks."

Fact: The elevators were slow. Fact: I wouldn't have hired the unresponsive Ralph as a kennel attendant. But the pay scale? The cost of living at the Gateway? The decline in the quality of staff and services? And the cockroach? As I returned my volunteer's badge to the bulletin board in the office and signed myself out, I inspected the area for signs of infestation. I found none. On the contrary, the linoleum floor looked freshly washed and waxed, the desks and shelves were free of dust, there was no odor at all, and nothing was crawling along the baseboards or anywhere else. And there were plenty of activities, weren't there? There had to be. Helen Musgrave was always attending something, wasn't she? But if Helen showed up to find that an event had been canceled or didn't exist, what would she do? With a sinking heart, I realized that she'd immediately forget her disappointment and happily bustle off elsewhere. The recent past disappeared from Helen's mind as swiftly and as completely as every trace of Nancy had vanished from her room within hours of her death. Passing through the lobby, stopping to let Rowdy say goodbye to the women gathered there, I realized that although a prominent section of the big notice board by the front doors was devoted to welcoming new residents, there was nothing there or elsewhere to acknowledge the departure of those whose beds the new people now occupied. On the way out, I studied the Polaroid photos of the new residents. Well, what did I want? A notice that read Bon Voyage? And underneath it, deathbed snapshots of people breathing their last?

So that was when the third incident really occurred. Studying the snapshots of the new residents, I realized that I'd learned of one death at the Gateway, Nancy's. In fact, people had been dying there all the time. I'd simply pretended otherwise. Althea was older than I wanted to acknowledge. The Holmes nonsense was make-believe. Fact: Jonathan Hubbell had been brutally murdered. Fact: Although we are all dying all the time, Althea was going to die sooner than most other people, sooner even than most other people at the Gateway. The complaining woman in the elevator had definitely been wrong about one thing. The Gateway had never, ever been *just* like a hotel. Here, almost no one had ever checked out alive.

Chapter Eighteen

AS I WAS CRATING ROWDY in the back of the car, Hugh and Robert suddenly appeared in the Gateway parking lot, hustled across, and abruptly demanded a sample of dog hair.

"Hugh intends to perform a few experiments," Robert explained. Half to Hugh and half to me, he added in the sort of voice people use when they're quoting, *"I gather we have your good wishes, Miss Winter."*

Lacking the correct Sherlockian reply, I just said, "Indeed you do, Mr. MacPherson. And if Rowdy were shedding, you could have enough hair to spin and weave into a deerstalker hat. But he isn't."

Producing a pair of manicure scissors, Hugh started to speak. I cut him off. No pun intended. "Rowdy is entered tomorrow," I said, shifting into what is literally my mother tongue—she bred and showed golden retrievers. "In a dog show," I explained. "I want someone chopping off a patch of his coat about the way you want someone hacking off the first paragraph of 'A Study in Scarlet.'"

"In eighteen seventy-eight . . ." Hugh began.

Robert cut in. "*In* the year *eighteen seventy-eight* . . ."

"The American Kennel Club had not yet been established," I said, "and it wouldn't have made any difference, but it does now. Besides, those scissors have sharp points." Softening, I conceded that Kimi was beginning to shed. "I'll send you some of her hair if you want." That's me: all generosity.

Like the proverbial bloodhounds on the trail, Robert and Hugh, however, insisted on following me home. As I drove there, I kept checking the rearview mirror in the hope that I'd lost them. But Hugh, at the wheel, stuck to me like the infernal paint that the villainous Stapleton applied to the unfortunate hound of the Baskervilles. With Rowdy entered the next day, I had grooming to do, and having spent the morning doing housework and then visiting the Gateway, I hadn't written so much as an indefinite *a* or *an* or the definite *the*, never mind the kind of article I could sell. Like every other freelance writer, I live in terror of having to get a real job. It was noon. Would Hugh and Robert hang around? Would they expect lunch?

Something about those two simple questions made me realize how little I knew about Hugh and Robert. They shared, it seemed to me, Holmes's fondness for disguise, but instead of adopting the Master's guises, they cloaked themselves in the identity he'd hidden beneath the persona of a drunken-looking groom or an old woman. What exactly was the quality of their devotion to Althea? Did they love her as a woman, a person? Or as *the* woman, the representative of Irene Adler? As to their relationship, was it a peculiar reenactment of what Holmes-lovers called "The Friendship"—the curious tie between Holmes and Watson? I thought of the tongue-in-cheek essay Althea had given me: "Watson

Was a Woman.'' Hugh and Robert were definitely men, brothers-in-law, men who had married sisters, yet who made no secret of having lived their lives in thrall to a third woman, Althea. They'd presumably been visiting the Gateway since Althea first moved there. Had the complainer in the elevator voiced her dissatisfaction to them? Had the Gateway's standards really declined? Had the cost increased? Jonathan had been Althea's heir. He'd had her power of attorney. He must have paid the Gateway's bills. Could he have planned to move Althea to a cheaper place? Could Hugh and Robert have taken decisive action to prevent the move?

As I pulled into my driveway, two crazy ideas arrived with me. The first was about Hugh's demonstrated capacity for violence. As quite a young man, Althea had told me, Hugh had disrupted a Sherlockian convention by taking his fist to the jaw of an opponent in the Oxford-Cambridge debate. The ardor of youth, I'd assumed, had overcome Hugh's judgment. But from Althea's perspective, Ceci was, and I quote, ''a young woman.'' Ceci was eighty. Hugh's episode of supposedly youthful violence might have taken place only a few years ago. Hearing about it, I'd facetiously reflected that Hugh's mistake, in the eyes of Sherlockians, had been to use his fist instead of the Master's favorite weapon, a loaded hunting crop. The weapon used to murder Jonathan Hubbell was only presumed to be the missing shovel that Ceci had abandoned by Simon's grave. Could it, in fact, have been a weighted hunting crop? The second crazy idea was about the cocaine on Jonathan's body. The Republican philatelist victim seemed as wildly improbable a source of the white powder as did his great-aunt, Ceci. Was it possible that in their Holmesian zeal, Hugh and Robert indulged in a seven-percent solution?

As I got Rowdy out of the car, I found it difficult to suppress the thoughts that had been burbling around during the drive from the Gateway, but when Hugh pulled the Volvo in behind my Bronco and the two men got out, I was oddly alarmed by the contrast between my suspicious fantasies and the Holmesians' appearance of normality. With his impressive height, his white hair, and his well-tailored dark topcoat, Robert was the kind of handsome and distinguished-looking man you see in Harvard Square on Commencement Day when he's just marched with a handful of other surviving members of the Class of Long Ago. I've never been near an M.I.T. commencement and have no idea what's comme il faut in the way of men's clothing, but Hugh's khaki pants and wool-lined tan jacket were practical-looking, and with his sturdy build, his jaunty mustache, and the outdoorsy glow on his face, he could've been about to accept an important scientific award for having invented an ingenious contraption that enabled researchers to investigate the center of the earth, the bottom of the sea, and other places with low potential for development as family vacation spots. Both men made ordinary remarks about my neighborhood. Yes, I agreed, the townhouses that Harvard had built on the opposite side of Concord Avenue were a big improvement, and it certainly was convenient to have a branch of the library right across the street. Furthermore, neither Hugh nor Robert asked whether I owned the house or rented my floor, and neither stooped to making any sort of ill-bred reference to the increase in property values that has accompanied the gentrification of the area.

As I was contemplating the happy prospect of raising my tenants' rent, Rita came down the back steps, and I felt ashamed of myself. When I performed introductions, Robert and Hugh were gracious and charming.

They said normal things like *How do you do?* and nothing at all about Sherlock Holmes. This phenomenon was, it seemed to me, a miracle on a par with my letting sixty social seconds elapse without mentioning dogs, not that it's ever happened, but, hey, if Robert and Hugh, why not me?

After explaining that she had to dash off to a meeting, Rita murmured to me, "You were right about that psychic after all. She got my poor patient's hopes all built up, and now, all of a sudden, she announces the dog is dead. I am outraged. Will you be around tomorrow morning?"

"No, I'm going to a show. Tonight?"

"I'm having dinner with someone. A person of the opposite sex, actually. A man."

"Rita, I know which is the opposite sex. You have a date," I informed her. "Well, have a good time."

Still without mentioning Sherlock Holmes, Dr. Watson, fog, gaslights, gasogenes, violins, cocaine, Jezail bullets, or anything else even remotely related to their obsession, Robert and Hugh seconded my good wishes and said what a pleasure it had been to meet Rita. Following their fine example, I refrained from asking whether the date owned a dog.

Once Hugh and Robert were in my kitchen, the availability of dog hair was embarrassingly obvious. I'd given Kimi a token, useless brushing that morning and vacuumed everything, including her. During my absence, a malamute storm had blown in to whip up whitecaps on the floor in the form of wisps of fluffy undercoat. Oblivious to the clumps of hair springing from her hindquarters, Kimi dashed up to welcome our visitors. "Robert, she'll get hair all over you!" I warned about a second too late. "I'm sorry."

"It doesn't matter in the least." A true gentleman!

His dark topcoat bore a long, wide swatch of white. "Is she suffering from some sort of condition?"

"No," I said. "This phase is the worst. The undercoat comes out first, this wooly stuff, and then the outer coat, the guard hairs. That part isn't quite so bad. Kimi, you are a good girl. It's not your fault, is it?"

Hugh, meanwhile, was crouched down collecting samples from the floor and transferring them to a small brown paper bag. The activity fascinated Rowdy, who has always taken a keen interest in the tools of housework, mops, brooms, vacuum cleaners, and dust cloths, all of which he apparently regards as rival dogs, and an even keener interest in people, especially people displaying peculiar behavior. Like a psychiatrist evaluating a potentially explosive patient, Rowdy quietly observed Hugh from a distance of a few feet. Then, reaching a benign diagnosis, he calmly gave Hugh a big, wet kiss. Hugh answered with a childlike grin of surprise and awkwardly thumped Rowdy's head.

I said, "Rowdy, enough. That will do. Kimi, here, let's get a nice clump of fresh hair from you."

Rising, Hugh reached inside his jacket to extract a pen from the array lined up in the plastic pocket-protector in the breast pocket of his flannel shirt. "I'll need to label this," he explained as he stepped toward my kitchen table, on which rested my one-volume Doubleday edition of *The Complete Sherlock Holmes*. The book lay open to display two pages of *The Valley of Fear*. I liked the beginning, the part about Fred Porlock, the Tragedy at Birlstone, and especially the cipher message that Holmes decodes by consulting an almanac. As I refrained from admitting to Hugh and Robert, however, whenever I'd tried to finish the story, I'd found myself bogged down in all that business about Vermissa Lodge and the bodymaster, mostly because it had nothing to do with Holmes and Watson. I'd left the book open in the hope of reminding myself to plod on.

"Ah hah!" Hugh exclaimed with great vigor and enthusiasm.

"Applying myself to the Canon," I said, hoping to avoid a trivia question about *The Valley of Fear* that I wouldn't be able to understand, never mind answer.

My vagueness succeeded to the extent that Hugh, after gesturing to Robert to keep his distance from the open book, spoke to his companion rather than to me. "Now, Robert, Holly presents us with an intriguing little puzzle. Open on her table is the volume you will certainly recognize."

Robert nodded solemnly.

"Open to a certain work that makes a *singular* yet cryptic allusion to her profession," Hugh continued, "and contains a *doubly* allusive line."

I was so mystified that I glanced at the book to see whether it had somehow turned its own pages from *The Valley of Fear* to *The Hound of the Baskervilles*. It had not. Furthermore, far from making a cryptic allusion, *The Hound of the Baskervilles* was explicitly about a dog.

Hugh was beaming. After depositing his evidence bag on the table, he jabbed a fist of dramatic challenge at Robert and demanded, "Quote the line!"

I know the answer now, of course. What I still find eerie is that in addition to containing a double allusion to my profession, the correct solution to Hugh's trivia challenge hints at the identity of Jonathan's murderer in a way that Hugh could not possibly have known. So, only if you consider yourself a genuine Sherlockian, I offer the challenge to you: What was the line?

Chapter Nineteen

THREE DAYS LATER, I presented Irene Wheeler with a close-up photograph of the cat. I'd taken the picture on Saturday after Rowdy and I returned from the show. About the show itself I will report almost nothing except that the stunning young malamute who went Winners Dog and Best of Winners had a name with eerily Holmesian connotations: Kaila The Devil's Paw. Devil's Paw? Devil's Foot. Yes, indeed, *Radix pedis diaboli,* devil's-foot root, the obscure African poison that the evil Mortimer Tregennis stole from Dr. Sterndale, the source of the toxin that left Tregennis's sister dead and his two brothers completely demented, the same poison that Sterndale himself used on Tregennis and that almost did in Holmes and Watson when the Master's experiment proved far more potent than he intended. Furthermore, Narly, as the dog is known, happened to be the grandson of a famous and utterly gorgeous top-winning malamute, Tracker, officially named, I swear, Ch. Kaila's Paw Print. Yes, *Paw Print,* as what was frozen in the mud near the scene of

Jonathan's murder. Paw Print, footprints, as in those of a gigantic hound.

What's more, when Hugh and Robert unexpectedly turned up at the show to collect samples of white dog hair, they embarrassed me less than my father had done at a few thousand previous shows. But everyone knows Buck, whereas Hugh and Robert expected introductions and kept announcing that they were friends of mine. I dealt with them rather well, I thought. I warned them not to go around brandishing scissors and not to demand great hunks of show coat. Instead of telling my friends that the newcomers were Holmesian lunatics, I described them as researchers, a term that Hugh and Robert happily accepted. The description went over well with the dog people, too. Show types being, by definition, a competitive crew, the exhibitors, once assured that only small samples were required, seemed pleased to have their dogs selected as subjects in a scientific investigation and proceeded to inundate Hugh and Robert with information about *correct* coat and color in breed after breed. The investigators, however, were disconcerted to discover that in addition to all-white or predominantly white breeds like the kuvasz, the Great Pyrenees, the Samoyed, the West Highland white terrier, and the bichon frise, there existed white-coated individuals in dozens of other breeds as well. In some, the boxer and the German shepherd dog, for example, an all-white coat was a disqualifying fault. In others, including the Alaskan malamute, it was perfectly acceptable in the show ring and, to my eyes, beautiful. Westies and bichons and such were obviously too small to have left the gigantic paw prints found near the scene of Jonathan's murder, but there remained many more possible breeds than Hugh and Robert had expected.

I had to admit, though, that in contrast to the looniness of Hugh and Robert's Sherlockian speculations about missing heirs and the secrets of illustrious personages, their methods were systematic and, in a wacky way, sensible. Every bit of hair was stored in its own clearly labeled envelope, and Hugh recorded everything in a database on his laptop. The dog hairs found at the scene of the murder had, after all, been exclusively white. Kimi had confirmed the presence of a large dog. And I'd seen the immense paw prints myself. As I pointed out to Hugh and Robert, the paw prints clearly predated the homicide: The dog had been at Ceci's during the spell of damp, mild weather we'd had during the week before the murder. On Saturday, we'd had a cold snap; by Saturday night, when Jonathan was killed, the mud must have been frozen solid. With considerable condescension, Hugh and Robert countered that preliminary experiments with Kimi's hair and samples collected at Ceci's indicated that the dog had been at the scene both before and after the freeze. I was skeptical. An ugly suspicion again crossed my mind. Hugh and Robert reveled in the Baskervillian features of the murder. Holmes himself had lamented the scarcity of interesting crimes. Was it possible that his disciples had turned to villainy to have something to investigate? Or were my own speculations taking a daffy Sherlockian turn? Real crime was what Kevin Dennehy investigated: the sordid slaying of Donald Lively, the drug dealer who had specialized in cocaine. I reminded myself to ask Althea what Holmes's source had been. "Watson Was a Woman"? Fine. But "Watson Was a Dealer"? Surely not! Hadn't he slaved to break Holmes of the terrible habit? If not Watson, who? Oh, no! Holmes's "dirty little lieutenant," Wiggins, and his gang—the Baker Street Irregulars. Highly irregular!

One final word about the show. Actually, three words. Gloria and Scott. They were not there. Even in their absence, I overheard four separate conversations about Irene Wheeler. Three I caught out of the corner of my ear; they were testimonials to her uncanny powers. Oddly enough, in all three cases, she had communicated canine concerns about teeth. So much for her psychic ability to intuit *my* dental troubles! The fourth exchange I heard clearly. "Now, make sure and tell her it was me that sent you," a woman emphasized.

The response interested me. It was made in jest. "You get some kind of kickback?"

Irene's advocate turned bright red. In a low tone, she said, "Yeah, if you want to call it that. She'll do the same for you. Free consult if you send someone. There's nothing wrong with it. So make sure and tell her it was me that sent you, okay?"

Sign on a friend. The cheap ploy would have put me off. Irene Wheeler had not tried it on me. Her accuracy in sizing up her clients riled me. Especially one client: Ceci. In the spirit of honesty, let me admit that what got to me was not any particular attachment to Ceci. If, for example, I'd seen Ceci being duped into paying the funeral expenses of an imaginary child who'd supposedly died of cancer or being wooed by some bigamous Lothario who'd vanish with her life savings, I'd have felt a sort of universal outrage with nothing personal about it. Furthermore, even if I'd known for sure that Jonathan had been murdered to prevent him from spoiling the scam, I'd have felt no sense of mission. In the eyes of the law, Ceci's beliefs were her own business, and she was entitled to spend her money as she chose. Jonathan's murder was, of course, police business. No, what got to me was the particular nature of the swindle: the promised resurrection of Lord Saint Simon. When it came to her dog, Ceci was a complete fool. I was the same kind of fool myself. I'd have given *anything* to see my Vinnie again. It drove me almost crazy to see Irene Wheeler prey on the same love and grief I felt myself.

On Sunday, when I made an appointment with Irene Wheeler, and again on Monday, when I kept it, I knew I was making a cowardly mistake. I live with Alaskan malamutes; I am an expert on predators. I knew I failed to act like prey. I wasn't weak, injured, or needy; there was nothing erratic about my behavior. Hiding the wounds I should have shown, I kept Vinnie's picture in my purse. Equal to equal, I offered Irene Wheeler a photograph of the cat.

If one of us seemed vulnerable that day, it was Irene Wheeler. Greedy spring sunlight ate its way through the closed blinds of her office. Lines showed around her eyes, and the whites were shot with red. Her hair had a damaged look, as if she'd overused a curling iron. She wore the kind of cream-colored outfit that's become popular in Cambridge since the allergy craze hit: a baggy top and loose skirt of what I guessed was organically grown unbleached cotton. Am I making this up? No. Seriously. There are people here who shop as if they're expecting a famine that will force them to eat their clothes. The fabric looked as nutritious as bed sheets, and it drained the color from Irene Wheeler's face. I wondered whether she might be recovering from a cold. Or maybe she'd recently awakened from an especially exhausting trance.

"I rescued it," I said as I reached across her desk to hand her the picture of the cat. "I didn't set out to get a cat, at least not this cat. If I had, I'd have gotten something big and tough that would stand a chance against the dogs."

"Let us concentrate on this image of the ideal cat," she suggested, closing her eyes. "The ideal cat is large."

Wow! I'd just said so, hadn't I?

"The color I see is gray," she continued. "And amber! A strong amber! Yes, *amber eyes*!"

My whole body gave an involuntary twitch. I was glad Irene Wheeler still had her eyes shut. But I'm a truthful person, especially when I'm in shock. "Yes."

She opened her eyes and studied me. "You are surprised," she remarked lightly. As if taking it for granted that she'd read my mind, she turned in businesslike fashion to the photo of the real cat. "You are obviously disappointed," she said.

I hedged. "Well, more or less. The problem is . . . Well, there are a couple of problems. One is that I never intended to keep this cat, but no one else will take it, so it has nowhere else to go."

"It?" she asked.

"It doesn't have a name."

"I meant the sex," Irene Wheeler said.

"It's a—" I started to say.

"Female," she said matter-of-factly. Focusing on the picture, she added, "I sense pain. Yes! An ear. I sense something wrong with one of her ears."

This time, I couldn't hide my astonishment. The cat's bandage had been removed. In taking the portrait, I'd zoomed to get a profile shot of the side with the intact ear. Irene Wheeler's eyes were on me. "She has a torn ear," I said. "How did you know that?"

"It's a gift. For example, this cat has double paws." The photograph, I remind you, was a close-up of the cat's face.

"Yes," I stammered.

"But let us move to what matters. This animal needs far more attention than she is getting."

The cat was still stuck in my office. Worse, I found myself doing most of my work at the kitchen table. I cleaned the cat's litter box. I provided food, water, and veterinary care. Now and then, for maybe ten seconds, I tried to make friends. If the cat had been a dog, she'd have learned the rudiments of obedience by now. If she'd been a dog, of course, she'd have liked me. They all do. There's nothing supernatural about the attraction. My pockets are always filled with dog treats. Also, I know how to talk to dogs, and I do it all the time. With the cat, I had made shamefully little effort.

"I have to protect her from the dogs," I said.

"This animal is frightened," Irene Wheeler told me. "What I feel from her is fear. Mistrust."

"In the case of my dogs, it's justified."

"Let us discover," said Irene Wheeler, "the dogs' perceptions of the matter." She reached a hand toward me.

I caught on. Digging into my purse, I found my wallet. Taking care to leave Vinnie's picture where Irene Wheeler couldn't see it, I pulled out a photo of Rowdy and Kimi that I'd once used on a Christmas card. In the background was a field of snow. The dogs wore red harnesses and were hitched to a dogsled. Irene Wheeler took the photo from me, studied it, and closed her eyes. I discovered myself annoyingly eager to hear what she'd say.

"They are naturally curious about the presence of the cat," she said. "Their curiosity is heightened by your attitude of alarm. They find your response extremely interesting."

"They probably do."

"They are used to being taught what to do," she

said. "They wonder why, in the presence of this new animal, they are given no guidance. They say that you ordinarily communicate your wishes. They wonder why you are not doing so now."

"Because I don't trust them, that's why," I said.

"They understand that."

"And the reason I don't trust them," I said, "is that when it comes to cats, they are not trustworthy."

"They are eager to learn," said Irene Wheeler. "Their feelings are hurt. They would like you to make an effort."

Thus I left Irene Wheeler's with the most improbable piece of advice anyone could have offered me: the sensible suggestion that I, of all people, start training dogs.

Chapter Twenty

I ARRIVED HOME FROM Irene Wheeler's profoundly unnerved. I was, among other things, peculiarly angry about having gotten precisely what I'd paid for: the all-too-real sensation of encountering genuine psychic powers. Having made their acquaintance, I didn't like them one bit. After greeting Rowdy and Kimi in an unusually perfunctory fashion, I pulled out my wallet, extracted the picture of the cat, held it up near the kitchen window, and examined it in the daylight. Did the cat look feminine in a way I'd missed? It didn't have the jowly look of an adult tom, but to my eye, it could still have been male. The double paws were, of course, out of the picture. Furthermore, in the photo, the cat looked misleadingly relaxed. I'd said that I'd rescued the cat. My tone could have alluded to sinister circumstances; Irene Wheeler might have guessed about the cat's fearfulness. And the ear? Nothing in the picture, nothing in my voice or my manner could possibly have suggested the torn ear. Unless . . . Could I have unconsciously raised a hand toward one of my own ears? As an experiment, I tried lifting my right hand, then my left, in the sort of movement I might have made. The gesture felt unfamiliar. To the best of my knowledge, I wasn't in the habit of talking with my hands. A lifetime of dog handling should have taught me to keep my body language to a minimum. My mother had always emphasized the importance of controlled handling. To this day, I'd hear her authoritative reminder to keep my elbows in. And if I'd become sloppy, an obedience instructor or a dog-training friend would have taken me to task. How on earth had Irene Wheeler guessed about the cat's torn ear? Or the double paws? How had she known that the cat was female?

And how could she possibly have known about the gorgeous gray cat with the huge amber eyes? I'd told Steve about the TV commercial right here in my own house. I'd seen the ad months ago, and I'd immediately asked Steve about the gray cat's breed. Even if Irene Wheeler employed spies to sneak around eavesdropping and ferreting out bits of obscure information about her clients, she'd hardly have sicced her agents on me long before she and I had ever heard of each other. She certainly didn't collect random pieces of inside knowledge about the entire population of Greater Boston just to be prepared for the clients who showed up in her office. Had I mentioned my ideal TV cat to anyone other than Steve? I remembered telling Leah about the gray cat, but we'd been in the car on the way to a dog show; no one could possibly have overheard. I might have mentioned the cat somewhere in public where, by weird coincidence, Irene Wheeler had happened to be listening in. I couldn't remember any likely occasion. I hadn't run into her anywhere since our first consultation. Then, I'd had no sense of ever having seen her before. And neither Steve nor Leah had any reason to go around talking about my infatuation with the beautiful gray cat. How had Irene Wheeler known?

From Ceci! Scrounging everywhere for a home for the damned little cat, I'd offered it to Ceci on the night Kimi had served as Hugh and Robert's supposed tracking dog. Just before leaving Ceci's, I'd stopped in at the house to thank her for her hospitality. In passing, I'd mentioned the cat. She hadn't been interested. Had I said anything about the torn ear? I'd been trying to foist off the cat, hadn't I? It would have been unlike me to stress its bad points. I must have described it as needy. I'd probably focused on what a wonderful home Ceci could provide for it. In my eagerness to place the cat in what really would have been a perfect situation, could I have gotten carried away to the extent of comparing it to the gorgeous gray cat in the television commercial? I didn't think so. But I just might have told someone at the Gateway about the big, handsome TV cat. A few of the people Rowdy and I visited preferred cats to dogs. I'd definitely discussed cats with Helen Musgrave, Althea's roommate. Althea could have been listening. There was a television mounted high on a wall in Helen and Althea's room. I constructed a little scenario. The TV is on. Ceci is visiting Althea. The cat-food ad appears. Catching sight of the beautiful gray cat, Ceci exclaims and gushes in characteristic fashion. Althea remarks that Holly, too, is enamored of the commercial's captivating feline star. Improbable? Yes, but less improbable than what I wanted to view as the outright impossible—mental telepathy.

I just had to know. I'd never talked to Ceci on the phone before. The musical tone of her voice had escaped me. She sounded happy to hear from me and asked about Rowdy and Kimi. She seemed in no rush to find out why I was calling.

I said, "I've had an odd experience."

"Oh," she said merrily, "you've been to Irene Wheeler!"

"Yes. I am really quite—"

"Unnerved!" She made the sensation sound marvelous. "I was myself."

"What I'm wondering is . . ." I faltered. "Do you happen to have seen a cat-food commercial on TV? With a, uh, beautiful gray cat with big amber eyes."

"I usually watch Channel Two. Or Forty-four." Those are our local PBS stations. "I am positively *addicted* to 'Wall Street Week in Review.' If the truth be known, I have a mad crush on Louis Rukeyser! Oh, and the evening news, but most of the commercials are for, well, not at all what I care to contemplate anywhere near dinnertime and, really, not the sort of thing that has any place in a public forum, and, well, by comparison, cat food would be appetizing. So if the commercial was on, I might not have been watching, although a dog might have been another matter—that would certainly have caught my eye!—because, as you know, I am essentially a *dog* person—it's a matter of the solar plexus—not that I have anything against cats, naturally, or anyone or anything else, for that matter, except this cold-blooded murderer whom Jonathan attempted to apprehend during the course of what would otherwise have been an armed robbery, and I find it very difficult to forgive myself for the unkind thoughts I had about poor Jonathan before I knew, although all is now forgiven, of course. And Jonathan is extremely sorry for the terrible things he said to Irene. Like most of the world, he simply did not understand."

Ceci's nonstop delivery had the odd effect of making me hold my breath until she paused, as she did not do until she'd finished. Her lungs, I reflected, must be extraordinary. Could she have had operatic training? Recovering from my anoxia, I asked, "A robbery?"

"Oh, yes. Althea didn't tell you?"

"No."

"Well, an attempted robbery it was. Both Irene and Jonathan have made that crystal clear. Objects, you see, speak to the gifted just as our seemingly mute creatures do, and the supposedly inanimate beings with whom we share the cosmos forget nothing, because, you see, time is meaningless to them, all is eternal, past is present is future, and it occurs to me that it must be terribly frustrating for them, poor things, to have so much to say and so few beings eager to listen, unless, of course, do they converse among themselves? I must ask Irene. In any case, after I retired, Jonathan heard a *noise* outdoors, you see, a sort of scraping sound, exactly the sort of sound a burglar might make, by mistake, naturally, not on purpose, and so Jonathan decided to investigate, because when all our neighbors installed these noisy alarm systems, well, Ellis said that a big dog was the best deterrent on earth, besides which pets, you know, are forever accidentally triggering those alarms, and then the police come, and it's really such a great nuisance that most people end up leaving the alarms turned off and . . . Where was I? Oh, yes, so Jonathan, surreptitiously, you see, went and got his parka and *crept* out through one of the French doors to investigate and *sprinted* after the burglar and finally *nabbed* him right by the sundial, where he did his best to subdue the man, but tripped, and was himself subdued." Sounding pleased with her turn of phrase, she added, "From a temporal perspective, it seems unfortunate that I had the bad judgment to leave the shovel lying there, but Irene assures me that far from being my fault, everything occurred as it was meant to occur, you see, and there was nothing anyone could have done to prevent it. Irene has reminded me that if fate had decreed otherwise, I might have been murdered in my bed."

"Has, uh, anyone said anything about who this burglar was?"

In dire tones, Ceci said, "A *stranger*."

"Anything more specific?"

"No, except that he is now far away, and I must say that I am extremely annoyed with him, whoever he is, because he went and frightened Simon away just when we were making such wonderful progress, and frankly, I am not pleased to have Irene diverted by this business of communicating with stones and fences and crocuses and blades of grass. After all, what's done is done, and we know what happened, and we know that it was meant to be, don't we? So, with Simon out there waiting, what do I care about listening to stones? I care nothing whatsoever for blades of grass. Simon is *there*, and I want him back *here* now!"

"I understand," I said inadequately. Selfishly switching back to the point of my call, I said, "So, I don't suppose you and Irene have ever discussed the gray cat."

As if explaining everything, Ceci said, "It has nothing to do with *me*."

"I just wondered."

"I've never heard of this cat before," Ceci said, "but clearly the animal has some sort of special meaning for you, which is, I must tell you, precisely the sort of thing that instantly communicates itself to Irene. I hope I'm not prying, Holly, but I must say that you sound rather upset, which is perfectly natural at first, I felt the same way myself, but really, when you think about it, haven't you known all along? Your own dear dog, for example. I've forgotten her name."

"Vinnie."

"Well, haven't you known all along?"

"That . . . ?"

"That she still *exists*? That her essential being did not simply vaporize?"

"This is completely different."

"Irene," declared Ceci, "loses sight of the effect she has on those who are unprepared." It hit me as a ridiculous statement to make about a clairvoyant, but Ceci went on unperturbed. "I see it all now. You had this gray cat in mind, and Irene's telepathic powers came as a shock to you, so naturally you are grasping for some sort of everyday explanation."

"Yes. Exactly."

"There is none," Ceci said. "And if I may be so bold as to advise you, I would suggest that you stop wasting Irene's powers on trivia. As you have discovered for yourself, Irene has great gifts. Don't you long for contact with your Vinnie?"

I made a soft noise.

"I assure you that you can tell Irene absolutely everything. I have done so myself, and I have found her utterly trustworthy. Holly, my dear, I can hear that you are frightened, but you really need not be. There is nothing at all to fear from your Vinnie, is there? Or from Irene, either. In your heart, haven't you known all along that your dear dog still loves you and aches to be with you?"

In a way, what Ceci said was true. I had never lost the magical sense of Vinnie's presence. During her existence in this sphere, she had behaved as if she read my mind. *As if?* Had she actually done it? Could she do it still? And Rowdy and Kimi? Were they, too, blessed with telepathic powers? I have to admit that I was crazy about the possibility. Dreams fulfilled! Nothing, I realized, would make me happier than knowing for certain that dogs could read my mind. It was simultaneously clear to me that I loathed the idea of having even one human being do the same. And if it had to be one human being, I didn't want it to be Irene Wheeler. I called her. We had a brief, businesslike conversation. I made an appointment with her for the next day.

Chapter Twenty-one

I N WHAT I VAGUELY sensed as a skirmish in the battle of the psychic's powers against mine, I sat at the kitchen table to plot my strategy for training Rowdy, Kimi, and the ill-tempered cat. My plan had everything to do with positive reinforcement and nothing to do with mental telepathy. Pushing aside the new issue of *The Malamute Quarterly*, I grabbed a pad and a pen, and started planning on paper. I devoted one page of yellow legal pad to the dogs and one to the cat. At the top of the dogs' page, I spelled out my goals. Did I want Rowdy and Kimi to love the little pussy cat? No. My goal was to teach them to ignore the cat. I broke the goal down into steps, and the steps into behaviors that I could reinforce: looking at anything except the cat, holding still, moving away from the cat, displaying relaxed ears and lowered hackles, doing nothing at all in the presence of the cat, displaying any behavior incompatible with attacking the cat or totally unrelated to the cat, first from a distance, then very gradually from closer and closer. On a fresh sheet of paper I rearranged my notes about training the dogs in a pyramid-shaped diagram. The goal was still on top. On paper, it looked easy to reach.

At first, the task of outlining a behavior-modification program for the cat stymied me. My goal, I admitted to myself, was not a trainable behavior: I wanted the cat to go away and live with someone else. Failing that, I wanted her to become a gorgeous gray feline TV star with huge amber eyes. Better yet, she could transform herself into a dog. And failing all that? The answer required a fresh sheet of paper. This sheet was for my behavior. The goal for myself was to establish a relationship with the cat, which in the language of behavior training meant a reinforcement history. So far, our relationship consisted of a negative history. To her, I meant the pillowcase, the stone, the approaching hand that scared her off the cozy mouse pad on my desk. To me, she was hisses, scratches, and the unwelcome message that here was one animal that didn't want me around. Within five minutes of taking in a stray dog, I'd have given it a name. The first step in breaking the negative cycle with the cat was to decide what to call her.

Cambridge places a heavy burden on anyone who sets out to name an animal. The expectations are dauntingly high. A respectable name for the cat, I feared, would allude to a character in some famous work of literature I'd never read and wouldn't want to. Hidden in an Icelandic saga or a Persian folktale was undoubtedly a maiden who'd suffered trauma to an ear and had six fingers on each hand. My cousin Leah would know, but it would defeat my purpose to get Leah to name the cat. In my entire life, hadn't I ever read anything sufficiently highbrow to enable me to name a Cambridge cat? Ah-hah! Sherlock Holmes! Somewhere in the Canon there had to be a cat. References to dogs sprang from every page. In "A Study in Scarlet," Watson, as a prospective roommate, warns Holmes that he keeps a bull pup. The pup never reappears, but other dogs do. Indeed, in the same story, in a passage I'd almost forgotten and didn't want to reread, Holmes actually kills a dog to test some poison, a dog, if I remembered, that was dying anyway. Even so! But in addition to canine characters are zillions of images of dogs. Lestrade is like a bulldog, and something or other—a dark mass?— is like a Newfoundland dog. Wasn't there a single kitty-cat in all Sherlock Holmes?

As *kitty* crossed my mind, it overturned a mental object that crashed with a *thunk.* In the aftermath of the fall, a sinister inner voice with an affected English accent whispered dark words: "He is everywhere!" There was indeed a Kitty in the Canon. She appeared in "The Illustrious Client." She was Miss Kitty *Winter*, of all things, the hurler of vitriol. But damn it, Sherlock Holmes or no Sherlock Holmes, and even if your name *is* Winter, here in Cambridge you just cannot call your cat Miss Kitty! The cat had caused me enough trouble already. She was not going to turn me into a social outcast. Damn her! And damn the abusive would-have-been cat murderer and his ugly bulbous forehead! Why couldn't fate have let me rescue a dog? Preferably an Alaskan malamute.

A second mental object tumbled after the first. This one, however, landed with what sounded remarkably like a familiar *woo-woo-woo* that seemed simultaneously to sing from the open pages of *The Malamute Quarterly.* On the right-hand page was an ad for the young show dog who'd taken the championship points at Saturday's show, Kaila The Devil's Paw. *Kaila,* I am relieved to report, has nothing to do with Sherlock Holmes, at least so far as I know. It's the kennel name of Chris and Eileen Gabriel, the breeders and owners of the dog, Narly, and of his illustrious grandsire, the late Tracker, Ch. Kaila's Paw Print. Inspiration at last! The nomen omen! I would name the cat after an Alaskan malamute, and not just any malamute, either, but a legend, a champion, a dog I'd admired at shows for years and years. The original Tracker, the famous dog, like my gourmet cat-food star, just so happened to have been big, gray, and gorgeous, and also happened to have been what this cat was not but should have been: an Alaskan malamute. And *Paw Print*? Arguably the most famous line in the Sacred Writings: *"Mr. Holmes, they were the footprints of a gigantic hound."* So you see? The ad, the cat, the devil, big, gray, and gorgeous. The original Tracker, the show dog, admittedly, had correct malamute eyes, dark, not amber, and his color was dark wolf gray. Even so! My cat: Tracker. I said it aloud. "Tracker." Then I said, "My cat, Tracker." Then I tried, "My cat, Kaila's Paw Print." I cheated: "My cat, *Champion* Kaila's Paw Print." Modestly, I added, "But she's called Tracker."

So I'd attained my first goal: Tracker had a name. And I'd broken the cycle of negativity. Tracker was a champion. She was a gorgeous gray legend with Holmesian connotations. She was virtually an Alaskan malamute. Fired up by the successful christening, I outlined a systematic-desensitization program designed to convince Tracker that I was a wonderful human being and to remind me that she was all but a champion Alaskan malamute. Then I put the program in operation. I entered my study and calmly took a seat on the floor. Tracker hissed at me. I showed no response. She remained on my mouse pad. I thought loudly and silently, *You, there, Tracker! You won three Best of Breeds at specialty shows, you have multiple group wins and placements to your credit, two awards of merit at Na-*

tional Specialities, AND you went Best of Breed twice at Westminster! Tracker was unimpressed with herself. I admired her humility. After five minutes, I quietly left the room. At a later stage, I'd need help in training the dogs. Steve, I was certain, would cooperate by holding Tracker at a safe distance from them, but still in sight. For today, I settled for rewarding calm canine behavior outside the door of my study. I made a start.

Only when I was congratulating myself on relying on my own rational methods instead of Irene Wheeler's mind reading did I recall in a sort of verbal rush that it had been Irene Wheeler who had insisted that the cat was frightened, that the cat needed more attention than she was getting, that the dogs were curious about the cat and about my attitude of alarm, and that they were used to being given guidance about the behavior I wanted from them. In other words, in applying my own rational methods as carefully as Holmes applied his, I'd done precisely what Irene Wheeler had suggested. The damn thing was this: The psychic had been absolutely right.

Chapter Twenty-two

A GREAT SPIRIT," PRONOUNCED Irene Wheeler. After examining the photograph, she'd kept her eyes shut for a long time. I'd stared at her lids to see whether she was cheating, but had seen no sign that she was peeking at me to gauge my response. My eyes had been damp. The muscles around my mouth had twitched.

"Vinnie," I said, "was perfection itself."

Vinnie could answer the telephone. If canine anatomy hadn't impeded her, she'd have issued a polite hello. She was as reliably and zestfully obedient in daily life as she was in the ring, where, I might add, she earned consistently high scores. Oh, and she loved cats. Introduced to Tracker, Vinnie would have played nursemaid by licking the poor creature's wound. In our obedience work, I'd slaved to deserve her. Was she flawless? Whenever she encountered a rotten fish on the beach or a decomposing squirrel in the woods, she'd flop down and wiggle in wild delight; her favorite perfume was Eau de Dead Thing. She carried herself with an air of moral superiority; she was an unreformed teacher's pet. Ours was not a relationship of equals: I was the teacher, and she was the pet. Steve's skill and my mercy spared her the last agony of cancer. She died in my arms. Now, I made no effort to hide my feelings from Irene Wheeler. If you want proof of cannibalism, the bait to offer is your own flesh.

Today, Wednesday, Irene Wheeler wore a navy linen suit, a silk blouse, and leather pumps. I hadn't taken off my anorak, which was cobalt blue, brighter than navy. I reminded myself that according to the L.L. Bean catalog, the anorak's polyester fleece was twice as warm as natural fibers. It was the second such anorak I'd owned. The first had been a present from Steve. After I'd worn it for a few years, the hood had started to come loose, and a tailor had informed me that the anorak couldn't be repaired. The tailor was new to this country and still learning English. What he actually said was that the garment had defected. On reflection, I decided that the tailor was right: In going to pieces, the anorak had committed treason against a great American institution. Consequently, I bundled it up and shipped it to Freeport, Maine, where, after what I assume were grueling hours under harsh lights, it evidently confessed its guilt, because L.L. Bean replaced it with the new and presumably loyal anorak I now wore. I hadn't asked for a replacement; I'd just wanted to snitch. But L.L. Bean is the real thing. Satisfaction guaranteed. Anyway, I'd worn the brand-new anorak in the hope of presenting myself to Irene Wheeler as the sort of prosperous person who can pay to raise the dead as easily as she can fill her closet with polyester fleece. Rita, I might mention, insists that in choosing to wear the anorak, I elected to garb myself in a personal symbol of reincarnation. As to the remainder of Rita's interpretation, well, it's true that Vinnie was the last gift my mother gave me before she died, the pick puppy from the last litter she bred, and I did, admittedly, grow up in Maine, but L.L. Bean as a *mother figure*? Therapists! Let me also point out that since polyester fleece is warm, soft, and cuddly, it has to feel like a baby blanket against your skin. What else could it feel like? It has no choice in the matter. I said that to Rita. She said, "Neither do you."

But back to Irene Wheeler. "A model of perfection," she said. "We do keep coming back to ideal images. The gray cat?"

I decided to keep quiet about the mystical transformation Tracker had undergone the second I'd named her after a breed champion malamute. "Vinnie was real," I said. "Besides, she was my dog." It didn't require a psychic to see our bond in the picture I'd offered Irene Wheeler. It was a color snapshot I'd had blown up. Vinnie and I are standing on the pier in Port Clyde, Maine, on a hazy summer day. The diffused light that radiates downward and bounces back from the ocean creates the illusion that her coat and my hair are exactly the same color. I am kneeling with my arm around her. We are smiling at each other. We are both young. Vinnie is obviously going to live forever.

"She was beautiful," Irene said tritely.

I stopped short of saying that I would pay anything to see Vinnie again. I settled for saying that I'd give anything. As I spoke the words, as I'd certainly done before, I suddenly felt as if I'd been blasted with loud noise. Sometimes when Rowdy shrieked in the bathtub or when Kimi roared in my ear as I bent down to put her food dish on the floor, my head would rock as if I'd been whacked hard on the skull. Whenever it happened, I wondered whether I might actually have sustained a mild concussion. Irene Wheeler's office, however, was quiet. What rocked my head were my own words.

"Your great dog is still available to you," said Irene Wheeler. "Is she not?"

I hesitated. "In a sense, she is." My head was still reeling. The office seemed like an echo chamber that distorted my own voice. *In a sense,* I heard myself say. The phrase ricocheted: *Innocence.*

"In a sense," Irene Wheeler repeated.

"Not in material form," I said carefully.

Irene eyed me with what looked like suspicion. "Perhaps your Vinnie is as close as she is ready or able to be."

"Vinnie was always ready for *anything*," I snapped.

"Her life was full? It was complete?"

"Absolutely," I said truthfully. I couldn't control my tears. "I gave her everything I had. She gave everything back a millionfold."

"Everything," said Irene Wheeler. "She gave you everything. She was more than willing to try anything you asked."

"Yes," I agreed.

"A cycle is complete. She gave you everything. She continues to sustain you. And you want *more*?"

I said nothing.

"The dogs you have now?" Irene Wheeler asked.

"Rowdy and Kimi."

"Would you trade them?"

"Not for anything."

"Not for Vinnie? Their lives for hers?"

My head rocked again. "Of course not." The prospect felt sick and grotesque: a bargain with the devil.

"You ask too much of everyone," Irene Wheeler said. "Of your dogs, past and present, of me, of yourself, and of the cycles that govern the universe. The full completion of a cycle is rare and beautiful. Just as you said, it is perfection itself.'' She let silence hang. ''Do you have any questions to ask of Vinnie? Is there anything you need to know? Any unfinished business?''

''None,'' I said. I saw Vinnie enter this world. I was the first human being to hold her. I was the last. I'd been holding her ever since. Now I finally let her go.

On the sidewalk outside Irene Wheeler's building, I paused and stood in an oddly peaceful daze. What awakened me was a brief flash of light from a third-floor window of the three-decker house across the street. Moving nothing but my eyes, I caught sight of a pair of binoculars in the window. Then an invisible hand drew a curtain closed. The neighborhood snoop? Or a confederate of Irene Wheeler's? But why observe clients as they left? Peering at me as I descended the steps of the psychic's house, a confederate could have learned less than Irene Wheeler had seen and heard for herself. And with a thousand confederates, how could she have known about the beautiful gray TV cat? About Tracker's ear? About her double paws?

Today's experiment had been a failure in the sense that Irene Wheeler has sized me up as a client entirely different from the wealthy, lonely, gullible Ceci. Anorak or no anorak, I was broke. And I'd have been hard to fool. Irene Wheeler chose her victims carefully. She had rejected me. Yet she'd demonstrated a power as uncanny as her inexplicable knowledge of my ideal cat and my real Tracker. She had challenged my sorrow. I felt healed by evil.

Chapter Twenty-three

THAT SAME WEDNESDAY KEVIN Dennehy and I had dinner at a restaurant on upper Mass. Ave. The place is a favorite of his. There's surf-and-turf on the menu, and "cheese" refers exclusively to a tremendous pool of warm goo so absolutely identical in color to the orange plastic that covers the comfortably padded seats of the restaurant's booths that I am always tempted to sneak a bite of the upholstery to find out whether it is, in fact, the solid form of the glop on the nachos. The more Kevin and I go there, the more difficult it becomes for me to decide what to order. There's a lot of cheese on the menu. Also, I rule out anything else I've had before. Tonight, in desperation, I'd splurged on broiled swordfish. It had arrived liberally sprinkled with an orange-colored powder that I labored to think of as paprika. As usual, Kevin had the surf-and-turf. Even with the aid of a serrated knife, Kevin had to work at the lobster tail and the steak, but far from complaining, he raved about the food the way he always does. Kevin enjoys a triumph over a tough opponent, and opponents don't come much tougher than that surf-and-turf.

Pushing the swordfish around in an effort to create the illusion that I was consuming my dinner, I said, "Kevin, the murder of Jonathan Hubbell? You're going to think I'm joking, but I'm perfectly serious. There really is a lot about it that ties in with Sherlock Holmes."

Chewing a piece of meat, Kevin was unable to do more than grunt.

"Especially," I continued, "with *The Hound of the Baskervilles.* You've read it, right? You probably read it in high school."

The gristle prevented Kevin from answering. He shook his head.

"You've seen the movie?"

He nodded.

"The old movie," I guessed. "With Basil Rathbone. And Nigel Bruce."

Irene Wheeler's office was only three or four blocks away, on a side street off Mass. Ave. It occurred to me that maybe having once eaten at this same restaurant with a companion who, like Kevin, had ordered surf-and-turf, she'd decided to set up shop nearby in the hope of capitalizing on the need for telepathic communication.

"Well," I said in response to Kevin's mute nod, "I just reread it, and there really are a lot of parallels. Listen, okay? The victim is Sir Charles Baskerville. Every night before he goes to bed, he takes a walk down a yew alley, meaning not our kind of alley, obviously, but a sort of pathway between two hedges. And on the path, there's a gate. Okay? And Jonathan Hubbell? In the evening, after dinner, he leaves his great-aunt's house and goes down a pathway that ends at guess what?

Evergreen hedges. And a gate. Now admittedly, Sir Charles Baskerville's body was found on the far side of the gate, and Jonathan's was found in his great-aunt's yard, and there are zillions of other differences. Even so, in both cases, what's found near the body?''

In his effort to swallow the lump he'd been chewing, Kevin turned so red that I was afraid it had lodged in his throat. A doctor once told me that a person who is choking can't speak; people who say they're choking are fine. ''Kevin, are you all right? Say something!''

He didn't.

Lucky for Kevin that I'd recently watched an excellent video on first aid! Rising swiftly from my seat, I said, ''Relax! I know what I'm doing. Stand up!'' I ordered. ''I can't reach you. Stand up!'' As Kevin started to comply, I added, ''I know everything about the Heimlich maneuver. I just watched a video about it. It was called 'How to Save Your Dog's Life.' I practiced on Rowdy and Kimi.''

I didn't have to touch Kevin. My words alone performed a sort of verbal Heimlich. As soon as they left my mouth, the lump of gristle flew from Kevin's and landed in the middle of my swordfish. Kevin gasped for air. By now, a crowd of waiters and concerned fellow patrons had gathered. Embarrassment turned Kevin's face a deeper shade of crimson than choking had done. Shooing everyone away, he glared at me.

Once again seated across from him, I said quietly, ''Now, Kevin, anyone can choke. There's nothing to be ashamed of. And it's the restaurant's fault, really.''

Between clenched teeth, he demanded, '' 'How to Save Your Dog's Life'?''

''I was trying to reassure you that I knew what I was doing.''

''With you around, who needs the Heimlich maneuver?'' he growled.

''You might have, for one,'' I replied with dignity. ''Anyway, as I was saying, in both cases, what was found near the body?'' Since Kevin seemed inexplicably disinclined to answer, I continued. ''The footprints of a gigantic hound. Or a giant dog, anyway. But there's more!''

A waitress appeared. ''Done?'' she asked.

''Yes,'' I said. I felt almost grateful to Kevin for ejecting the lump into the dinner I'd otherwise have had to make a show of finishing.

Nothing ruins Kevin's appetite. As the waitress removed his plate, he ordered strawberry shortcake and asked whether I wanted dessert. I asked for chocolate ice cream. How could even the worst restaurant ruin that? By repeatedly thawing and freezing it until it's a mass of ice crystals. Or that's my guess, anyway. I picked at the ice cream. Kevin devoured what looked like strawberry jam topped with shaving cream.

''So we have the yew hedge, the gate, the evening stroll, paw prints near the body,'' I persisted. ''The paw prints of a giant dog. And, Kevin, *and*, it so happens that the entire neighborhood where Jonathan was murdered, where his great-aunt Ceci lives, in a fancy section of Newton, has gaslights. Gaslights! Sherlock Holmes, right?''

''Invitation to crime,'' pronounced the voice of Law Enforcement.

''Well, they don't provide much light,'' I admitted. ''But they're very charming. And the traces of cocaine on the body? Holmes again.'' Echoing Althea, Hugh, and Robert, I said, ''*He* is everywhere.''

''What's God got to do with it?'' Kevin asked sourly.

"Not God. Sherlock Holmes."

"Cocaine." Kevin's voice was ripe with disgust. "I keep telling you, I got no use for—"

"And I keep telling you! Neither did Dr. Watson. Anyway, there's more. Over and over in the stories, there's this theme of the victimization of the innocent. *The Sign of Four,* 'The Speckled Band,' 'The Engineer's Thumb.' In probably half the stories, maybe all of them somehow or other, there's some innocent person who's being taken advantage of by the forces of evil. Here, it's Ceci who really is being victimized by Irene Wheeler, okay? Even if nobody but me seems to give a damn about it. Except Jonathan Hubbell. And Jonathan was murdered, maybe because just like Sherlock Holmes, he was trying to protect his great-aunt. Maybe. And the particular con game is also very Holmesian. Halfway through the stories, what happens to Holmes? He plunges to his death at the Reichenbach Fall. Supposedly. Except, of course, that Holmes was *resurrected.* Really, Conan Doyle made the mistake of killing him off, but the public just wouldn't tolerate losing him, so Conan Doyle had to bring him back. And resurrection is Irene Wheeler's con game: bringing Ceci's dog back from the grave."

"You want to know what I think?" Kevin asked.

"Yes."

"You're letting your imagination run away with you. Look, Holly, you work hard enough at it, you can always make something out of nothing. Take this case we got now. Donald Lively. Drug dealer. Dealt in what? Among other things, cocaine. Sherlock Holmes! The guy victimized the innocent. Not all that innocent, but you can look at it that way."

"Was there a yew hedge? A gigantic dog? Were there—"

"The point is, Holly, what you see depends on what lens you look through."

"Lens! There, you see? Lens. Magnifying glass. Sherlock Holmes."

Kevin was unimpressed. "If you want to treat this case like it was a Sherlock Holmes story, you look hard enough, and you're going to find something. I don't know what, 'cause I haven't looked, but in his closet, you're going to find a funny-looking hat with flaps over the ears, or you're going to find that the guy who lived next door was named Watson or—"

"Was he?"

"No. But if he had been, it'd be a coincidence. Like I said, it all depends on the lens you look through."

"There it is again!"

This time, Kevin had the grace to smile. A few minutes later he had the even greater grace to insist on treating me to dinner. As we were leaving the restaurant, I offered polite protests. "And I'm sorry I embarrassed you," I added.

"Hey, I was the one who spoiled half your dinner," Kevin said.

"That wasn't your fault." Kevin held the door for me. He does that. I don't mind. Stepping onto Mass. Ave., I said, "You couldn't control where—" I broke off. Passing directly in front of me on the sidewalk, clearly visible in the light of a streetlamp, was a tall, thin man with brown hair cut in a peculiar but fashionable-looking style. His most prominent feature was a bulbous forehead. Tonight, he wasn't wearing the green suit. Rather, he had on an expensive-looking brown trench coat. As he'd done the first time I'd seen him, though, he carried a white bundle. Actually, he carried two. Neither was a pillowcase. This time, he was clearly returning from an innocent errand. In each hand, he held a plain white plastic shopping bag.

"Kevin!" I whispered. "Kevin! Get that man!" I lowered my voice another notch and pointed. "Kevin, *that's* the man who tried to drown my cat! Get him!"

Instead of bolting after the villain as he'd normally have done, Kevin opened his mouth to ask what I assume would have been a question. I now understand that just having recovered from the humiliation I'd inflicted on him in the restaurant, he was eager to avoid tackling the stranger only to have me announce that, gee, sorry, but this wasn't the same guy after all.

I'll let Kevin hold doors for me, but if he doesn't, I somehow miraculously manage to open them myself. Abandoning Kevin to his second bout of mortification, I sprinted after the man, who had apparently overheard my whispered accusation. As if to confirm his guilt, he was fleeing up Mass. Ave., his progress impeded by the two heavy-looking shopping bags. "You!" I hollered at him. "You! Stop!"

What did I intend to do with the cat-drowner when I caught him? I had no plan in mind. As I hurtled past parked cars, shop windows, and window-shoppers, it occurred to me that collectively, Rowdy and Kimi outweighed this scrawny cat-murdering bastard. And they were all muscle. If I could handle two Alaskan malamutes in prime condition, I should be able to manage one skinny bit of human scum. "You!" I yelled in a breathless-sounding version of my best bossing-dogs-around voice. "Stop! Or I'm going to get you, and I'm going to rip you to shreds!"

Without the plastic bags that bumped at his sides, the man might have outdistanced me almost immediately. Running the dogs around Fresh Pond keeps me in decent shape, but in addition to a head start, he had the advantage of long legs. Neither he nor I, however, was a match for Kevin, whose burliness is deceptive: He's been a long-distance runner since high school. A short sprint barely gives him time to warm up, but once he gets moving, his mass and muscle kick in, and he can keep going forever. When he barged past me, I'd covered a block. My quarry was a good half block ahead. I knew Kevin would lose me. I might as well have stopped to catch my breath. Pride kept me going. Ahead, the thin man made the mistake of looking back. Catching sight of Kevin, he must have felt like a retreating soldier who turns to see whether he's shaken a lone pursuer and discovers a rapidly approaching tank. Or maybe he felt like a snowball in the direct path of a plow. Panic must have impaired his judgment. On the sidewalk ahead of him, eight or ten people had congregated to wait for tables at a tiny, brightly illuminated storefront bistro. Instead of sensibly detouring, the thin man tried to cut straight through the little crowd and ended up tripping on a woman and knocking her to the concrete. The group that immediately gathered around the fallen woman blocked the sidewalk and brought Kevin to a momentary halt. Just beyond the human blockade, the man paused, gasping, to regain his balance. As I started to catch up with Kevin, I heard him holler, "Police!"

Instead of bringing the chase to an end, Kevin's bellow of authority acted like a bullet that missed its mark. With sudden energy, the man veered around and launched the only weapons he had. Raising his right arm, he swung one plastic shopping bag backward and sent it flying over the fallen woman and a companion who knelt next to her. Kevin caught the bag before it hit his face, but as he did so, the man flung the second bag at him, turned, and raced away.

Kevin and I again took up the chase. This time, we didn't stand a chance. Working our way around the crowd, we had to squeeze between a parked car and a bicycle chained to a meter. By the time we did, our quarry was whipping around the corner of a distant side street. When I reached it, Kevin was dimly visible far ahead of me, and the man was nowhere in sight. Sucking in air, wrapping my arms around my aching ribs, I finally gave up. Along both sides of the street were typical Cambridge three-deckers, with here and there a brick apartment building or a big single-family house. Our prey could have vanished into any of the yards or down any of the driveways. He could have been hiding between or even under any of dozens of parked cars.

I waited for Kevin, who'd been ahead of me and might have seen where the man had gone. After ten minutes, Kevin still hadn't shown up, and I began to retrace my steps to the sidewalk in front of the tiny bistro. When the cat murderer had flung the white plastic bags, I'd noticed that he was wearing gloves. Even so, fingerprints might be all over the contents of the shopping bags. It now seemed to me that I should have left pursuit to Kevin and made myself useful, as even Hugh and Robert would have done, by protecting the evidence. And, indeed, I returned to the spot to find that well-meaning members of the group waiting for tables at the bistro had gathered the spilled contents of the two white bags. The crowd was animated. The woman who'd been knocked to the sidewalk hadn't been seriously hurt, someone told me. In fact, having waited for a table, she was now inside seated at one. Had I eaten here? someone asked. The food was wonderful, well worth the wait. Of course, you didn't always get entertainment like tonight's.

"Entertainment?" I asked.

Everyone laughed.

The cause of merriment, I learned, was the contents of the white plastic bags. On close inspection, the bags turned out to be imprinted with the interlocking red circles that were the logo of a chain of discount drugstores. Now repacked with the man's purchases, the bags were propped up against the front of the bistro. When I was first told what they contained, I didn't believe it. I'd assumed that the man had been toting the usual variety of odds and ends that people buy when they run ordinary errands: milk, coffee, toothpaste, a can of tomato sauce, microwave dinners. Those who'd picked up after the man, however, wondered aloud whether he was the sort of kleptomaniac who makes the newspapers by succumbing to a bizarre compulsion to shoplift large numbers of items that could serve only to meet some deranged and evidently symbolic need—the pitiful man caught filching a hundred pairs of ladies' underpants, the wealthy woman who wears her diamonds and pearls while stealing cheap costume jewelry from cut-rate establishments where she'd never stoop to shop.

But the white plastic bags did not contain lingerie or costume jewelry. And the man hadn't stolen anything. In one of the bags was his receipt for the bags' contents—two dozen packages of women's hair coloring. All in the same shade: jet-black.

Chapter Twenty-four

GIRL SCOUT COOKIES? I was far too old. Vacuum cleaners? Because of the dog hair, I burn them out all the time. There were two broken ones in the cellar, but neither those nor the one that was still working would pass as a demonstration model. Besides, did anyone still sell vacuum cleaners door-to-door? Magazine subscriptions? I could legitimately present myself as a representative of *Dog's Life,* and we're always eager for new subscribers, of course, but for once, I preferred to avoid the subject of dogs. So much for collecting donations to Alaskan Malamute Rescue. But what about another charity? Or better yet, Cambridge being Cambridge, a political organization? I owned a clipboard, and could easily fake a petition of some sort and forge the signatures of imaginary people ardently in favor of such-and-such or adamantly opposed to this-and-that. But no matter how Cantabrigian the cause I selected, around here, I'd be doomed to encounter a devil's advocate or possibly a Cambridge misfit who'd keep me stuck for hours listening to the case for global nuclear armament or the imminent destruction of the rain forests. But solicitors for charities and lobby groups needed licenses. I didn't have one. And solicitors always handed out literature.

The availability of props thus determined my role. I already owned a Bible. My possession of the collection of leaflets and tracts was mainly the dogs' fault. I'd opened the door without knowing who'd rung the bell. To prevent the dogs from getting out, I didn't open the door all the way, but held it a little ajar. Standing there was a sweet-faced, dowdy woman accompanied by a guy in his twenties with hair so oily and skin so red and clean that he looked as if he'd been submerged in hot fat, like a fried clam, but not for long enough to turn brown. As I was about to say politely that I wasn't interested and then swiftly shut the door on my callers, Rowdy and Kimi poked their noses out, thus making it entirely unnecessary for my callers to get a foot in the door; I couldn't shut out the Jehovah's Witnesses without simultaneously squashing the dogs' muzzles. The woman caressed the Bible she carried and, instead of telling the blunt truth ("I'm a Jehovah's Witness here to plague you"), said brightly, "We're Jehovah's Witnesses, and we're sharing some Good News from the Bible."

The woman and her underfried clam wasted forty-five minutes of their time and mine sitting in my living room trying to convert me, of all people, to a sect that would've required me to do an awful lot of walking without being able to take a dog. I'm serious. I asked whether dogs could go along. Why I bothered, I don't know. I mean, have you ever opened the door to find a Jehovah's Witness standing there with a dog? It's obviously a good idea. With gorgeous dogs along, these poor people would have a lot fewer doors slammed in their faces than they do now. Greenpeace should also consider the possibility. As to vacuum-cleaner salespeople? Yes, imagine! With long-coated dogs trained to shake hair all over the houses of likely prospects, who'd then have no choice but to agree to have the mess cleaned up? Indeed, a foot in the door no more. From now on, it's a paw. A nose. Or an awful lot of fur.

Anyway, I retrieved the sheaf of religious tracts that I'd put with the newspapers and other recyclables. Then I worked on my disguise. After taking a hot shower, I put nothing on my face except moisturizer, and with the aid of a blow dryer, I did my best to convince my hair to curl conservatively under. As a costume, I selected a white blouse, a gray wool skirt, black flats, and my navy blue wool coat. The finishing touch was a white rayon scarf fashioned into a wide headband that held my hair back from my face the way mothers always like. The only missing element was a second Jehovah's Witness. It seemed to me that like the legs of panty hose, they always traveled in pairs. A man and a woman? I couldn't remember for certain. It didn't matter. The only person I could think of who'd join me in the charade was my cousin Leah, whose red-gold curls would create an undesirably pagan appearance and who, in any case, had classes to attend. Men? Steve and Kevin would've been equally opposed to the project. I toyed with the idea of enlisting Hugh or Robert, who'd have enjoyed emulating the Master by traipsing around in disguise, but I was afraid that either of the Holmesians would overcomplicate what I meant as a simple piece of research. Besides, I didn't really need an accomplice.

Dressed in my costume, armed with my Bible and tracts, I paused briefly in the hallway to brush dog hair off my coat. Then I got into the car, cut down Walden Street, turned onto Mass. Ave., passed the bistro where the cat-drowner had abandoned his many packages of hair dye, covered a few more blocks, and parked at a meter. Making my way on foot toward the street where Irene Wheeler had her apartment, I naturally hoped that I wouldn't run into her. If I did? Well, maybe for all she knew, I *was* a religious fanatic, as in a sense, of course, I am. The thought proved useful. Ascending the wooden steps of the house opposite Irene Wheeler's, I allowed the sincerity of my devotion to dogs to flood my face with an expression of fervor and holiness.

From the outside, the building looked like a mirror image of Irene Wheeler's, except that hers had fresh paint, new windows, and other signs of renovation. The outside door to this one was battered. More to the point, it was unlocked. The entryway was dirt brown and stank of cats. In the light of what must have been a twenty-watt bulb, I examined three ancient mailboxes set in the wall by three paint-encrusted doorbells. Lying on the cracked linoleum was a ton of junk mail: ads for supermarkets and discount hardware stores, and sad blue-and-white postcards with blurry photographs of children who asked, "Have you seen me?" The mail on the floor was addressed to "Resident." The first-floor mailbox bore a strip of masking tape on which someone had printed "Schultz." The other two mailboxes were unlabeled.

I decided to practice my performance. My goal was the third-floor apartment, the one with the window where I'd seen the binoculars. I chose Schultz as the audience for my dress rehearsal. On a door opposite the mailboxes and bells was a pink plastic numeral *1*. After adjusting my holy smile, I rapped on the door. Inside, feet shuffled. Then the door eased open an inch. A wizened yellow face peered at me through the crack. I'd intended to address whoever answered as Mr., Mrs., or possibly Ms. Schultz, but found myself unable to guess whether the creature was male or female.

"Good morning!" I announced sweetly. Prominently displaying my Bible and my tracts, I said, "I'm a Jehovah's Witness, and I'm sharing some Good News from the Bible."

Success! The door slammed in my face. Confident now that I had, indeed, played my role to perfection, I climbed to the second floor. Rapping on the door, I felt eager to repeat my performance. To my disappointment, no one came to the door. After once again knocking and waiting, I made my way up the stairs to the third floor. The effort of ascending one short flight of steps wasn't nearly enough to make my heart pound. Rather, the extra beats were from second thoughts. Jehovah's Witnesses, I decided, did well to go in pairs. In lieu of an animate companion—preferably canine, but I'd have settled for a mere person—maybe I should have protected myself with something other than a disguise that left my face readily recognizable. There was a Sherlock Holmes story called "The Veiled Lodger." For a second, I couldn't remember anything about it except the title. Who was the lodger? Oh, yes. A woman who'd been mauled by a lion. Too bad that Jehovah's Witnesses weren't required to cover their faces. But whatever awaited me in the third-floor apartment couldn't be worse than a hungry lion. Could it? *A living dog is better than a dead lion,* I thought. Two living dogs would've been twice as good. The villain who'd tried to drown Tracker was obviously no animal lover. Maybe he was terrified of big dogs. Maybe my impersonation was a terrible mistake. Last night, after hurling the white bags of hair coloring, the man had vanished down a side street only a few blocks from this shabby building. Was it possible that . . . ?

Slowly inhaling and exhaling, I rapped on the door. This time, it took courage to paste on the smile of joy. Clutching the Bible, I felt tempted to raise it directly in front of my face.

I heard brisk footsteps. Maybe because the yellow-faced creature on the first floor had opened the door, I somehow expected this door, too, to open, if only an inch or two. It did not. Cambridge is, after all, a city, and few city dwellers simply open their doors to strangers.

Through the closed door, a male voice inquired, "Who is it?"

Once again mimicking the dowdy woman, I repeated the line about sharing Good News. In my own ears, I sounded nervous. I felt like an actress who has lucked into a small part only to botch her one line.

The door opened nonetheless. It opened wide. Before me, binoculars dangling from a strap around his neck, stood Robert, looking, as usual, as if he ought to be wearing a kilt. At his heels was Hugh. I felt like a total flop. If I recalled correctly, on not a single occasion had Watson ever come close to penetrating any of the Master's disguises. Robert and Hugh, of course, recognized me instantly.

"Good News," repeated Robert, cocking his distinguished head.

"A religious term," Hugh informed him, "referring to—"

"I am familiar with the expression," Robert replied impatiently.

I yanked off the headband and wiped the sappy look off my face. *"I never was more glad to see anyone in my life,"* I quoted.

Robert responded with the quickness of a well-trained dog. *"Or more astonished, eh?"*

"Well, I must confess so," I said.

"Confess to it." Having set me straight, Robert added, *"The surprise was not all on one side, I assure you."*

Except for my misquote, the dialogue was straight from *The Hound of the Baskervilles*. I was disguised as a religious fanatic, right? It made sense to quote the Bible. My tactic worked. Hugh and Robert invited me in.

Perhaps I should make it clear that the grubby apartment opposite Irene Wheeler's was the abode of neither Hugh nor Robert. Rather, they'd rented it, as Robert explained to me, as an aerie in which to perch while casting eagle eyes on everything that went on across the street. The place was such an ugly, depressing mess that my first response was relief that no one had to live there. From the walls cascaded strips of hideous flower-patterned beige wallpaper inadequately coated with a primer of white paint that had also been applied to the woodwork. Paint chips leaped from the window frames, doors, and baseboards. Bare lightbulbs hung from the stained ceilings of some rooms. Other ceilings sprouted spidery masses of electrical wire. Scattered on the dirty, worn wood floors were coat hangers, crumpled bits of paper, and other debris that neither the last tenant nor the landlord had bothered to sweep up. I didn't see the kitchen or the bathroom. And didn't want to.

In tidy contrast to the rest of the place was the observation post that Hugh, I suspected, had set up in the living room near the front windows, which formed a little bow that overlooked the street. I could now see that what I'd mistaken for curtains were, in fact, brand-new white sheets, their creases visible, nailed across those front windows. Right by the shrouded windows, mounted on tripods, stood a powerful-looking spotting scope and a camera. Nearby were two aluminum folding chairs and a narrow folding cot on which lay a rolled-up sleeping bag. Between the chairs, a big cooler served as a makeshift table that supported two stainless-steel thermos bottles. Hugh's laptop computer rested on the floor by one of the chairs. If I hadn't known better, I'd have assumed that Hugh and Robert were avid birders who'd camped in this improbable location in the hope of adding some exotic species to their life lists.

"You've made yourselves very comfortable here," I remarked. "Just like the Man on the Tor."

That, too, is from *The Hound*. The mysterious Man on the Tor turns out to be Holmes, who has camped out in an abandoned hut on the moor. Naturally, Watson doesn't connect the mystery man with the Master until Holmes reveals himself: *"It is a lovely evening, my dear Watson,"* said a well-known voice. *"I really think that you will be more comfortable outside than in."* The inside of the hut, however, is pretty comfortable. Holmes has blankets, cooking utensils, food, and water. For the sake of fidelity to the Canon, I should add that he also has a half-full bottle of spirits and a pannikin, but since I have no idea what a pannikin is, maybe I'd better skip that part. Anyway, in that part of the story, Holmes is all excited, and so were Robert and Hugh, who described themselves as hot on the trail.

"Could we back up a little?" I asked. "I don't understand why you decided to, uh, observe here to begin with."

With the air of one who quotes, Robert pompously announced, *"These strange details, far from making the case more difficult, have really had the effect of making it less so.''*

Hugh came to my rescue. "In this case, the jarring feature is the presence of the psychic."

"So," I said, gesturing toward the curtained windows, "what have you observed?" I paused. "Besides me."

"We confess ourselves," replied Robert, "at something of a loss as to how to account for your presence there."

"Let's say that my mission was more or less the same as yours," I said. "Among other things, it seems clear to me that Ceci Love is the victim of a con game, and that the con artist"—I pointed toward Irene Wheeler's house—"is preying on Ceci's grief about her dog. That bothers me a lot. In itself, that's an evil thing to do. I've also wondered whether Jonathan Hubbell had the same idea and whether that's why he was murdered. It's also a little more complicated. There's a friend of mine who's also being victimized, in a minor way."

Hugh and Robert exchanged glances.

"And would your friend," asked Robert, "be a *tall* man?"

"A lot of men are tall," I said to Robert. "You, for example." Steve, of course, is tall, lean, and muscular.

Hugh took his turn. "Thin?"

"Lean."

"Hair color," said Robert. "Brown."

"Yes."

Hugh and Robert held another silent conference.

"The owner," Hugh said, "of a large dog."

Steve's pointer, Lady, is medium size, but India—no slight intended, far from it—is a good-sized bitch. "Yes," I said.

The privilege of making the final, magical Holmesian pronouncement fell to Robert. "Your friend drives a black panel truck," he proclaimed, as if pulling a rabbit from a hat. "His most prominent facial feature is an exceptionally bulbous forehead."

Chapter Twenty-five

*H***IS MOST PROMINENT FACIAL** *feature is an exceptionally bulbous forehead.*

The statement transformed my vision of Hugh and Robert. They seemed suddenly frail, elderly, and hopelessly innocent, as vulnerable as a poor, sick cat tied in a pillowcase weighted with a large stone. I had spotted the binoculars from the street. Anyone else might do the same.

"You are," I asked them, "strictly limiting yourselves to *observing* what goes on?"

Has there been a male yet who wants to be a man of *inaction*? My remark had an unintended consequence. Hugh and Robert, instead of assuring me that they were doing nothing except monitoring comings and goings, thanked me for reminding them of the need to return to their duties. Then they politely showed me to the door. Patting his pocket, Hugh informed me that he had his revolver. Robert, he said, was also prepared to defend himself. Like Holmes, Robert preferred to arm himself with a stick. I felt anything but reassured. In parting, I did, however, extract the promise that Hugh and Robert would desert their post for long enough to visit Althea the next morning. Reluctant though I was to burden a ninety-year-old woman with worries about matters she could do nothing to control, I counted on Althea's intelligence and common sense and on her influence with her old friends. She, at least, understood the Great Game as a strictly literary pastime. To Robert and Hugh, she was *the* woman. With luck, their Irene Adler would divert them with some purely Sherlockian puzzle or send them safely back to another dog show to collect yet more harmless tufts of show coat.

I now realize that in counting on Althea's intelligence and influence I made a serious miscalculation. She proved herself as sharp as I'd expected. I now see, however, that far from persuading Hugh and Robert to diverge from the hot and dangerous trail they were on, she set me on the same hazardous track. If I'd been clever, or maybe just irresponsible, I'd have taken care to arrive at Althea's room at the Gateway ahead of Hugh and Robert. As it was, Rowdy and I got to the Gateway that Friday morning at our usual time, ten-thirty, the earliest hour at which visitors were welcome, and we fulfilled our obligations to the people awaiting the regular visit of their therapy dog. More than ever, I felt caught between the desire to give each person ample time with Rowdy and the sense that we needed to press on. Ordinarily, what hurried me was my empathy for the remaining people who looked forward to Rowdy's weekly visit. Today, in my impatience to get to Althea's room, I hustled Rowdy from person to person.

By the time we finally entered Althea's room, the three Sherlockians were deeply involved in a collaborative analysis of the evidence. Pausing briefly just inside the room, I felt my view of the three undergo yet an-

other transformation. Through my newly Holmesian
eyes, I'd previously seen Hugh and Robert as coopera-
tive actors who shared the roles of Holmes and Watson
in a long-running performance of the Great Game. In
appearance, the tall, distinguished, keen-eyed Robert
was a natural for the part of the Great Detective; Hugh
made a rather short and hefty Holmes. It was Hugh,
however, who'd have conducted the stinky chemical experiments that had absorbed Holmes, Hugh whose
laptop computer was the present-day version of the al-
bums in which Holmes had stored and catalogued his
files. Or did the laptop also cast Hugh in the role of
Watson? The computer was, after all, the ultimate recorder. And it was Robert who armed himself with the
Master's favorite weapon. Hugh, like Watson, favored a
revolver. As for Althea, I'd accepted Hugh and Robert's
plain assertion that for both of them, Althea Battlefield
was Irene Adler. She was *the* woman. And who was I?
At most, I was the anonymous Reader. In the world of
Sherlock Holmes, I was no one at all.

Now, pausing before entering the drama, I sensed a
reassignment of the immortal roles. Ignoring Althea's
near blindness, Hugh and Robert were presenting her
with photographs. Hugh stood on one side of her, Robert on the other.

"Is this woman attractive?" Althea asked.

"Moderately," Robert replied grudgingly.

"Moderately," Hugh agreed, stroking his pale mustache.

"A man," said Althea, "visits an attractive woman.
What further explanation is required?"

"The man," said Hugh in ominous tones, "is the
owner of a large dog."

"An inference," Robert continued, "drawn from the
creature's response when we approach the vehicle in

which it is incarcerated. The vehicle is a windowless van of sorts.''

"A panel truck,'' Hugh said. "The cargo area at the rear has no windows.''

"Just so,'' Robert agreed.

"What Robert is trying to say,'' Hugh said, "is that we attempted to observe the dog on two occasions, last night and the night before, but each time, the dog created a ruckus that would have drawn attention to our presence.''

"How disappointing,'' Althea commented. "How ordinary! The *incurious* incident of the dog in the night-time.''

The story was "Silver Blaze.'' There, *the dog did nothing in the night-time*—and *"That,''* as Holmes remarks, *"was the curious incident.''* When someone approached, why did the dog do nothing? Because the intruder was no stranger to the dog. And Nicole Brown Simpson's Akita? Ponder it. "Silver Blaze''?

"The depth and volume of the dog's barking,'' Robert reported, "were sufficient to establish the size of the animal.''

"Data,'' Hugh said, "consistent with evidence collected at the scene of the murder concerning a tall white male dog with exceptionally large feet.''

As Hugh and Robert took turns presenting information to Althea, I continued to ask myself who was who in this Holmesian scenario. Speaking almost with one voice, Hugh and Robert were two halves of Holmes: Robert, the contemplative thinker; Hugh, the scientific analyst. I thought of Rex Stout's lighthearted essay. If Watson was a woman, had Althea now become Watson? Clearly not. It was she who was being presented with the evidence, she who was apparently expected to make something of it. Ah hah! Hugh and Robert, the men of action, collected the evidence and were now reporting to Althea, who never left the Gateway. Mycroft Holmes! Sherlock's brother, need I inform you? Yes, Mycroft, who, according to Holmes himself, possessed better powers of observation than Sherlock, but lacked ambition and energy, and only in times of crisis left his lodgings in Pall Mall for anywhere other than the Diogenes Club, where every member was forbidden to take any notice whatsoever of any other member. So, Althea was now Mycroft: the great brain lodged in a largely immobile body. The Gateway was her club. The murder victim was, of course, the unfortunate Jonathan Hubbell. The client, albeit an unwitting one, was Ceci. I felt a strange satisfaction in having squeezed the present situation into the Holmesian mold.

Again, who was I? In real life I was the professional writer in the group. In unconscious imitation of Watson, I asked, "Are we intruding?"

"Of course not!" Althea assured me. "You and your colleague"—she smiled—"are more than welcome."

Althea used words carefully. "Colleague?" I smiled. "Isn't that Holmes's word for Watson?"

"Indeed," said Althea, accepting Rowdy's paw. *"My friend and colleague,"* she informed Rowdy. Shifting her gaze from Rowdy to me, she said, "We could use your expertise. Would a puzzle interest you?"

"If it's a question about the Sacred Writings," I said, "I'll have to pass. I'm not in your Red-headed League."

Althea was delighted. "A dog puzzle," she said. "A game."

"I'll try."

"Gigantic paw prints," Althea said, "which I am told that you observed for yourself. The evidence of the sundial, so to speak: a tall dog, probably a large male dog. White hair and white hair only. Let us put that description together with a protective dog, at any rate, protective of the vehicle in which he rides. A dog that gives a deep, loud bark when strangers approach his territory.'' To Hugh and Robert, she said, ''Now, the two of you say not one word! What I'm after here is an expert opinion independent of the conclusions you have drawn from your data. Holly?''

''I can't give you a definite answer,'' I said. ''But—''

''Holly, for heaven's sake, stop hedging!'' Althea ordered.

''Okay,'' I conceded. ''There are three likely breeds. One: komondor. Hungarian sheepdog. Guard dog. Big and white, with a corded coat.'' In response to expressions of bafflement, I elaborated, ''The hair forms long, uh, ringlets, I guess you'd say. So the dog looks as if his coat is made of hundreds of thin ropes. Second, kuvasz. Big white dog. Also developed in Hungary. Guard of the nobility. More popular than the komondor, but still pretty unusual. But I think it's neither of those breeds. Among other things—''

''Holly!'' Althea chastised.

''Okay! Great Pyrenees,'' I said. ''On raw probabilities, a giant white dog is more likely to be Great Pyrenees than a komondor or a kuvasz because there are more of them. There are about as many Pyrs as there are malamutes.''

''Forty-fourth,'' Robert said.

''What?'' I asked.

''We consulted the registration statistics of the American Kennel Club,'' Robert explained. ''The Great Pyrenees ranks forty-fourth in popularity, whereas the kuvasz is one hundred and fourth, and the komondor one hundred and twenty-first. As you undoubtedly know.''

''The three coats are fairly distinctive,'' I said. ''You must have gotten samples at the show. The sample from a Great Pyrenees was the best match for the hair you found in Ceci's yard. Right?''

The two men still flanked Althea. Rowdy had sunk to the floor and lay at her feet. Althea's expression was gentle. Robert's, however, was now inexplicably hostile or suspicious. Hugh, in contrast, seemed to be gloating. I felt mystified.

The task of challenging me fell to Hugh, who now held the sheaf of photographs. With no warning, he suddenly thrust one at me. ''The time has come!'' he announced melodramatically. ''We know that this man, the owner of the presumed Great Pyrenees, is, as you admitted to us yesterday, a friend of yours.''

I tried to cut in. ''My friend—''

Hugh went on as if I hadn't spoken. ''We know that this same man, the driver of a dark panel truck, regularly visits the psychic, Irene Wheeler. You, too, have called on her. We further know that *you*, while accusing others of efforts to dupe the innocent Mrs. Love, have gone out of your way to ingratiate yourself with her as well as . . .'' He glanced briefly at Althea.

Robert took up the task. Pointing to the picture Hugh had thrust at me, he said severely, ''We demand to know the precise nature of your relationship with this individual.''

The photograph had obviously been taken from the Holmesians' aerie opposite Irene Wheeler's house. It showed the dark panel truck. Opening the driver's side door was the man with the bulbous forehead.

''My *relationship* with this man,'' I growled, ''is that he tried to drown my cat.''

Conflict is of immense interest to dogs. Rowdy, suddenly alert, rose to his feet and shook himself all over. I expected him to move neatly to my side. Instead, after conducting what looked like a swift survey, he planted himself next to Althea, raised a paw, and rested it on the arm of her wheelchair.

Ignoring Rowdy's implicit comment on the situation, I battled on. "My *relationship* with this man is that two days ago, on Wednesday evening, when I spotted him on upper Mass. Ave., he recognized me. And the second he did, he bolted. He knocked some innocent person to the sidewalk, and then he threw the shopping bags he was carrying at someone else who was chasing him. And he got away. My *relationship* with him is that I went back and looked at the shopping bags. They contained two dozen bottles of women's hair coloring. Black hair dye. And *that* is a full account of the precise nature of my *relationship* with this *fiend*, whose name I do not even know!"

Althea brought the dispute to an end. She spoke with tremendous dignity. At first, I thought she was addressing me. "My home," she said in low, patrician tones, "now consists of half a shared room, a bed, a nightstand, a handful of books and objects, these few chairs for guests, and the wheelchair in which I spend my days. It is my home nonetheless." She raised a long, big-boned arm in what looked like a gesture of blessing. Her arm descended. With her huge hand, she covered Rowdy's paw. "Thank you," she said to Rowdy. "Thank you for remembering."

Chapter Twenty-six

I F MY LATE MOTHER happened to tune into the episode while on a break from her labors as Head Trainer at the Celestial School of Dog Obedience, she must have felt proud of Rowdy. Robert, Hugh, and I, in contrast, would arrive at the pearly gates of my martinet mother's obedience ring to find ourselves preregistered for an ultra-sub-novice class in the rudiments of civilized conduct. I could hear her. Truly, I could. *You got into a shouting match?* She, of course, was not shouting. She was whispering in tones of horrified incredulity. *A scrap? With two elderly men? While making a therapy dog visit? To a ninety-year-old woman in a nursing home? Young lady! You may have been raised at a kennel, but your were not raised in one. Or am I mistaken about that? Do correct me if I am wrong, but . . .*

"Althea," I said, "I am terribly sorry." She looked so thoroughly the retired schoolmistress that I had visions of being required to stay for an hour's detention at the Gateway.

Before I could continue to grovel, Robert drowned

out whatever apology Hugh was uttering by saying, "Unpardonable of all of us."

"You are forgiven," said Althea, "provided that the three of you come to your senses, sit down, and reason this entire matter out. Holly, it is perfectly all right to sit on the bed." To Hugh and Robert, who still flanked her, she said, "I do not require an armed guard. Please *sit!*"

In response to the familiar word spoken in an authoritative tone, Rowdy squared himself. If Hugh, Robert, and I had been dogs, we, too, would have earned the reinforcement I gave him. "Good dog, Rowdy," I said, popping him a treat from my pocket.

"Bad people," said Althea. "With good intentions. The road to hell is paved with efforts to protect elderly ladies from things that might upset them. As a consequence, a great many elderly ladies die of nothing more complicated than *boredom*. Now, I take it that this affair began with my sister."

"It began, really," I said, "with the death of Ceci's last dog, Simon. She couldn't accept Simon's death. She was lonely and vulnerable. She began to consult a psychic, a woman named Irene Wheeler. At first, the psychic channeled messages from Simon."

"Oh, dear God," sighed Althea. "How much of Ellis's money did this psychic get her hands on?"

"At first, not much," I replied. "Your sister went to Irene Wheeler's office in Cambridge. She probably saw her once a week or so. Then Irene Wheeler started going to Ceci's house in Newton. She built up to what I gather are daily or almost daily visits. My impression is that to keep her customer satisfied, she had to come up with something that went beyond simple messages from the dog. I think she started by cultivating the hope of closer contact with him."

Althea shook her head sadly. "My sister has always been such a tightwad."

"She got offered something she thought was worth paying for," I countered. "And the psychic, Irene Wheeler, is . . ." I broke off. "She seems," I reluctantly admitted, "to have genuine, uh, telepathic gifts."

"Piffle," said Althea. "Holly, I must ask you to move your account along. Lunch will be served rather soon now."

Institutional life, I'd noticed, had a peculiar way of turning people into dogs. Like Rowdy and Kimi, everyone at the Gateway lived for mealtimes. But I complied with Althea's request by summarizing what I'd worked out. A week ago Monday, I said, Irene had staged the appearance of a spectral dog in Ceci's yard. I emphasized that there had certainly been a real dog there, a white male of a giant breed.

"Ah hah!" Althea exclaimed. " 'The Copper Beeches'! But I am leaping to conclusions. Proceed."

In "The Copper Beeches," a young woman, Violet Hunter, is offered a position as a governess and consults the Master for advice about whether to take the job. What worries Violet Hunter is that to accept the offer, she will be required to cut her long, beautiful hair very short. She must also agree to wear any dress given to her by her prospective employers. She takes the position, cuts her hair, and wears the dresses. As it turns out, what her evil employers really want isn't a governess, but an unwitting impostor to be used in ridding the household of a devoted and persistent suitor.

"A white dog," I said. "A Great Pyrenees. At first, the color was all right, because after all, this was supposed to be a ghostly dog. But Lord Saint Simon was an entirely black Newfoundland. Eventually, he'd have to begin looking like himself. The black hair dye."

"Elementary," said Robert rather snottily.

Althea ignored him. "Chronology, please? Holly?"

"Simon first, uh, appeared on the Monday before Jonathan was murdered. Ceci was so utterly convinced that Simon had come back that she couldn't keep the news to herself. She told me about it when I first met her. She just couldn't contain herself. Anyway, on Tuesday, Jonathan happened to phone Ceci, and she blurted out the joyous news. I think she made him promise not to tell you."

Althea nodded.

"I think," I continued, "Jonathan realized she was being conned. And he decided to come to Boston and stop the whole business."

"Jonathan was a rational soul. He must have been livid. He'd have had blessed little patience with Ceci's blather about the reincarnation of a dog. Oh, my, no. No patience whatsoever. No more than I have."

"Once he got here, on Saturday, he had his fears confirmed. He was anything but tactful with Irene Wheeler. The two of them met. Ceci told me so. As I work it out, Jonathan arrived on Saturday, heard what Ceci had to say, and went . . ." I caught myself. "Became very angry. But he didn't shake Ceci's faith in Irene Wheeler. So maybe Ceci insisted that he meet the psychic and judge for himself. Or maybe Jonathan insisted. In either case, Irene Wheeler would hardly have refused the request to meet Ceci's grandnephew. Ceci must be one of her best clients. Irene is sharp. She must have, uh, intuited that this was a major threat. And she probably thought that she could pull it off. I'm almost surprised she didn't."

"Not everyone," Althea said censoriously, "swallows poppycock. What on earth has this woman done to convince *you*? And don't tell me she hasn't! I always used to tell my students, 'I have eyes in the back of my head.' Now, they're virtually the only ones I have left, but their vision remains as unclouded as ever. I have no difficulty in seeing through this paranormal malarkey and no difficulty in seeing that a web of it has been spun over your eyes."

Reluctantly, I said, "She told me things she couldn't possibly have known except . . . Althea, she told me things that I would have sworn on Rowdy's head that she couldn't possibly have known."

"Indeed," said Althea.

I described my infatuation with the beautiful gray cat. "Irene Wheeler described that cat perfectly." I gulped. Yes, *purr-fectly*. Sorry. Rita informs me that punning is a symptom of anxiety. "I've thought of every possible way she could have found out about that cat. I don't really believe in mind reading, but . . . Althea, every other possibility is totally farfetched, practically impossible. And when you eliminate the impossible . . ."

"Half the residents of this facility," Althea cut in, "were identically infatuated with that foolish cat." Sweeping an arm toward her roommate's empty bed and toward the television, she added, "Helen used to ooh and ahh whenever that commercial was on. She even managed to remember the cat from one moment to the next. Gray thing. With big yellow eyes."

"Yes."

"That commercial ran incessantly. Every animal lover who has turned on a television during the past year is smitten with that cat. This so-called psychic took a guess. You were an animal lover. Therefore, you, too, were enthralled with that cat. What was true of you was true of millions of people, especially people *like* you.

Did you happen to mention a cat to her before she produced this bit of mind reading?''

"Yes," I admitted.

"Well, there. So much for *that* bit of mumbo jumbo."

After a silent consultation with Robert, Hugh picked up the interrogation. "We are wondering," he said, "what prompted you to bring up the subject of cats. It has been our observation . . ."

"That I am obsessed with dogs," I finished. "You aren't the first to notice. I asked Irene Wheeler about a cat because I rescued one." Here, I gave a succinct account of saving Tracker. I described the man who had tried to drown her and the episode of the bottles of hair color. Robert and Hugh were bug-eyed. "So I showed Irene Wheeler a picture of the cat," I continued, "a close-up shot, in profile. The damaged ear didn't show, and neither did the double paws. And without being told, she knew that the cat was a female, and she knew about the ear and the paws and a lot else. I was bowled over. It seemed like a genuine miracle."

"But it was not," Althea said sympathetically. "She knew the cat."

I felt really, really stupid. "She conned me. She knew the man, she knew the cat, she saw the picture. Presto! Clairvoyance."

"Almost from the beginning," Robert interjected, "we have viewed the existence of a confederate as a logical necessity."

"Acting alone," Hugh explained, "the woman could not have staged the appearance of the spectral dog."

I'd had the same idea myself. But my candidates for the role of accomplice had been Gloria and Scott.

"The seances," Robert said, "took place in Ceci's house, yet the dog appeared outdoors."

"The evidence was plentiful," Hugh added. "Dog hair, paw prints, footprints, tire tracks."

"Moreover," Robert pointed out, "this psychic, this medium, knew that Lord Saint Simon was black. The portrait hangs over Ceci's fireplace. Therefore, the someone else, namely, the confederate, made the initial error of miscasting a white dog in the role of Simon."

"But with a big white dog on hand," I said, "the two of them made the best of the initial mistake. When Simon first came back, he was a spectral dog—a white dog. Gradually, as he materialized, he was going to get darker and darker."

Althea nodded. "Yes, 'The Copper Beeches.' But the need was not to cut the hair. Rather, it was to change the color."

From the hallway came the sound of food carts. A heavy odor drifted in. Lunch at the Gateway always smelled like overcooked broccoli.

"Let me summarize," Althea said. "With the aid of the confederate photographed by Hugh and Robert, Irene Wheeler duped my sister into believing that her late dog was materializing. What do we know of this man, this confederate? That he almost succeeded in drowning a cat, a cat known to Miss Wheeler, perhaps her own cat. We know that communication between Miss Wheeler and this man is somewhat disturbed, shall we say. Instead of supplying the black Newfoundland she needed, he provided a large *white* dog. The evidence suggests that he is a somewhat unstable, perhaps impulsive, individual. He could have done away with the cat under cover of darkness or in a secluded area. Instead, he tried to drown the creature in daylight on a stretch of the river where there was a fair chance that he would be observed. When Holly spotted him in Cambridge, did he act rationally? No, on the contrary, he panicked and thereby drew attention to himself.''

"My companion in Cambridge,'' I said as much to myself as to Althea, Hugh, and Robert, "was a Cambridge police lieutenant, Kevin Dennehy, whose picture has been in all the papers. And he's been on TV. His appearance is distinctive. He's a big, tall guy with red hair. And the reason he's been in the papers and on television is that he's one of the people investigating the Donald Lively murder. He was the Cambridge drug dealer whose speciality was—''

Hugh couldn't let me finish. In deep, dire tones, he proclaimed, "Cocaine!''

"I assumed,'' I said, "that the man panicked because he recognized *me* and was afraid of being charged with animal abuse. Hah! The one he was scared of was actually Kevin.''

"The traces of cocaine on Jonathan's body,'' Hugh said.

"My grandnephew,'' Althea said smugly, "was not at all that sort of person.''

"But this man is,'' I pointed out. "His behavior is erratic. And the cocaine connection accounts for something else, namely, Irene Wheeler's desperation. We've been . . . Well, I, at least, have been assuming that her motive in conning Ceci and everyone else is purely mercenary. But maybe there's a reason for her greed. One day when I saw her, she looked terrible. I thought she had a dreadful cold. But now . . .''

Althea was impatient. "Jonathan was all that stood between this scheming pair and my sister's money. I have no doubt that they had plans that reached far beyond the payments made for daily consultations. And when this woman visited my poor, gullible sister and failed to convince Jonathan of her supposed psychic powers, her confederate listened in.''

"The footprints in the flower beds," Hugh informed me.

"And," Althea continued, "lured Jonathan outside and murdered him, leaving behind minute traces of—"

"The solution!" Robert cried dramatically.

"Of course," Althea calmly pronounced. "The seven-percent solution."

Chapter Twenty-seven

I CAN'T BE BLAMED for playing Sherlock Holmes. The impulse is irresistible. When Rita came home for lunch, I sprang on her the astonishing deduction that her patient's missing dog was a male Great Pyrenees stolen while the owner was running on Greenough Boulevard. Whenever Holmes made a comparably staggering proclamation, the victim was always gratifyingly stunned: *"How the deuce did he know I came from Afghanistan?"*

Rita, in contrast, just said, "I already told you that."

I was childishly put out. "No, you didn't. I deduced it. Just like Sherlock Holmes."

"This Sherlock Holmes obsession of yours is getting to be worse than dogs," she sighed.

I continued. "The man who stole the dog is the same one who tried to drown Tracker."

"Tracker?"

"The cat. I finally got around to naming her."

"Tracker," Rita said ungenerously, "is a stupid name for a female cat."

"Positive reframing," I said, lapsing into the psychotherapeutic jargon I'd picked up from Rita herself. "And you know what? It works. It's totally transformed my feelings about her. And Tracker is only her call name. Her real name is Kaila's Paw Print. Actually, it's Champion Kaila's Paw Print. I named her after a famous malamute. I'm teaching her to live on top of the refrigerator. That's from Holmes, more or less. 'The Empty House.' *From this convenient retreat, the watchers were being watched and the trackers tracked.''*

Rita, for once, refused to listen. In fact, she interrupted me by shrieking. When she'd composed herself, she said, "I was right! The Holmes obsession is getting to be worse than dogs. So, who is this mystery man?"

Succumbing to the Holmesian fondness for theatrics, I let silence linger before making my dramatic pronouncement. "He is Irene Wheeler's partner in crime. He has drug connections. Greenough Boulevard is one of his haunts. Kevin is always warning me about that stretch of the river. I just never took him seriously."

Rita's patient's dog had been stolen just before the spectral Simon, the giant white dog, made his first appearance. Later that week, Irene told the owner that the dog was fine. After Jonathan's murder, however, Irene, in uncharacteristic fashion, gave the owner unwelcome news: All of a sudden, Irene channeled the information that the dog was dead. In other words, once the situation took a deadly turn, Irene wanted the owner to quit searching for the dog. She wanted it even more than she wanted to keep a client.

Unlike Holmes's creator, who investigated a couple of real-life murders, I tried to limit my imitation of the Master. It was one thing to make astonishing deductions, even if they didn't produce the intended effect, it was quite another to meddle with a double murderer. Jonathan Hubbell had been murdered in Newton, but

Donald Lively, the dealer, had been killed on Kevin's turf, in Cambridge, right near the courthouse. In the early afternoon, I tried to reach Kevin. I left a phone message at the station. Then I ran next door. His mother said that he'd barely been home for two days. He'd stop in to eat, catch a nap, and take a shower. Then he'd be off again. I emphasized to Mrs. Dennehy that I absolutely had to talk to Kevin the next time he showed up, no matter when it was. As I didn't tell Mrs. Dennehy, I just couldn't face trying to explain matters to the Newton police or to any of the other authorities involved in the whole business. I imagined the reception I'd get if I phoned the police or the D.A.'s office and outlined the story to some stranger: Hugh and Robert's application of Holmes's methods, the use of a stolen Great Pyrenees to impersonate a dead Newfoundland, my conviction that a man vicious enough to attempt the murder of a pitiful cat would stop at nothing. Kevin and his cop buddies alternately joked and complained about nuts who wasted police time by propounding loopy conspiracy theories. Especially if I failed to censor what I am informed is a slight tendency to punctuate narratives with the occasional extraneous detail or two about dogs, I'd be mistaken for a paranoid lunatic. Kevin Dennehy knew the full extent of my madness, but understood that it was strictly limited to matters canine.

And to a lesser extent, feline. Tracker's physical condition, I might mention, was improving. As part of my plan to integrate her into my household, I took advantage of the two big dog crates I'd set up in the guest room. The crates occupied most of the floor space, but anyone who'd visit me—my father, for example— would view the crates and their occupants as a welcoming touch of hospitality designed to make the visitor feel right at home. So I crated the dogs, closed the guest-room door, and closed off my bedroom, too, before opening the door to my office and tempting Tracker off the mouse pad and out of the room. My personality held no charms for her, but she was now wild about canned tuna. I succeeded in luring her into the kitchen. Sensing somehow—ESP? my dog instincts?—that she was ready, I gave her a boost to the top of the refrigerator and promptly ladled out more tuna. Before the kitchen was redone, Kimi had been able to leap up and snatch food from the top of my old refrigerator, but the old one was small, and most of it was recessed under a cabinet. Tracker, I thought, should be safe from predation on top of the new, deep refrigerator, at least if she stayed away from the front.

Have I digressed? God help me! First it was dogs, then Holmes, now cats. Stop me before I love more! The point is that after returning from the Gateway, chatting with Rita, and trying to reach Kevin Dennehy, I puttered around implementing the program I'd designed for my breed champion Alaskan malamute cat, Tracker, before returning her to my study, releasing Rowdy and Kimi, and settling down to earning our daily kibble by writing the beginning of an article about the dogs of Sherlock Holmes.

As I was about to finish the first sentence, the ring of the doorbell interrupted me. On my back steps I found a young neighborhood friend of mine, a ten-year-old boy who loves dogs and misses his own. The separation is temporary. The kid's parents are on a one-year stint as visiting scholars at Harvard. Meanwhile, the family dogs live in air-conditioned splendor with the boy's uncle back in the United Arab Emirates. The kid arrived in Cambridge speaking fluent American English, but his classmates apparently made fun of his name, whatever it is, so he insists on being called Billy. Although he speaks four or five languages and has traveled all over the world, he is wonderfully unassuming about his accomplishments and background, and is friendly to the point of brashness and refreshingly unspoiled. Indeed, he's the only child on the block who can be hired to perform such traditionally all-American-kid tasks as shoveling sidewalks, taking out trash, and walking dogs. Every few weeks, Billy showed up at my door in the hope that I'd finally relent by letting him add Rowdy and Kimi to his canine clientele. As I did not tell Billy, he was way too small to manage one malamute, never mind two. Instead, I explained, as he already knew, that I walked the dogs myself. Rowdy, Kimi, and I ran into him all the time. Anyway, when I saw him on my back steps, I assumed that he was there either to repeat the request for employment or to stop in for a visit. As he promptly announced, however, he was running an errand.

Handing me a sealed envelope, he gave me a big grin and said shamelessly, "I'm not supposed to deliver this to you until tomorrow."

I grinned back. "Then why are you delivering it now?"

"Because," Billy replied with commendable honesty, "the man said you'd pay me for it, and I don't want to wait until tomorrow."

"And how much did the man say I'd give you?"

"He *said* a dollar, but then I said it would be better to leave it up to you, and he said that was all right."

We settled on two dollars plus another two for the rush delivery. When Billy had departed, I examined the envelope. It was plain white. My name and address were written in legible, old-fashioned script. There was no return address. Inside was a single sheet of white typing paper. Hand-printed on the sheet was what I instantly recognized as a cryptic message. It inevitably reminded me of the one Sherlock Holmes receives from Porlock at the beginning of *The Valley of Fear*. I didn't bother dashing out of the house and down the street to snag Billy and get a description of the man who'd arranged the delivery. The cipher message? Delivered by a child? And an Arab child no less, albeit one rather different from the urchins, the *dirty and ragged little street Arabs,* who formed the ranks of the famous Baker Street Irregulars. The man had to be Robert, who took an interest in vowels. Only a trained ear could have heard the Middle East in Billy's fluent American English.

To refresh my memory, I got out my copy of the Canon and looked up the story. Porlock's message to Holmes, I remind you, begins:

534 C2 13 127 36

The Great Detective realizes that he has received what he calls *a cipher message without a cipher.* In other words, he needs to discover the particular cipher—presumably a book—that will let him break the code. He eventually concludes that the cipher is something called Whitaker's Almanac, chosen because Porlock assumed that Holmes would have no difficulty in finding it. After a false start (Holmes first consults the new Almanac instead of the previous year's), the Master decodes the message by going to page 534, column two, and reading the thirteenth word, the one hundred twenty-seventh word, and so on.

My message also began with the number 534. Next, however, came the letters L and W, separated by a comma, and then a series of numbers.

534 L,W 24,13 36,3 5,17 38,10 9,7 25,2 14,2,3,4

5,1,2,3 25,2 43,11,12 7,4 43,15 44,1,2,3,4

23,14,15 43,11 41,14 30,10 1,7 7,4 4,11 29,6 40,8 11,6

1,12 4,5 15,16 4,5 37,6 3,5 45,12 13,12 29,6 14,1

32,1,2 25,10 7,4 1,4 45,4 39,9 14,13 4,13 33,14 4,5 25,11

35,18!

In *The Valley of Fear,* Holmes reasons that *C* stands for *column.* Therefore the book he seeks is one with columns. It seemed to me that if the cipher I needed had columns, the *C* would appear at the start of my message. It didn't. So I needed a work without columns. Not the Bible, for example. Instead of a *C,* my message had *L,W*—lines and words? So, the message began with the thirteenth word of the twenty-fourth line on page 534 of *some* book without columns. With a minimum of 534 pages, it was a long book. And as Porlock had done in sending his encoded message to Holmes, Hugh and Robert must have chosen a work that would be easy for me to find. An almanac? The men had commented that my house was right across the street from the Observatory Hill branch of the Cambridge Public Library. As I was about to sprint over there, I had a sudden inspiration.

Of course! Hugh, Robert, or almost anyone else would correctly assume that I owned the latest edition of the American Kennel Club's *Complete Dog Book.* Consulting it, I found that page 534 was devoted to the beginning of the write-up of the Tibetan spaniel. A photograph occupied about half the page. Consequently, there was no line twenty-four. Dead end. What other long book without columns would I be certain to own?

The Merck Veterinary Manual! Flipping to page 534, hurriedly counting lines, I found that the twenty-fourth had only twelve words.

Then, like Holmes, I suddenly realized my mistake. The correct cipher had to be *The Complete Sherlock Holmes.* It was long. It lacked columns. Furthermore, Hugh and Robert not only knew that I owned it, but had seen my one-volume Doubleday edition the day they'd trailed me home from the Gateway. Yes, of course! What story had we discussed? Which adventure had Hugh's little Holmesian puzzler been about? Indeed, *The Valley of Fear.* Robert and Hugh had known for certain that I'd read about Porlock's cryptic message.

Turning to page 534, I found myself in ''The Solitary Cyclist.'' Grabbing a pencil, I hurriedly marked the numbers of the lines. With a yellow legal pad at hand, I started to locate the lines in the message and count the words. Like Holmes, I got off to a false start; *coal-black* counted as one word, not two. I tried again. ''Line twenty-four, word thirteen,'' I said to Rowdy and Kimi. ''Hm. The end of the line. A word division. *Con.* Fine. *Con* it is. Line thirty-six, word three. *Lady. Con lady!* There! The game really is afoot!'' I explained to my two Watsons. ''What do you think of that?''

Decoded, the cryptic message read:

Con- lady and blackguard up to Heaven knows what!
We hastened onward to the marks of feet upon the muddy
    path
close to the hedge down half no or wood road.
If we blunder we shall meet with abduction or murder.
Quick, clear eyes of a young friend now see where we
    were.
Help!

"No or wood," I said with sudden alarm. "Norwood. Down half. Lower. Lower Norwood Road. They've gone to Ceci's!"

This message was supposed to reach me tomorrow. It was a precaution sent in case Hugh and Robert vanished; in case, as the message said, they were abducted or murdered. After leaving the Gateway, they must somehow have learned that something was to happen tonight at Ceci's house. Their plan, I decided, was to hide on Lower Norwood Road, the dark dead-end street at the bottom of Ceci's property. Did Ceci have an appointment with Irene Wheeler tonight? And did the men hope to nab her confederate as he and his stolen dog staged another appearance of the late Lord Saint Simon? Like Holmes and Watson in "The Speckled Band," Hugh and Robert were keeping a night watch. But Holmes and Watson were young and strong. Watson carried a revolver. It was of no comfort to me to realize that Robert and Hugh, too, would be armed.

Chapter Twenty-eight

I DIDN'T PANIC. A stolen Great Pyrenees wasn't exactly the hound of the Baskervilles, and unless Watson had failed to mention the excellence of the Grimpen Mire school system, the suburb of Newton, Massachusetts, was a far howl from the evils of the famed Baskervillian moor. Furthermore, I had learned of Hugh and Robert's plan in what I trusted was plenty of time to intervene. In dog training, low-key prevention is always a better strategy than dramatic after-the-fact confrontation and correction. As in dog training, so, too, in life. And when it comes to training dogs, I'm not in the habit of screaming for help. If I persuaded the Newton police to block off Lower Norwood Road, there'd be a hullabaloo that might culminate in Hugh's arrest for what I suspected was illegal possession of a handgun. A trivial offense? In Massachusetts, it carries a mandatory one-year jail term. The frivolous thought crossed my mind that at least Hugh would have an advantage over his fellow prisoners: He'd entertain himself by endlessly rereading Sherlock Holmes. Then the reality of prison hit me: harassment, assault, drugs, bitter loneliness, and shame. Hugh was an old man. Jail would kill him. Furthermore, although possession of Holmes's favorite weapon was probably legal, I didn't trust Robert to use the hunting crop exclusively as a harmless Sherlockian prop. And Holmes, like Watson, sometimes carried a revolver. What if, God forbid, Hugh and Robert mistook some innocent dog walker for Irene Wheeler's confederate? What exactly was Hugh and Robert's plan? Some Sherlockian scheme, no doubt, to lurk in the shrubbery and then spring a surprise attack on the villain. The end of the Hound of the Baskervilles came when Holmes emptied five chambers of his revolver into the beast. Dear God! What if Hugh and Robert shot a dog?

But with a minimum of fuss, I could foil the scheme. If Irene Wheeler's confederate arrived to find Lower Norwood Road other than dark and deserted, he'd simply postpone the reappearance of the spectral dog and depart, thus depriving Hugh and Robert of the opportunity to get themselves in trouble. And if my own plan went astray? Newton, as I've said, was not the Grimpen Mire. If need be, I'd scream: I'd ring doorbells or lean on the horn of my car until some outraged suburbanite called the police. If I hurried, I'd beat Hugh and Robert to Lower Norwood Road.

I gave Rowdy and Kimi their dinners at ultra-fast-forward. Instead of walking them, I let them out in the yard for a few minutes. To avoid once again losing my bearings in the tangle of gaslit streets on Norwood Hill, I consulted my scribbled directions to Ceci's and studied the Newton map in my atlas of eastern Massachusetts. Then I crated Kimi, threw on my parka, snapped a leash on Rowdy, and tore to my car. I told myself that Rowdy was my camouflage: If for some unforeseen reason I needed to pass unnoticed in Newton, I'd become yet another suburbanite exercising another suburban dog. Like Sherlock Holmes lingering outside Irene Adler's house, right? Disguised as a drunken-looking groom—of the equine variety, of course, although when you consider Holmes's admiration for *the* woman, you naturally have to wonder about his unconscious motivation in casting himself as a groom. And about mine in taking Rowdy with me. Camouflage? Oh, sure. Any excuse would do. The truth? As the Bible says, ''Yea, though I walk through the valley of the shadow of death, I will fear no evil.''

Instead of meandering along Greenough Boulevard, I cut across the river to Soldiers Field Road. A sharp left took me under the Mass. Pike, and a right led me to Oak Square in Brighton. Turning left, I crossed into Newton and, consulting my refreshed mental map, made my way up Norwood Hill without getting lost. The challenge was greater than on my previous trip. The night was mild and foggy. I seemed to ascend into a cloud. Twenty minutes after I'd left home, I was on Norwood Road. A block ahead of me, I knew, the road split. Upper Norwood forked to the right and continued past Ceci's house, and Lower Norwood veered left to dead-end near the bottom of her property. On my previous trip here, I'd had to get out of the car to search for a street sign. The neighborhood had intimidated me and made me feel vaguely angry and resentful, as if the invisible inhabitants of these immense houses had conspired to maintain exclusivity by insisting on charming gaslights that failed to illuminate hidden street signs.

Now, on this Friday evening, one of the houses on the block of Norwood Road before the fork was visibly and brightly inhabited. Fog-softened light radiated from every window of the three-story colonial; cars lined both sides of the narrow street. About half were big, new four-by-fours: Jeeps, Blazers, a Land Rover. Honestly, to judge by what's driven in prosperous suburbs, you'd assume that free-roving lions and elephants posed a constant threat to people running errands and ferrying children to soccer practice. If not, why prepare for a safari? Anyway, parked between a Mercedes and a vehicle suitable for off-road adventure in Africa was a familiar old Volvo from which the bumper sticker had been removed. Hugh and Robert had evidently decided that when the game actually was afoot, it was best not to advertise the news. Had their quarry also arrived? I scanned for a dark panel truck. Its presence here, I realized, would be unremarkable; anyone would assume that it belonged to the caterer hired by the hosts of the party, or perhaps to an electrician, plumber, or locksmith responding to a household emergency. But the panel truck wasn't there. It could have been on Lower Norwood Road, of course, or somewhere else nearby. And the man with the bulbous forehead could have driven anything: a rental car, a fancy new four-by-four borrowed from a friend. Was he here? Or had I arrived in time?

Rowdy's comforting presence offered a reliable way to find out. At shows and at dog training, I seldom have to worry that Rowdy will start a fight. What I do have to worry about is that a dog with warped judgment will decide to take him on. Also, when trouble breaks out between other dogs, Rowdy feels compelled to join the fun. If he's loose in the back of the car, he has a slight tendency to roar at any dog we pass. And, naturally, he won't tolerate having his turf invaded by canine strangers. When I first brought Kimi home, he exhibited a certain amount of rivalry. Now, of course, he adores her. The two of them won't fight about anything except food, and even when a battle breaks out, there's more noise than actual bloodshed. So for a dominant male malamute, he's remarkably good with other dogs. But if Irene Wheeler's confederate had arrived here with a male Great Pyrenees, Rowdy would let me know.

Backing carefully along the car-lined block of Norwood, I reached an empty space and parked. Would the villain remember my car? Probably not. He'd seen it for only a few seconds. Outside the restaurant, it had been Kevin, not me, he'd recognized. Would he know my face again? Maybe. But Lower Norwood Road was dark. I hoped that no one had repaired the broken gas lamp. I certainly hoped that no one there was giving a party. And Rowdy and I wouldn't go all the way to the end of the street; we'd just reconnoiter and backtrack.

As soon as Rowdy and I began to stroll up Norwood Road, I discovered a new and powerful reason to object to the damned inadequate, elitist gas lamps. It was one thing to be unable to read a street sign, quite another to be virtually unable to see Rowdy. Now, in the fog and darkness, when subtle changes in Rowdy's body language were supposed to signal the presence of Simon's spectral stand-in, I could see little more than a burly, white-faced mass with a plumy white tail. Running my hand down Rowdy's neck and back, I felt no sign of hackles. Trotting along, he paused now and then to lay casual territorial claim to a tree trunk in the name of the Sovereign Nation of the Alaskan Malamute. We reached the fork in the road without incident and turned left onto Lower Norwood. The dim glow of a gas lamp showed a sidewalk stretching along the left-hand side and, on the right, the kind of wide strip of grass and tall shrubbery I'd seen at Ceci's. The map of Newton had shown me that Lower Norwood Road was only one short block long. The few houses facing it were on the left; on the opposite side were the ends of large lots like

Ceci's with addresses on Upper Norwood. The dead-end road was even darker and more deserted than the last time I'd seen it. In addition to the gas lamp near the fork, two others were visible, one on the right, then one on the left. The broken one I'd noticed near Ceci's still hadn't been fixed. On my previous visit, the house opposite Ceci's lower gate had been dark. The carriage lamps and other bright lights of the brick Tudor next to it, I now realized, had been the principal source of illumination for the street. Ceci had remarked that its owners must be home from Florida. Maybe they'd gone back. How was I supposed to reconnoiter when I couldn't see anything?

But if I couldn't see, I couldn't be seen, could I? Especially if I avoided the small circles of gaslight. Crossing to the right-hand side of the road, I hoped that local dog walkers carried plastic bags and invariably cleaned up after their dogs.

I stopped for a moment. In the house across from me, a glowing first-floor window suggested a television. The house beyond it had a car parked in the driveway and a bright window on the second floor. I listened. Prosperous suburbs are supposed to be peaceful and quiet. In the daytime, all year long, they are, in fact, cacophonous. As soon as snow vanquishes the din of lawn-service equipment, snow blowers start roaring. Furthermore, house-proud people with money are always renovating, putting up additions and garages, or having driveways and sidewalks deafeningly repaved. Politicians eager for reelection make sure that the streets get swept, plowed, and newly blacktopped by machines obviously designed by hearing-aid manufacturers bent on causing mass hearing loss and thus generating business for themselves. Face it: This kind of noise is beyond the reach of the poor. Even now, Newton was far from silent. In the distance, traffic swept along the Mass. Pike. I heard a plane overhead. Blocks away, cars and trucks rumbled. To avoid the gaslight, I crossed to the left-hand side, stopped to listen again, and went on. Rowdy gave no indication of sensing the presence of another dog. Reaching the last illuminated gaslight, we crossed back to the dark side. Opposite us was a deserted-looking house. Beyond it was the Tudor with the carriage lamps set on big pillars. The last house looked as empty as on my first visit. With the exception of the car I'd seen in a driveway, there wasn't a single vehicle in sight. No one else was walking a dog. It was easy to imagine that a nuclear attack had destroyed all the people, but left their houses and possessions intact. I'd intended to glance down this street. According to my plan, if I found it dark and empty, I'd return to my car and drive back here with the headlights on high beam. Just as I was about to make an about-turn and carry out the plan, Rowdy quit sniffing the ground. I couldn't see the expression on his face or the hair on his back. I couldn't even see his face. His white tail wagged merrily in the air above an apparently nonexistent dog. He was pulling me toward someone or something near the gate to Ceci's yard. There'd been no nuclear attack here, of course. There wouldn't be now. And the murk was just that, a meteorological phenomenon, fog, neither toxic nor otherworldly. No one has succumbed to it or been wafted here enshrouded in its vapors.

Chapter Twenty-nine

ON A DESERTED DEAD-END road on a dark, foggy night, men lurk in the shrubbery only yards from the scene of a recent murder. They are ready to spring at me. Rowdy approaches them. He approaches in the hope of a tummy rub. He threatens wet kisses. My deduction? "Silver Blaze."

Only one of the two men sprang out: Robert. He was far from glad to see me. In fact, his stage-whispered greeting was, believe it or not, "Go home! This is no place for the weaker sex."

Truly. But when I'm dealing with a person of Robert's age, I always strive to take generational differences in attitude into account. Most of the time, there aren't any. Now there were. "I'm sorry," I answered at normal volume. "Kimi would have liked to come along, but I'm afraid we'll just have to make do with a male." Without pausing, I added, "Your message arrived ahead of schedule. If I deciphered it correctly, you *did* ask for help."

"You," Robert whispered in disgust.

"I don't know what you're talking about."

"You have alarmed Althea. You should never have done that."

"I haven't seen Althea since this morning. I don't know how I'm supposed to have alarmed her. Wait! Yes, I do. You thought I'd have to take the message to her, didn't you? You didn't think I'd be able to figure it out for myself. Well, if I'd had to take it to her, then she really would've been alarmed, wouldn't she? You should've—"

From the bushes came a wordless injunction to be quiet. I heard the sound of a car engine. The beam of distant headlights glowed through the fog. Before I could decide whether to vanish into the shrubbery or resume my disguise as a dog walker, the lights faded as the car turned onto Upper Norwood. Popping out of the unpruned hedge by Ceci's gate, Hugh took Robert and me to task so severely that Rowdy plunked his bottom on the ground and listened, too. Although Althea had largely disabused me of my newfound flirtation with the belief in thought transmission, I realized that Rowdy was watching me. It was too dark to see him. But I could feel his gaze. I reached down to rest a hand on his head.

According to Hugh, Robert and I were making a mockery of a serious situation. He was, of course, right.

"How serious is it?" I asked. "Do you have some reason to believe that something is going to happen tonight? Now?"

"I warned you of this!" Robert told Hugh. "The cipher message was *your* idea, I remind you, and—"

Ignoring Robert, Hugh informed me that after leaving the Gateway, the men had discussed the entire matter and decided to interrogate Ceci. In a phone conversation, they'd learned that she was eagerly expecting a reunion with Simon this very evening. Indeed, she'd been so thrilled by the prospect that they'd obtained only a little information from her about the events preceding Jonathan's murder. It had been Jonathan, not Ceci, who had called Irene Wheeler to insist that she meet with him. On the phone, and later in person, Jonathan had demanded that Irene return every cent Ceci had ever paid her. According to Ceci, Jonathan had said terrible things to her and to Irene as well, but the men had been unable to discover exactly what the terrible things were.

"When Robert challenged her on the point," Hugh whispered indignantly, "she had the audacity to hang up on us."

"Ceci is afraid of ending up at the Gateway," I ventured, "or in another nursing home." It seemed to me, too, although I didn't say it, that Irene and her confederate, the man with the bulbous forehead, might, after all, be guilty only of conning Ceci. Irene's psychic powers might not be genuine, but her powers of persuasion were real. And the man who'd tried to drown poor Tracker had certainly conspired with Irene to create the credible illusion of Simon's return. Moreover, Ceci depended exclusively on Irene for her sense of contact with Simon and for the wondrous prospect of earthly reunion with him. Simon, Ceci had told me, was "coming home." She'd meant the words literally: coming home to his house and his yard on Norwood Hill. To Ceci, Simon was as real as Rowdy was to me right now. But I could rest my hand on Rowdy's head. In the darkness, I could feel his gaze. Jonathan, I thought, had threatened to deprive his great-aunt Ceci of precisely the kind of contact I had at this moment with my own living dog. But I needed no help to reach Rowdy. Ceci needed Irene. And to see and touch Simon she needed to be at home on Norwood Hill, not at the Gateway, not anywhere else on earth. If Jonathan had threatened to drive Irene away? If he'd questioned Ceci's mental competence and threatened to move her from Simon's home? If so, he had, in effect, threatened to kill her dog. And Irene and her confederate had unwittingly set Ceci up to commit murder.

"The *Gateway*," Robert said with scorn. "The Gateway! Death and roaches!"

"I've never seen roaches there." I didn't mention that I'd heard about them, looked for them, and found none.

"According to our research," Hugh countered, "there are five superior facilities in the area."

"There are probably hundreds of inferior ones," I loyally replied. Then I did a mental double take. Research? Had Hugh and Robert been visiting nursing homes? I hadn't done comparative shopping. When Rowdy and I had begun to volunteer, my expectations of nursing homes had been so low that almost any half-decent facility would have been better than I'd feared. For all I knew, the Gateway had roaches I hadn't seen. I remembered the unresponsive attendant, Ralph, the one we'd met by the elevators, the one I wouldn't have hired as kennel help. The roaches might be imaginary. Ralph was real. Rowdy and I arrived at the Gateway at ten-thirty one morning a week. What went on when I wasn't there? And it was true that the Gateway offered Althea no intellectual companionship. Almost no one else showed any interest in books, and Althea had never shown the slightest interest in any of the social activities that drew Helen Musgrave. Helen was pleasant and cheerful, but wouldn't Althea happily trade her roommate for the luxury of privacy and the space for more than a handful of personal possessions? Maybe Althea would be better off at one of the five superior facilities.

But the Gateway simply had to be a better-than-average facility. There was nothing cheap-looking about it. It occurred to me that I had no real proof that Jonathan's visit here had anything to do with Irene Wheeler, spectral dogs, con jobs, or the great-aunt at whose house he had been murdered. Maybe the purpose of his visit had concerned his other great-aunt, Althea. According to Ceci, Jonathan had Althea's power of attorney. It had been Jonathan who'd written monthly checks to the Gateway. It might not meet Hugh and Robert's standards as a suitable place for Althea—would any institution?—but those checks must have been for large sums. Any nursing home was expensive. Could Jonathan have come here not to protect Ceci from a con job, but to *move* Althea from the Gateway to some cut-rate place?

Another possibility occurred to me. On the Saturday when Jonathan had arrived here, he had talked on the phone to Irene Wheeler, and she had come here to meet him. What else had he done? Had the psychic been the only one he'd talked to? Althea had known of his impending arrival. She must have told Hugh and Robert. Had they presented Jonathan with information about the five superior facilities? Hugh, I felt certain, had carefully entered tons of data on local nursing homes in a file on his laptop. With research data available, Hugh and Robert could have presented Jonathan with the demand that Althea be moved to a facility of their choice. Or perhaps they'd insisted that she at least have a private room. If Jonathan had refused? Ceci had told me that she was positively not going to take over Althea's finances; with Jonathan dead, someone else would have to assume the responsibility. Hugh and Robert had known Ceci for decades. They'd surely have been able to predict that response. They were the obvious people to take over from Jonathan. Perhaps one of them already had Althea's power of attorney. Perhaps plans were now under way to move her. But did Althea have the funds to pay for a palatial nursing home? The sister who did was Ceci. Could this entire Holmesian investigation of Jonathan's murder be an elaborate smokescreen? With Jonathan dead, Althea was Ceci's heir. Oh, yes! Althea would inherit not only Ceci's money, but her house on Norwood Hill. The money would be more than sufficient to pay for round-the-clock care. And unlike any institution, this grand and beautiful house would be a suitable residence for *the* woman.

Irene Wheeler was supposed to visit Ceci this evening. Were Hugh and Robert really here to set a trap for Jonathan's murderer? Or to frame the psychic and her confederate for the murder they themselves intended to commit? Hugh, I reminded myself, had sent one man to the hospital. And another to the morgue?

Chapter Thirty

IF HUGH AND ROBERT had murdered Jonathan, they were here tonight to reenact their Baskervillian drama. This time, however, Ceci would play the victim. Rowdy, I imagined, would find himself miscast as the demonic hound. Did I, too, have a role? Or was I caught not in a Holmesian play, but in a psychic con game? Irene Wheeler had already duped me. I didn't blame myself. Gaining misplaced trust was how she made her living. Violence was not her game. It was, of course, her confederate's. He'd tried to drown a sickly, aging cat. He'd fled at the sight of Kevin Dennehy, a cop whose face had appeared in the papers and on television in connection with the murder of Donald Lively. If the man with the bulbous forehead had murdered Jonathan, he'd made an unexpected move in Irene's game. Then there was Ceci's metaphor, the one she'd borrowed from Conan Doyle: the joyous image of the gates that were not shut, the great news that the dead were not lost to us, but eager to communicate, ready to speak, to listen, and even to return to those who loved them.

But the Holmesian drama was a game, wasn't it? The

Great Game: the pretense that fiction was history. And Irene's con game was her drama. The people of the drama: Irene as the grifter, Gloria and Scott as her shills, and Ceci as the perfect chump. And the content of the game, the theme of the play, was the illusion of reality, or perhaps the reality of illusion. To Conan Doyle, who was, after all, in a position to know, Holmes and Watson were creatures of the imagination; to Hugh and Robert, the Great Detective, the Friendship, and the Sacred Writings were overarching realities. Conan Doyle's true mission was not to create a Canon more real than reality, but to awaken the world to the reality that was the substance of Irene Wheeler's con game, the same illusion that was now Ceci's reality, the splendid news that death itself was an illusion and that its gates swung open in both directions. Until Jonathan tried to lock that gate.

The actual gate to Ceci's yard, the iron gate, was shut but unlocked. When it came to spectral dogs, mundane security precautions evidently did not apply. For all I knew, maybe the gate had never had a lock. And if it had been Ceci who'd murdered Jonathan, she obviously had no need to protect herself against the murderer's return. As to Simon's access, Ceci must credit him with the power to undo latches or maybe to pass through material barriers. When I pushed the gate inward, it squeaked on its hinges. Why had Jonathan left the house? Because he had heard something outside: the squeal of this gate.

Robert made genteel noises of objection and asked what I thought I was doing.

Hedging my bets, I wanted to say. *Heading away from violence: the two of you. The man with the bulbous forehead.* Even if Ceci had killed Jonathan, she was morally innocent of murder. Besides, she was no physical threat to me. Furthermore, she knew I was the last person in this world or any other to stand between a loving owner and a beloved dog. Far from trying to hurt me, she might tell me what she'd done. She'd already have spoken about the deed to Irene Wheeler. Ceci would have wanted to communicate with Jonathan. She'd have required Irene's help. And in any case, Ceci would have assumed that the psychic would know without having to be told. If so, Ceci needed another kind of help. Violence was not the psychic's style. But blackmail was.

When I closed the gate behind me, its hinges gave another horror-movie squeak. The noise reminded me to remove Rowdy's rolled-leather collar with its collection of jingling tags. I pulled him close to my left side, held still, and found my bearings. The fog was still thick. I had to rely on my memory. The sundial, Simon's grave, and the scene of Jonathan's murder must be to my left and four or five yards uphill. Directly ahead of me, I remembered, a long bluestone walk led to a flight of steps that gave access to the terrace at the rear of Ceci's house. Like the edge of a stage, the patio was dark. Center stage glowed hazily. Then a breeze stirred, and the fog briefly cleared. The French doors that formed the big alcove were transparent curtains. Flanked by tall fronds of potted palms, two chairs had been drawn close to the edge of the stage, almost as if their occupants were acting in the sort of so-called experimental play that forces actors and audience to reverse roles. So-called: If the result of an experiment has been replicated zillions of times, the experiment isn't exactly experimental anymore, is it? I mean, if theatergoers wanted to be actors, they'd audition, wouldn't they? They wouldn't buy tickets. And that, of course, is the zillion-times-replicated result. Tonight, for example, the entire audience consisted of a woman and a dog who'd sneaked in without paying and occupied standing room near the rear exit of an otherwise empty theater.

On another night, another gate-crasher had made it all the way to the edge of the stage. Crushing flowers and foliage beneath his feet, the man with the bulbous forehead had stood in the wings, where he had eavesdropped on the action. But which side of the footlights had he really stood on? Was he a sort of stagehand or animal assistant who awaited Irene Wheeler's cue to send the dog onstage? Or perhaps he was a vigilant and mistrustful director who wanted assurance that Irene was speaking her lines correctly. What was she saying now? What was Ceci saying?

To approach unobserved, I couldn't stride up the bluestone path with a big, flashy dog. No, I'd need to take a circuitous route. I wished I'd seen the yard in daylight. Looking uphill, I could see the bright alcove, of course, and the silhouettes of the house and, to its left, the low roof of the garage. The sundial was to my left. Near it was the semi-excavated resting place of Simon's ashes. Jonathan Hubbell had not, of course, caught a foot in the grave and taken a mortal fall onto the sundial. If I tripped or bumped myself, I'd survive. But not necessarily in silence. I moved to my right. With Rowdy's leash in my left hand, I stretched out my right and inched along until my fingers brushed the hedge. Ceci had said that the yard was fully fenced. We'd follow the perimeter. Any hazardous pieces of garden sculpture would be on display in prime locations, not tucked in the boundary shrubs. I'd let Rowdy move ahead of me. Dogs have excellent night vision and, of course, that uncanny sense of smell. I'd keep an eye on Rowdy's white tail. If he moved to avoid an object, I'd avoid it, too. And if we needed to vanish, the shrubbery would offer hiding places. If we needed to bolt, we could run like mad for the stretch of fence to the right of the house, and in seconds we'd be through the gate and on the sidewalk of Upper Norwood Road.

The plan worked perfectly for about thirty seconds. We followed our course to the right, turned left, and were starting uphill when the bright lights in the alcove suddenly went out. In the blackness, I heard the simultaneous sound of a door and the wail of Ceci's voice in the open air. "Simon, come!" she screamed. Her voice had the high-pitched musical quiver that you hear when elderly women sing hymns. "Simon, come! Here, Simon! Here! Simon, come!" Caroling to her dead dog, she was heartbreakingly eager and desperate. "Simon, please! Please come back!" Then impatience crept in, as if the long-gone Newfoundland bounced and pranced just out of reach, happily engaged in some infuriating game of catch-me-if-you-can. "Simon!" Ceci scolded. "Simon, *come! Come here right now!*"

Although Ceci's behavior now strikes me as ludicrous and pitiful, its immediate effect was bizarrely convincing. On visits to the Gateway, I often took part in present-tense conversations about dogs who had left this world decades earlier, but lived on in the lives of their owners. There was a woman named Gladys who always perked up at the sight of Rowdy and announced to me in the familiar tones of canine fellowship, "I have two French bulldogs!" The first few times Rowdy and I visited Gladys, I assumed that her dogs lived nearby with a relative and that she got a chance to see them every week or so. I started to catch on when she happened to mention that she drove a Studebaker. I also learned that Gladys was an enthusiastic gardener. She complained about how hard it was to get the soil out from under her nails. To prove her point, she held out a clean hand. Gladys and I nonetheless continued to discuss her French bulldogs. I couldn't bring myself to ask a brittle, cheerful, "And how are your dogs?" Rather, on each visit, I let Gladys reestablish the present-day reality of the two French bulldogs and all the rest. Once she did, I always felt perfectly comfortable. Relativity didn't freak out Einstein, did it? On the contrary, he enjoyed it. So did I.

Gladys's Frenchies lived where she did, in an internally consistent past made present by physiological change, which is to say by a merciful act of God. Her relationship with them was thus as harmonious as mine with Rowdy and Kimi. Gladys and I had been blessed by coincidence: Temporal relativity had granted us the comforting good fortune of coinciding with our dogs. Furthermore, as surely as I could have driven Kimi to the Gateway to introduce her to Gladys, Gladys could not have presented her dogs to me, because they existed with her in her time, not with me in mine except during brief visits when Gladys, Rowdy, and I coincided in space. Is this getting too cosmic? The point is that in listening to Ceci's expectant, melodious calls to a dog whose ashes lay buried nearby, I entertained the fleeting fantasy that there were two spectral dogs: one the unwitting impostor, the other the true Simon, who might triumph over time, space, death, and human fakery to leap over the heavenly and earthly gates to sail past me and into Ceci's arms.

Rowdy stirred. From the house, I heard soothing murmurs: Irene. The French door closed; the lights came back on. Rowdy and I resumed our uphill course, reached the level of the terrace, and inched our way from the shrubbery to the corner of the house, and from there toward the spot where Hugh and Robert had found the crushed flowers. Light spilled onto the terrace from the French doors at the center of the alcove, but the immense pot and lush foliage of the tropical plant at this corner of the little conservatory created an ideal post for eavesdropping. I could already hear soft voices. As I've mentioned, dogs have good night vision, and the long down had always been one obedience exercise that Rowdy performed quite reliably, if rather more noisily than the AKC obedience regulations allowed. Even if he hadn't been able to see the downward sweep of my right hand, he'd have sensed the familiar signal to drop to the ground and stay put. Mindful that malamutes are malamutes, I repeated the signal to stay. I knew he wouldn't get up. And in the absence of an AKC judge and a crowd of entertainment-hungry spectators, he probably wouldn't howl.

An obedience dog knows that when you start with your left foot, you expect him to move with you: Heel! Consequently, when you leave a dog on a long down, you start off on your right foot. I took three small steps in front of Rowdy, squatted, and peered into the alcove. A plant entirely blocked my view, but I could hear everything. Irene was, however, speaking about a topic so unexpected that I was tempted to put my ear to the glass to make sure I was hearing correctly. I'd assumed that Ceci and her psychic would be discussing Simon, of course, and Ceci's impatience for his return. I'd hoped to overhear talk of Jonathan and his murder. Or evidence of blackmail? What I got instead was, of all things, a damned travelogue. Irene Wheeler was discussing California.

"The climate," she said with emphasis, "in all senses of the word, is naturally appealing. The atmosphere is wonderfully receptive."

"According to the papers," Ceci replied, "the smog is absolutely terrible, you can hardly breathe, and police brutality, and the cost of real estate is simply sky-high, you pay millions for a dismal little hovel of a place, and the people! Thinking of nothing but making movies and riding on surfboards and sending some harmless man to jail for life because he forgot to pay for a slice of pizza pie. And what do you call it? Silicon! Everywhere! It's terrible! I can't imagine why anyone, certainly not you, would want to live in such a place.''

After softly clearing her throat, Irene confessed that finances were a consideration. ''The foundation,'' she said in a reluctant tone, ''is not on the solid footing I had hoped. The endowment campaign''—she let the phrase hang for a moment—''has fallen short of my goals.'' Without giving Ceci a second to respond, she added, ''I must remain focused on the crucial importance of the work as a whole. I cannot sacrifice my greater mission. The global possibilities simply must take precedence over my ability to meet the needs of a few individuals, no matter how deserving.''

''But Simon is so close!'' Ceci protested. ''You can feel his presence! You felt it only five or ten minutes ago!''

''This very evening, he may yet appear,'' Irene said.

''I have waited and waited! I have done everything!''

''Perhaps there remains some small impediment we have overlooked.'' Irene was stalling. Had Simon's impostor failed to turn up for a scheduled appearance? ''The impediment may be my own discord,'' she confessed. ''My worldly worries are perhaps creating a field of negativity.'' In an unusual burst of what sounded like genuine frustration, she exclaimed, ''How I loathe and despise being weighted down by these petty material concerns!''

Ceci was not to be diverted. ''Could Jonathan be

interfering again?" She made her murdered relative sound like some bothersome character in a soap opera.

"Jonathan has repeatedly assured us," Irene reminded his great-aunt, "that he is at peace. Now that his eyes are open, he fully understands and appreciates our earthly efforts to awaken him to beauty and fullness."

"And," Ceci added, as if speaking a line that Irene had absentmindedly forgotten, "he has forgiven me completely."

"He has passed beyond blame. If he forgives you, you must forgive yourself."

"If I'd had the least idea that he'd go wandering out chasing away the burglar, I'd have warned him not to trip and fall on the sundial. But whoever would have thought that he'd go out?"

"The workings of the universe are just that," Irene said firmly. "Accept his messages of love and peace."

"Oh, I do, but I still can't help blaming myself, not enough to drive Simon away, but I keep wondering—"

Irene interrupted. "Yes! We are making progress now. Listen to yourself! Keep *wondering*! Maintain the sense of wonder! It is the great secret of childhood and the great secret of animals! The *wonder* of it all! Remind yourself of what Simon has told us. He has brought us messages of the wonder and awe of eternal love."

Irene, it seemed to me, had gone a bit further than she had intended. Ceci was now crying audibly.

But Irene knew what she was doing. "We must not be selfish about those messages. We must not be miserly. It is our duty to share this miraculous reality with everyone. By temperament, I am drawn to helping individuals, spirit by spirit, to using my gifts to unite and reunite all creatures. But these gifts are not mine to keep to myself or to share with the few I can help directly. A foundation is not my personal wish. As you know, the notion goes against my grain. But I am a very small part of the cosmos. It is only my mission that is large.''

''My only mission,'' replied Ceci, ''is to see my Simon again. I would give anything, *anything at all,* to see my Simon again.''

Neither woman spoke explicitly. Neither needed to. Irene's threat? No check, no dog. Unless Ceci funded her foundation, she would move to California, taking with her the messages from Simon and all hope of his material return. And Ceci's reply? No dog, no check. Stalemate.

Chapter Thirty-one

I **HAD HEARD ENOUGH.** Ceci had not murdered her grandnephew. She blamed herself for Jonathan's death, but only because she had failed to warn him about Simon's half-open grave. Irene was conning her victim on a grander scale than I had realized. In assuming that Irene was a small-time operator, I had greatly underestimated her ambition. Irene didn't want to spend the rest of her life grinding away at dog-photo thought transference, diagnostic hocus-pocus, and kitty-cat spirit rapping. Rather, her daily labor was a way to establish trust in her and in her psychic powers. All along, I'd thought of her as a *con* artist, but I hadn't understood that the conning I'd observed was only a preliminary step in a true con game, the necessary phase of gaining a victim's *confidence*. Irene wanted Ceci to endow a foundation. Ceci and how many others?

Rowdy had been a good, quiet boy. Transmitting unspoken words of praise, I stepped carefully back to him and rubbed his head in gratitude. Then I silently patted my leg to signal him to get up. As he rose, I took long strides away from the alcove in case he decided to treat himself to the kind of full-body shake that might be audible through the panes. Distracted by my eager steps, he trotted with me to the corner of the house. When we reached it, I turned left, slowed my pace, and walked toward the fence in confident search of the gate to Upper Norwood Road. Why head back down through Ceci's yard, where we would certainly have another encounter with Hugh and Robert, and might almost literally run into Irene's confederate? Instead, we'd follow Upper Norwood to the fork. As we did, I'd make a new plan.

Confidence was my word of the moment. Self-confidence, that is. I now knew that Ceci was innocent. And for the first time, I understood exactly what Irene was up to. Con artists, Kevin had insisted, are never violent. Irene, I now saw, was a true con artist on the verge of a major sting. Would a bona-fide grifter have allowed violence to ruin everything? But how much control did she have over her violent confederate? Watson had cured Holmes of the cocaine habit. The man with the bulbous forehead was no Dr. Watson. Did Irene depend on him for the means to commit violence against herself? Even if he had murdered Jonathan without her foreknowledge, she was an accessory after the fact. But had he murdered Jonathan at all?

Hugh and Robert remained a mystery to me. They were human snails: I knew their shells, but had only glimpsed the animals inside. Effective armor, I thought, always created an appearance of caricature. Armadillos, for instance, were foolish-looking, although probably not to one another. And real dog people? I'd known thousands of men and women almost exclusively as collie fanciers, top obedience handlers, AKC judges, Akita breeders, active members of kennel clubs, or Doberman people, for instance. I was equally at ease with presenting myself dog first, so to speak. I was as malamutian as Robert and Hugh were Holmesian. In my case, the persona and the soul were one. A chromosomal examination would undoubtedly reveal that I possessed the canine complement of thirty-nine pairs instead of the human twenty-three pairs. If you scratched Hugh and Robert, what sort of Study in Scarlet would flow? Did the fluid run only along the surface of the extremities? Did it gush through the heart? Were their hearts set on Althea? Or on the character she represented to them—the former lover of the King of Bohemia, *the* woman in someone else's life? The woman with *a face that a man might die for*? Had they killed for her? If so, for the person or the persona?

Hugh and Robert lurked downhill. Both were armed. The spectral Simon was apparently late for his scheduled appearance. He and his handler would approach from Lower Norwood Road. Reaching the fence that separated Ceci's yard from Upper Norwood, I searched for the gate. Her house was to my immediate left. The kitchen was on the opposite side of the house. I had no idea what room lay beyond the dark windows on this side. The gate should be *here*, shouldn't it? Midway between the house and the property line. The fence that ran along Lower Norwood was of some expensive variety of coated chain link. The gate there was iron. Here, a wooden fence that matched the style of the house presented an attractive face to Upper Norwood Road. I'd noticed it when I'd brought Kimi here. On the other side of the house, the wooden fence and gate that ran between the big colonial and the garage were topped with a foot or two of handsome latticework that I'd admired. Now, a gas lamp on the street let me see the same latticework atop the fence on this side. Shouldn't the same light creep around the outline of the gate? But this was a solidly constructed fence. Holding Rowdy's leash in my left hand, I explored the heavy boards with my right. The gate could be anywhere, really, I told myself, here in the middle of the fence, next to the house, or next to the adjoining yard. Its latch was probably at waist level. I slowly worked my way from the center of the fence toward the house and found no latch, no handle, no hinges, no indication of a gate. Backtracking, I did a thorough search. Latches were sometimes set high up, weren't they? My fingers felt for metal, for wooden contraptions, for any break in the uniformity of board after board. They found none. On inspiration, I dropped to the ground in the hope of finding a bluestone walk, a series of flagstones, or anything else that might mark a path to the gate. The grass ran right up to the fence. I hadn't actually seen a gate on this side. I'd just assumed that there must be one here. In fact, there was no gate.

Annoyance with myself. Mild claustrophobia. No big deal. Avoiding the lights of the alcove, we'd circle around below the terrace. Then we'd head for the gate between the house and the garage, the gate that was definitely there. For the first time ever, I regretted the whiteness and prominence of Rowdy's beautiful tail. I was supposed to be able to do anything with dogs, wasn't I? There was no way to persuade him to carry his tail down. No, he was going to wave it over his back like a big white flag. And Ceci was expecting a ghostly dog. Enough of this inching along, I decided. We'd just get out fast. I was impatient anyway. At best, Ceci would be delighted to catch sight of her Simon. At worst, she'd be disappointed that he'd fled. So, Rowdy and I would run a little downhill, dash across the yard below the terrace, bolt uphill, and sprint through the gate, down the driveway, onto Upper Norwood Road, and away from this all-too-securely fenced yard.

I had no way to foresee what would go wrong with the plan. The night Kimi and I had been here with Hugh and Robert, no one had mentioned anything about motion sensors. Ceci had once referred to her neighbors' alarm systems and said that she didn't have one. Furthermore, only minutes ago, Rowdy and I had made our way from Lower Norwood to the spot by the French doors. In search of the nonexistent gate, we'd gone back and forth along the wooden fence without triggering anything.

But we hadn't put a foot or a paw in the area directly in front of the terrace. When we did, the powerful lights mounted high on the house suddenly flooded the terrace with what felt like a tidal wave of foggy illumination that rushed directly downhill at us. It didn't lap at my feet or Rowdy's paws. Before we could escape, the light engulfed us. And as it did, a French door banged open and Ceci flew out screaming piteously for Simon. Expecting to see her dog, she saw him in his entirety in Rowdy's white tail, and she took in nothing else. Listening to her call her dog's name—"Simon! Simon!"—I again shared Ceci's longing for the impossible reunion. This time, I envisioned a bank of fog that would suddenly weave itself around Rowdy. Seconds later, after a rapid metamorphosis, the misty cocoon would open to reveal a huge black Newfoundland who would run to his mistress, cover her with slobbery kisses, and let her hold him, warm and young, in her loving arms. Rowdy wouldn't have minded. Neither would I, provided that I could immediately have had my own dog back.

The lights and the fantasy slowed me. Fighting off a massive startle reflex, I tried to stick to my plan of getting to Upper Norwood Road. I was a half century younger than Ceci, I reminded myself. Rowdy and I were in good shape. We could beat Ceci to the gate and sprint off into the mist. But instead of making directly for her spectral dog, Ceci astutely headed for his apparent destination; she didn't dash down the steps from the terrace, but hustled along the path toward the gate between the house and the garage. Of course! The real Simon had probably learned to enter the house through the kitchen. Ceci was exactly the kind of person who keeps a monogrammed towel at the back door for wiping a dog's muddy paws. Rowdy and I were taking Simon's route. If we kept going, we'd run directly into Ceci. I had no choice. Turning tail, I started downhill toward the iron gate to Lower Norwood Road.

For the first few steps, Rowdy and I chased our own shadows. Mine was an amorphous lump. Rowdy's incorporeal self was more interesting than mine. So what else is new? His body was half its usual length, his ears twice their normal height. Bounding ahead of us, the shadow Rowdy was a hefty fox. When we passed beyond the area illuminated by the floodlights, our phantom selves vanished. Nothing appeared to replace them. Heading downhill, we were somewhere to the right of the bluestone walk that led to the iron gate. Rowdy's white tail must still have been visible. To our left and behind us, shoes slapped the bluestone. As if straining to reach the high notes, Ceci wailed, "Simon, wait! Simon! Simon, please don't go! Simon! Come to me! Simon, come!"

A voice hushed her. "Stop!" Irene Wheeler cautioned. "You are driving him away!"

Rowdy pulled ahead of me and veered to the left. Too late, I saw that he was skirting the sundial. My right foot dropped into a pit, and my left leg threatened to go out from under me. Tightening my grip on Rowdy's leash, I scrambled for balance. Just as I regained my footing, the iron gate gave a painful squeal. Rowdy replied with a low rumble. Framed by the masses of high hedge on either side of the gate, a gigantic form appeared. It passed through the gate and entered the yard. Rowdy's leash carried his tension to my hand.

"Simon!" Ceci cried. "Simon!"

The phantasmic creature made no move toward her, but with a sudden surge of power and a low growl lunged toward Rowdy and, to my amazement, came to an abrupt and inexplicable halt. Hauling Rowdy to my left side, I took involuntary steps away from the aggressor, but I'd moved no more than a few feet when the strong beam of a flashlight in Ceci's hand suddenly explained the inexplicable. Revealed at last was the spectral Simon, the giant dog who had left the enormous prints. A thin cord ran from his collar and disappeared in the darkness beyond the gate. Caught in the light, he was bewildered and grotesque. The white of the Great Pyrenees is so distinctive that even I had difficulty in recognizing this mutant bear as a once-white dog. He wore a hideous piebald coat of white splotched with black and gray. Ceci gasped. The beam of her flashlight moved to Rowdy.

With sudden vehemence, Ceci swung around. As if she were jacking a deer, she directed the light into Irene Wheeler's eyes. I'd have expected Ceci to fall to pieces. In fact, she had never sounded more dignified than she did now. "You have deceived me," she declared flatly. "Do you imagine that I should have known better? Is that your excuse? Do you suppose that all of this is my own fault for being such an old fool? You are a vicious, cruel woman, Irene Wheeler! What you have done to me is beyond forgiveness.''

She moved the beam back to the false Simon and slowly traced the cord that ran from his collar. The cord, I saw, was caught in the top hinge of the iron gate. The light rested briefly on a gloved hand that held the plastic handle of a retractable dog leash. Then it crept upward to reveal the face of a man. Pressed to his oddly bulbous forehead was Hugh's revolver.

Robert emerged from the darkness into the beam of the light and cleared his throat lightly as if preparing to deliver a speech. I had no doubt what its central theme would be. Before Robert uttered a word, however, the man who had tried to drown Tracker dropped in appropriately catlike fashion to the ground, where he must have seized Hugh's ankles. I heard something hit the ground: Hugh's revolver. And something else: the plastic case of the retractable leash. In seconds, the revolver was in the hands of Irene's confederate, who pressed it against Hugh's temple. Until Robert moved, I had forgotten that he, too, was armed. An unseen object whizzed upward and cracked down on the revolver and the hand that held it. The man screamed and bent double in pain.

''Holmes's favorite weapon,'' Robert declared smugly. ''For good reason. Hugh, the handcuffs, if you please. Thank you. Ceci, dear, some light? May I have the mixed pleasure of presenting Arthur Moore? We knew as soon as we heard the name. He goes by a nickname. Artie, he is called. Artie Moore.''

''Is that your proof?'' I burst out. ''Artie Moore? Moriarty? He happens to have a name that sounds like the name of Holmes's arch villain? That's not proof. It's just coincidence.''

''Rather *m-o-o-re* than that,'' replied Robert.

Chapter Thirty-two

NO ONE, INCLUDING *YOU*," I told Kevin Dennehy late that same evening, "took that crime seriously. Not that I'm letting myself off the hook! If it had been a dog, I'd have done something. But the point is that cruelty to animals is *not* some peccadillo."

"Watch your language there," Kevin replied. He was sitting at my kitchen table. For once, he wasn't drinking Budweiser or anything else.

"Kevin, please! You're just being defensive. I asked you to send this rock and the pillowcase and the twine to the police lab. But did you listen? No, you didn't even bother looking at them."

He was looking at them now. They were sitting between us on the kitchen table.

"Mea culpa." Thumping his beefy chest, he looked like a Catholic gorilla.

At the risk of sounding like Irene Wheeler singing a combined commercial for Coca-Cola and the phone company, let me say that the cosmos is, after all, a harmonious system in which people, animals, and objects really do communicate with one another all the time. But I have leaped ahead of myself. Robert's application of the Master's favorite weapon to the revolver in Artie Moore's hand ended what I am tempted to call "The Norwood Hill Melodrama." As you may have noticed, however, Robert's intervention did not resolve the question of who had murdered Jonathan Hubbell. As I had been quick to point out, the name *Artie Moore,* although reminiscent of *Moriarty,* offered no proof of the man's guilt. In the Canon, the nomen omen was a literary device. In the real world of the dog fancy, of course, the phenomenon carried a divine message. But just as there were Mrs. Breedloves and Mr. Bassets who didn't even like dogs, never mind show them, so there must be upstanding, law-abiding Artie Moores who bore no resemblance to the evil Professor Moriarty. Holmes, I felt certain, would have agreed with me. The Newton police did. And when the police asked who owned the revolver, Hugh and Robert, in an outrageous betrayal of the loyal Watson, fingered Artie Moore, who truthfully said that he had never seen the weapon before.

It was Ceci who called the police. What impelled her was the discovery that Irene Wheeler had taken advantage of the brouhaha at the gate to slip away. Soon after the police cruiser arrived, I wished that I, too, had had the sense to flee. Or maybe what I wished for was the power to dematerialize at will. The surreal scene took place in Ceci's living room. Having recovered her volubility, Ceci issued nonstop complaints about being the victim of fraud. The con artist who'd duped her, she reported in urgent tones, was at this very moment attempting to reach California, which Ceci apparently viewed as a small country with border crossings staffed by customs officials whose duty it was to keep normal people out. Her argument had admirable internal logic.

She was convinced that a fraudulent animal psychic was just the sort of person who'd be welcome. Meanwhile, Hugh and Robert attempted to follow Holmes's example by repeatedly assuring the two bewildered patrolmen that popular applause was abhorrent to them and that orthodox officialdom would be given full public credit for apprehending Jonathan Hubbell's murderer. Indeed, the Holmesians claimed no personal credit. Rather, they attributed their success to the diligent applicant of the Master's methods.

"The great thing," Hugh informed one of the uniformed officers, *"is to be able to reason backwards."*

Robert was scornful. *"The* grand *thing is to be able to reason* backward."

Slumped in a corner of one of Ceci's mile-long couches, Artie Moore confined himself mainly to rubbing his knobby forehead and keeping his mouth shut. He'd been walking his dog, he mumbled. He didn't know anything about anything else. Hugh and Robert promptly produced the snapshots of him and his van taken outside Irene Wheeler's. I added to the clarity of the account by reporting that Moore had abused and tried to drown my cat and should be arrested for cruelty to animals. He should have been informed of his rights by now, I advised. I also contributed a note of normality by demanding to know the whereabouts of the piebald dog, which, I said, was stolen property and belonged to a patient of a psychotherapist friend of mine. I didn't know the owner's name, but I was sure that she was frantic about her dog. Consequently, her therapist should be called immediately. As an aside, I mentioned that Artie Moore was wanted by the police in connection with the highly publicized murder of Donald Lively. Would the officers *please* call Lieutenant Kevin Dennehy of the Cambridge police?

Summoning help struck them as a good idea. Before long, a couple of detectives and more uniformed men arrived, as did an emergency medical vehicle with E.M.T.s who examined Hugh for injuries and led Artie Moore away, under police supervision, to have his bruised and swollen right hand treated.

It was during Hugh's absence that Robert made what I took to be a gentlemanly effort to distract a member of the fair sex from the distressing circumstances in which she found herself. By then, I had withdrawn to the alcove and was sitting in one of the rattan chairs. On a loose lead, Rowdy eyed the potted palms. Watching him, I reflected that it didn't take an animal psychic to read his mind. At the moment, he was reminding himself that the greenery, being indoors, was off-limits for leg lifting. He was also contemplating the prospect of taking a swift, satisfying bite of palm leaf.

Seating himself opposite me in the other rattan chair, Robert said, in tones suitable for making small talk at a dull party, "Well, have you solved Hugh's little puzzle yet?"

"What puzzle?" I asked.

Robert looked offended. "While visiting you," he reminded me, "we observed the one-volume Double-day edition."

"Yes."

"And Hugh issued a challenge."

"He challenged *you*," I replied. "I'm no expert. It would be a waste of time to ask me about Holmes trivia."

"Now, now," Robert said soothingly. "You underrate yourself."

"I can't even remember what the puzzle was."

"As Hugh was close enough to see, and I was not, the volume was open to . . . ?"

I searched my memory. "It was open to *The Valley of Fear*."

"Excellent!" Robert cried.

"Elementary," I responded.

Robert was overjoyed. "Open to a certain work that makes a *singular* yet cryptic allusion to your own profession," he informed me. "And contains a *doubly* allusive line. Quote the line! That was the challenge."

"Well, I'm afraid I'm not up to meeting it. *You* were supposed to be able to answer it. It didn't have anything to do with me."

"It certainly did," Robert replied. "*Your* profession?"

"Dog writing? Dog training? I don't think there's even a dog in the story."

"Ah, but the allusion is *cryptic*."

"Well, it's too cryptic for me."

"Consider the tools of your trade," Robert hinted.

"Pens? Paper? A computer? There aren't any . . . Well, in the story, there's that business about the dumbbell, but it's a different kind of dumbbell. It's the kind people use for exercise. It isn't the kind that dogs retrieve."

"Cryptic," Robert said, well, cryptically.

"Okay, so a dumbbell is an allusion to my profession," I admitted. "Sort of."

"And singular? A *singular* allusion?"

"There's one dumbbell, isn't there? The other one is missing. Oh, I remember. It turns out that the missing dumbbell was in the moat. It was used as a weight to sink something in the moat."

"Excellent! *The case hangs upon the missing dumbbell.* One dumbbell. The singular allusion. And the doubly allusive line?"

"Robert, I'm sorry, but I have no idea."

Robert tried to prompt me by quoting the beginning of the line. *"This is what we are after . . ."*

"This is what we are after," I repeated. "And I don't have a clue what comes next."

Hugh suddenly appeared. "Ah hah! The doubly allusive line!" With a look of triumph, he added, *"This is what we are after, Mr. Barker—this sodden bundle, weighted with a dumbbell, that we have lifted from the mud of the moat."*

"No, no!" Robert almost shouted. "Your own challenge, and you've botched it! *This is what we are after, Mr. Barker—this bundle, weighted with a dumbbell, which you have just raised from the bottom of the moat."*

"Mr. Barker," I said to Hugh. "And dumbbell. Doubly allusive. My profession. Very clever." Then I remembered the other line that Robert had just quoted: *The case hangs upon the missing dumbbell.* In a certain sense, this case did, too. It hung not on a dumbbell, but on a heavy object used to weight something that was to be submerged in water. I had to get home. Abruptly excusing myself, I cornered one of the detectives and demanded to be allowed to phone Kevin.

"Or call him yourself," I went on. "He's my next-door neighbor. Call him at home. If he isn't there, talk to his mother. She'll tell you that it's perfectly all right to let me go."

The detective rolled his eyes.

"Okay, I can see that you might not want to take his mother's word," I conceded. "But would you at least try to reach *him*? I swear that I'll answer any questions anytime you want. Just not now! Would you please call Kevin Dennehy?"

I won. As it turned out, the detective knew Kevin,

whose idea of speaking up for me was to assert that I was a complete dog nut.

Eavesdropping on the detective's end of the conversation, I said, "Tell Kevin that I absolutely have to see him tonight."

The innocent request generated a lot of guffawing back and forth. I didn't try to straighten out the misunderstanding. I just wanted to get home to Cambridge so I could finally hand over to Kevin the crucial evidence that rested at the back of a closet.

And as I'd begun to say before leaping backward, when I finally reached home and again presented Kevin with the evidence, he got understandably defensive. But then I explained that the cosmos is, after all, a harmonious whole in which people, animals, and objects communicate with one another all the time. I didn't actually need to explain the phenomenon to a cop. Kevin understood it already. Cops know more than I do about trace evidence. You know that old saw about killing two birds with one stone? Well, maybe Artie Moore had it in mind when he tried to drown Tracker. The stone he'd used to weight the pillowcase communicated its history. It spoke to the police laboratory. The stone said that it had been in contact with the scalp of Donald Lively. And with Artie Moore's hands. Oh, and the missing shovel used to bludgeon Jonathan Hubbell? Where would you guess it was? I guessed right. Kevin believed me. The police had no difficulty in dredging up the weapon in almost the exact spot where Artie Moore had tried to dispatch Tracker. Kevin was smug about the discovery. He'd always told me to beware of that lonely stretch of Greenough Boulevard.

Chapter Thirty-three

I RENE WHEELER WAS APPREHENDED not in California, but at Logan Airport in Boston. She was, however, about to board a flight for San Francisco. In her possession was a large amount of cocaine. She was evidently making off with her confederate's entire stash. Its value, I am told, was enough to endow a small foundation. Charges were also brought against her in connection with the murder of Jonathan Hubbell. In the apparent hope of saving herself, she tried to place all blame for the slaying on Artie Moore. Artie, she maintained, had acted entirely without her knowledge or consent. She was perfectly open about having enlisted Artie to manage Simon's "appearances." Indeed, she took pride in having made every effort to gratify an old woman's wish for earthly reunion with her departed pet. Her instruction to Artie had been to acquire a Newfoundland. Until informed by the police, she had no idea that the dog had been stolen. Or so she claimed. When Artie showed up with a dog of the wrong breed, she was unhappy with him, but soon realized that the substitution of a live Great Pyrenees for a dead New-foundland was nothing more than a kindly white lie.

As to the murder of Jonathan Hubbell, Irene insisted that Artie alone was guilty. He had made a full confession to her, she stated, just before her final visit on Norwood Hill. As she had been horrified to learn, on the Saturday of Jonathan's death, Artie had violated her client's confidentiality by lurking outside the alcove during the discussion she'd had with Ceci and Jonathan. After her departure, Artie had returned to his van, which was parked on Lower Norwood Road, and had mulled matters over with a dusting of chemical assistance. From Artie's point of view, nothing would look more natural than the apparently accidental death by overdose of the yuppie grandnephew. His boring old aunt goes to bed. He turns to coke. What else? To Artie's stoned amazement, however, Jonathan spared him the trouble of breaking into the house or luring his victim out. Armed with a flashlight, Jonathan appeared in the yard. The beam slowly made its way down toward Lower Norwood Road. Cocaine had a less beneficial effect on Artie Moore's reason than it did on Holmes's. Artie impulsively revised his plan. Now, the yuppie grandnephew leaves the house to do his coke, he overdoses outdoors instead of inside. As Jonathan neared the bottom of the yard, Artie got out of the van. His eyes apparently focused on the vehicle unexpectedly parked on the dark street, Jonathan stumbled, dropped the flashlight, and fell, striking his head on the shovel that his great-aunt had abandoned on the ground after her abortive attempt to disinter Simon's ashes. In response to Jonathan's soft cry of pain, the false Simon, the Great Pyrenees incarcerated in Artie's van, gave a low growl. The twin sounds threw Artie into a panic. He neither fled nor carried out his revised plan. Rather, he rushed at Jonathan, grabbed the shovel, and silenced him forever. Taking the murder weapon with him, he departed. Until reading the newspaper, he had no idea that he had inadvertently left traces of cocaine on the body. That was Irene's story, anyway. I have wondered whether the police challenged her about the obvious inconsistency in her account. If I'd had the opportunity, I'd have wanted to know why a *psychic*, for heaven's sake, had had to wait for her confederate's admission. If she could read dogs' minds just by looking at photographs, couldn't she read guilt on a human face?

So far as I know, no one questioned Irene Wheeler about Tracker, either, and I know for sure that the numerous charges brought against Artie Moore were limited to drugs and murder, and included nothing about animal cruelty. Not that Artie is innocent of the official charges! But viciousness is viciousness. I witnessed his myself. Lacking Irene Wheeler's paranormal gifts, I do not know whether she asked her confederate to rid her of her unwanted cat. Perhaps she asked him to dispose of Tracker at a shelter, where the ugly, old, sick little animal would immediately have been put to death. I do know that Althea was right about Tracker's ownership. According to Irene Wheeler's neighbors, the cat I saved from drowning—my cat—was definitely Irene's.

Irene Wheeler and Artie Moore made the Boston papers, which seized the opportunity to commit to print a countless number of headlines about Wheeler and the Dealer, Wheeling and Dealing, and so forth. Indeed, the nomen omen again. Gloria and Scott—remember Gloria and Scott? Steve's accusers? Irene's shills?—remained loyal to Irene for a few days after the story broke. Once word spread throughout the world of dogs, however, Gloria heard from a number of people she'd referred to Irene who were furious that Gloria had recommended a con artist. What turned Gloria against Irene wasn't resentment about those complaints or disenchantment with the psychic's paranormal powers. Rather, Gloria discovered that she'd received her kickback for only half the people she'd sent to the psychic. According to a rumor I heard at a show, Gloria is planning to take Irene to small claims court to recover the money she says Irene owes her. I really don't care how that case turns out. I'm just glad that Gloria is now so focused on Irene Wheeler that she has apparently forgotten all about Steve.

Speaking of Steve, I should report that he has forgiven me for interfering with what I now admit was none of my business. In fact, he accompanied Rowdy, Kimi, and me to the celebration held at Ceci's house a month after the arrests of Artie Moore and Irene Wheeler. The festivities were not some sort of tasteless celebration of incarceration. Indeed, the party was notably tasteful. It took place on an exceptionally foggy spring evening. Hugh and Robert were there. So was the false Simon, as I still thought of him, the Great Pyrenees, whose name was, in fact, Bear. With him was his owner, Rita's patient, Mary Kingsley, who kept apologizing about the terrible state of Bear's coat and who pinned Steve in a corner to interrogate him about whether dogs suffered from Post Traumatic Stress Disorder, and if so, whether Bear now had it. Rowdy and Kimi behaved remarkably well in Bear's presence. Both were perfect angels during dinner, but only because I took the precaution of crating them in the car just before the food was served. Ceci offered them the run of her fenced yard, but I declined. I just didn't trust the place. Also, I harbored a neurotic fear that they might desecrate Simon's newly restored grave. Accepting the finality of his departure from this life, Ceci had filled in the hole and planted it with spring flowers. The dog had been unearthed too many times already, I thought. He didn't need living dogs digging up his grave.

Tracker was also invited. Ceci understood completely when I explained that the cat was happiest in my study and was only beginning to make brief, carefully supervised trips to the top of my refrigerator. For the obvious reason, car trips had unfortunate associations for her. Also, she wouldn't enjoy the company of three big dogs. Bear might be fine with her, for all I knew, but Rowdy and Kimi had yet to complete my love-the-little-kitty retraining program. In fact, they still haven't graduated. I persist nonetheless. After all, everyone assures me that I can do anything with dogs. I can't, of course. For instance, I can't keep the dead alive. With Vinnie, I no longer try as I once did.

Rowdy now has his Rx.D. title. We continue to visit the Gateway. We have lost a few of our people. We have gained a few. One is a woman who speaks to no one except Rowdy. Another is a man who used to run a dog team in Alaska. We see Helen Musgrave now and then when she isn't bustling to or from her activities. She has a new roommate, a woman who is afraid of dogs. Helen does not miss Althea. She doesn't remember her. Every time Rowdy and I visit the Gateway, I miss our visits with Althea. We still enjoy her company, of course. Now, we see her at home. The celebration at Ceci's was a homecoming of sorts. Althea has moved. When we visit, we sometimes find her in her own private room, which is on the ground floor and was originally her brother-in-law's library. The bookshelves that line the walls hold the late Ellis Love's collection as well as Althea's own volumes and the bits of Sherlockiana she kept at her bedside at the Gateway. On chilly days, however, Althea sometimes sits beneath the portrait of Lord Saint Simon to enjoy the warmth of a cozy fire.

And speaking of fires, kindled by Hugh and Robert, my own interest in the Master is blazing. I have even been invited to present a paper at the Red-headed League of Boston. The paper isn't finished yet, but I am working on it. The evidence is overwhelming. Let me summarize for you the detailed presentation I made to Althea one sunny April morning as she and Rowdy and I sat among the potted palms in the alcove, which Ceci has thoughtfully rearranged to accommodate her sister's wheelchair.

So here's the gist: In "The Resident Patient," Holmes says to Watson, *"What would you say to a ramble through London?"* And this is how Watson describes his walk with his Master: *I was weary of our little sitting-room and gladly acquiesced. For three hours we strolled about together. . . . His characteristic talk, with its keen observance of detail and subtle powers of inference, held me amused and enthralled.* The walk together? Master and . . . ? For three hours, during which Watson, instead of getting bored or irritated the way a person would, remains amused and enthralled in the manner of a . . . ? Or let me quote Holmes to Watson. Off on a little adventure, Holmes says to his loyal companion, *"There is no prospect of danger, or I should not dream of stirring without you."* Then there's Watson's unusually keen sense of smell. "The Devil's Foot"? And in that same adventure, his declaration that helping the Master is *his greatest joy and privilege.* The clues are everywhere. In "The Illustrious Client," Watson comes close to spilling the truth. *By long experience,* he informs us, *I had learned the wisdom of obedience.* And the telegram that Holmes sends to Watson in "The Creeping Man"? *Come at*

once if convenient—if inconvenient come all the same.
From whom does Holmes demand a reliable recall, for
heaven's sake? From a woman? Surely not. And look at
the dialogue! In "The Naval Treaty," Holmes says,
"Come along, Watson." The response? The telling response? A human, "Oh, no, I don't feel like it"? Of
course not. What the loyal Watson replies is, *"Where
are we going now?"* I know that response perfectly. I
get it every time I pick up a leash. I know that eagerness
to accompany me, that enthrallment with my every
word, that attitude of unconditional loyalty. I virtually
speak the words Holmes spoke: "Rowdy, come! Kimi,
come!" Except, of course, that Holmes doesn't call
Rowdy or Kimi. No, no. He calls his own Best Friend:
"Come, Watson, come! The game is afoot."

That bull pup that appears in "A Study in Scarlet"
and never again? *"I keep a bull pup,"* Watson tells
Holmes. Watson *keeps* a bull pup? He assuredly does.
He keeps that pup well hidden between the lines of
every adventure. Watson was a *woman*? Certainly not!

When I had finished my presentation, Althea nodded
solemnly. *"When you have eliminated the impossible,"*
she quoted, *"whatever remains,* however improbable,
must be the truth." And the truth is . . . ? Watson
was the bull pup! Elementary? "Indeed," agreed Althea, "Watson assuredly *was* a dog."

About the Author

Susan Conant, three-time recipient of the Maxwell Award for Fiction Writing, given by the Dog Writers' Association of America, lives in Newton, Massachusetts, with her husband, two cats, and two Alaskan malamutes—Frostfield Firestar's Kobuk, CGC, and Frostfield Perfect Crime, CGC, called Rowdy. She is the author of eleven Dog Lover's Mysteries and has just completed the twelfth, *Evil Breeding*.